LAURA BRADBURY

OXFORD
Star

BOOKS BY LAURA BRADBURY

OXFORD SERIES

Oxford Wild

TRANSPLANT ROMANCE

Unlikely Match

THE WINEMAKERS TRILOGY

A Vineyard for Two

Love in the Vineyards

Return to the Vineyards

~ MEMOIRS ~

GRAPE SERIES

My Grape Year

My Grape Québec

My Grape Christmas

My Grape Paris

My Grape Wedding

My Grape Escape

My Grape Village

My Grape Cellar

Published by Grape Books

Paperback ISBN: 978-1-989784-29-7

eBook ISBN: 978-1-989784-28-0

Visit: www.laurabradbury.com

Oxford Star is for my fellow anxiety and panic warriors.

You are forking rock stars.

OXFORD
Star

Every star may be a sun to someone.

Carl Sagan

NOTES TO READER

» In *Oxford Star* the royal family is fictional, with a King who has three sons.

» The terms at Oxford University are divided into eight weeks. Each week begins on a Sunday.

» The week before the beginning of term is referred to as Nought Week.

» Oxford University is made up of 44 separate colleges scattered in and around the city. Each college is its own little universe.

» Beaufort College is fictional (with a wink to Colin Dexter's Inspector Morse) but largely inspired by New College, Oxford.

» Sub fusc is the formal outfit Oxford students have to wear for important University occasions such as Matriculation, Exams, and Graduation.

» *Oxford Star* involves anxiety and panic disorder and the death of parent in the past. Avoid if you feel either of these could be triggering. Take care of your precious self.

NOUGHT WEEK

OXFORD UNIVERSITY, BEAUFORT COLLEGE
HILARY TERM (JANUARY 15TH - MARCH 11TH)

CHAPTER ONE

Lucy

If limbo had a smell, it would be freshly cleaned airplane. I made my way down the aisle of the CanadaJet Dreamliner, my heart lodged in my throat.

The canned air and the soft muzak playing over the speakers were aggressively neutral but not enough to numb my doubts.

Should I have given into my mother's begging and stayed at home in Newfoundland? Or was going to Oxford to get an accelerated law degree the best way—the only way, really—I could make good on the promise I'd made to my father?

Crap. I double-checked my phone. I was sure I'd booked a window seat, but in the airline's infinite wisdom they'd put me in the aisle of the two-seat configuration. A hunched form in jeans and a black NASA hoodie was slumped against the window that should have been mine. I checked the ticket on my phone. Goddamn CanadaJet. They never failed to live up to their unofficial motto: "We're not happy unless you're unhappy."

People who hopped on airplanes the way I walk by the harbor

to check out icebergs wouldn't care about things like window seats but this was my first time crossing the Atlantic. I wanted to see everything, even if it was just six hours of clouds.

I shoved my tattered backpack in the overhead compartment and sat down. The armrests dug into my hips. Economy seats, just like most of the world, were not designed for size-sixteen bodies.

I couldn't help but admire the long, denim-clad legs of the sleeping guy beside me, but the hood around his face was pulled so tight I wondered if he was in the process of suffocating. What a waste of a window seat.

The saving grace with him being catatonic was it lowered my chances of getting trapped in small talk about World of Warcraft or Elon Musk or whatever guys wearing NASA gear were into. I hated chitchat, but as a Newfoundlander, it was pathologically impossible to cut someone off. Small talk was our way of life, just like fishing, swearing, and music-filled kitchen parties.

Silence meant I could spend the whole flight daydreaming about what Oxford was going to be like—if I could just get past my guilt at leaving.

My mother's tears were hard to bear, but I'd expected those, even though the scene she created at the airport made people look at me like my pastime was spitting in people's coffee cups.

She was a woman who'd always been looked after in life—first by her indulgent parents, then by my father, then by me—and there was nothing that terrified her more than having to fend for herself, even the tiniest bit.

Still, it was my ten-year-old sister, Alice, who'd almost made me cancel my flight. She'd wrapped her skinny arms around me in a tight hug and whispered in my ear that she was going to miss me, her blue eyes shiny with tears, but stoic. Even now I wasn't quite sure how I'd managed to tear myself away.

A familiar scent of vanilla and lemon wafted past my nose. What fresh hell was this? Where did CanadaJet find an air freshener that smelled like him, the absolute last person I wanted to be reminded of? Considering how famous Jack was now, he'd probably bottled his smell and sold it for a hundred dollars to all his screaming fans—as well as to airlines worldwide. For all I knew, there was probably a line of bestselling Jack Seary potpourri.

The announcement came on for the cabin crew to take their seats for takeoff, and the engines revved up until the vibrations rattled my teeth. I gripped my seat rests so tight my knuckles turned white.

I was doing this law degree because it was a stunningly efficient plan to provide a good living for my mother and little sister sooner rather than later. The fact that it also gave me a temporary escape from my life in Newfoundland? I was looking forward to that part so much that guilt was pushing me back against my seat as much as the forward momentum of the plane as it roared down the runway.

Was I sticking my neck out too far again? The only time I'd been truly self-indulgent in chasing my dreams had bitten me in the arse so hard it still stung.

Nobody I knew was living their dream. Okay, one person—the same person, Jack, who smelled like vanilla and lemon—but I'd banned myself from ever thinking about him again. Besides, the last piece of gossip I'd seen about him said he was self-destructing despite all the riches and fame he'd been handed. It almost made me believe in the existence of karma after all.

The wheels left the ground.

The decision was made now. I was on my way to England. There was no turning back.

An hour into the flight, a crew member came by with a trolley to serve lunch. His name was Angus, according to his name tag.

"Do you think he wants some?" He nodded at my comatose and/or deceased neighbor as he placed a tray of food in front of me.

I shrugged. "Your guess is as good as mine."

"You're not traveling together?"

"Never seen him in my life. He hasn't moved a hair since I sat down. You don't think he's dead, do you?"

Angus blanched. "No, no, I'm sure ..." He trailed off, studying him. "Actually ..."

We both stared at the inert body, searching for a sign of life.

Angus leaned farther over my seat. "I can't see his chest moving at all. Can you?"

I looked. Nothing. "No. Do you think we should poke him or something?"

"I guess." Angus didn't sound thrilled about the prospect, but he stretched out a finger. It was an inch away from my neighbor's shoulder when he reached up and scratched his nose.

I clutched my chest. Angus yelped.

"So that's what a heart attack feels like," Angus gasped. "I was really starting to think he was dead."

After that brief sign of life, the guy went back to being completely inert.

"I'm going to assume he's not hungry," Angus concluded and hurried off.

My airplane meal was hardly a gourmet feast, but I happily picked away at it as I started a good detective movie on the seatback entertainment system.

I was taking my first bite of my espresso cheesecake square when my seatmate did a full body jerk—the kind I sometimes did when I was falling asleep—and sat bolt upright. I almost stabbed myself in the eye with my fork.

He loosened the strings around the hoodie pulled tight over most of his face, just enough so he could see. He didn't make any move to slide it off his head.

"Do you mind if I get up?" he asked in a Newfoundland-accented voice I would have recognized anywhere.

My fork clattered down to my tray. Blood roared in my ears as I was snapped back in time to four years before.

A sob from someplace deep within me pushed up so there was no room left in my lungs for oxygen. I tried to swallow back the sudden tears.

Of all the times I'd imagined this moment, I never thought for a second I would have to blink fast to keep tears from gathering in the corners of my eyes. In my imagination, I was going to be disdainful and majestic, not this disintegrating, weepy mess.

Get it together, Lucy. Focus on the rage. "You?" I infused my voice with every last shred of scorn in me.

"Lucy?" Those unforgettable sage green eyes met mine. One of his expertly tousled waves of red hair peeked out from the circle of his hoodie drawstring. At least he looked just as shaken as I felt.

"What in God's green fuck are you doing here, Jack?" I emphasized the fuck part *hard*.

He bit the inside of his cheek. He looked good. That was always one of my biggest beefs against him. He always looked good, even now—pale, thin, and with tiny pleats of exhaustion at the corners of his eyes. Instead of looking like crap, he resembled a romantic poet with tuberculosis.

He cleared his throat. "Hello again to you too, Lucy. I'm going to England to take a bit of a break."

Spare me. "Life of fame and fortune too much for you?"

He yanked his hoodie strings tighter, covering the edges of his distinctive copper hair again. "Still have a tongue like an ice pick I see. You don't know how happy that makes me. Look, can you keep it down?" His eyes darted around us, and his face took on a hunted expression. "I can't deal with attention right now, Luce."

How dare he talk to me like nothing had happened. Did he seriously think I'd forgotten how he'd betrayed me four years earlier?

"You lost the right to call me Luce four years ago," I said, my voice so arctic I wouldn't have been surprised to see hoar frost appear on the armrest separating our seats. "Right around the time you lost the right to ask me favors."

He rubbed his forehead, wincing. "I've tried to apologize a hundred times."

Maybe, but nothing could make up for Jack's betrayal. He'd confirmed my deepest fear—I would always be Cinderella without the glass slipper.

My nose stung like it always did just before I started to cry. Hold on to the rage, Lucy. He doesn't deserve your grief.

"You could have chosen another guitarist and singer to accompany you," he insisted. "They were a dime a dozen at that audition. You have the most incredible voice I've ever heard. You sure as hell didn't need me to show it off."

Four years had gone by, and Jack's life had changed in every conceivable way, so how could we still be here? "You bailed on me at the last minute!"

"And? You didn't need anyone. You could have gone out on that stage and sung acapella, and you still would have won by a landslide."

Indignation burned in me. How could he still not realize that life didn't just magically work out for me the way it did for him? "So that's what you tell yourself to assuage your guilt?"

"You. Did. Not. Need. Me." He enunciated every syllable, a muscle in his jaw jumping.

It really pissed me off that I remembered all his little tells. "I was depending on you, and you let me down."

The finely-shaped nostrils of his stupidly perfect nose flared as he inhaled. "Yeah, well, take comfort in the fact you were just the first in a long line of people I've been letting down. Can you please let me get out? I was mainlining coffee in the airport lounge so I wouldn't miss this flight. Do you want me to pee all over my seat?"

I arched an eyebrow.

"Lucy…"

"I'm thinking about it." Letting him embarrass himself in public had a certain poetic justice to it, but it wasn't the revenge I'd dreamed about.

"Fine." I struggled out between my food tray and the arms of my seat, heat creeping up my neck. I was resigned to my body now—or at least more resigned than I used to be—but things like getting out of narrow plane seats were nevertheless made harder by my wide hips and strong thighs.

If I'd been born with the unconscious ease that Jack had, I wouldn't be stuck in this airplane seat beside him, still picking up the pieces from when he'd stolen my dream four years before.

He climbed past me, the painfully familiar scent of lemon oil he used for his guitar strings and the vanilla from his trusty Gibson guitar case lingering behind him.

He disappeared down the aisle, his head bowed and his hood

pulled tight. I flopped back into my seat, trying to recover from the shock that reverberated through my cells. Of all the things stressing me about my move to Oxford, being stuck on the plane beside Jack Seary—my ex-crush and now a world-famous rock star—had not been on my bingo card.

CHAPTER TWO

Jack

I kept my head bowed and my eyes downcast as I made my way down the narrow aisle to the bathroom. If anyone recognized me, it was game over. I'd be the object of stealth photos and TMZ posts about how I'd been rude and uncommunicative.

The exhaustion in my face would be picked apart by fans and the media. The speculation I was on drugs would gain even more momentum. They always ended up there, one way or another.

Why couldn't they make up some story about me becoming part of a cult in the Alps where I'd married a goat? Was a little bit of creativity and originality too much to ask? The thing that bothered me most about the drug theory was its sheer journalistic laziness.

And Lucy ... fucking hell. She was acting like I'd ended up on the same plane as her—in the seat beside her, no less—just to thwart her. The worst part was the last four years hadn't lessened the effect she had on me. My body crackled back to life the second I'd heard her hiss *'you?'*.

Apparently, my weakness for a lush body combined with a sharp tongue was as strong as ever.

The bathroom was vacant, so I slipped inside.

What was Lucy doing on my flight to London anyway? It was the last place I would've expected to bump into her.

Even though these new Dreamliners were far more spacious than other planes, I'd forgotten how small the bathrooms in economy were. I did the necessary, then washed my hands and pulled my hood back. I gulped in the fresh air. Well, not fresh—airplane bathroom air was a far cry from the off-the-icebergs breeze back home in Newfoundland.

It was stifling with my hood pulled tight, but there was no way I could cope with being recognized on this flight. I ran my hands through my hair, closing my eyes to better enjoy the cool water against my aching skull.

I'd bought a ticket to London at the last minute and the only remaining seat was in economy. It was probably better for remaining undetected anyway. People expected Jack Seary, music idol, to be flitting around in private jets or at least in first class.

But sitting next to Lucy? As if my life wasn't messy enough already. I'd longed to see her again, but not when I was in the midst of a complete meltdown, and not with her looking like she wanted to rip my head off and bowl it down the airplane aisle.

I leaned against the sink and rested my forehead against the cool mirror. If only I could stay like this, locked in here, the whole flight.

The whole point of my trip to England was to straighten out my head and get a handle on my panic attacks. To do this, I knew I had to escape everything rock star related, yet beside me on the plane was the person who'd been the catalyst for the whole thing.

The worst part was Lucy was right—I shouldn't be complaining about anything. I had everything people dreamed about—money, luxury, opportunity, fame. It was pathetic I couldn't get out of my own way enough to enjoy it. I'd tried everything. This eight-week Oxford sabbatical was my last-ditch effort.

If I could only find the cause of it all. Maybe karma was an actual thing. I should be reveling in my luck like my bandmates, but I was so miserable that most of the time I wanted to climb out of my body.

My fingertips tingled, and a familiar tension spread between my ribs. I pressed my fingers in the middle of my chest and coughed, trying to push it back down. *Christ.* I couldn't have a panic attack in a plane. I'd medicated myself enough before take-off to prevent this from happening, but if I had a public meltdown everyone in the world would know about the terrified boy behind the strutting singer.

I rolled my shoulders back, trying to rid myself of the sensation my skin was too tight and too loose at the same time.

"Are you done in there?" Someone knocked on the door. *Stupid, stupid, stupid.* I should've been in and out of the bathroom quickly to avoid attracting any unnecessary attention.

I pulled my hoodie tight around my face again and hunched over. Looking down at my feet, I shuffled out of the bathroom.

"Sorry," I mumbled, but the man waiting was too busy grumbling to take any notice of the disgraced rock star in his midst.

I headed back to my seat, both dreading and anticipating another sucker punch from the girl I'd never been able to forget.

LAURA BRADBURY

Lucy's glacier blue eyes were full of resentment as she stood up to let me pass. Her gaze burned, like touching ice for too long with bare fingers.

It wasn't pleasant to be the object of her hostility, but something in the fierceness of her anger felt solid. I could hold on to it so reality wouldn't slip away if my panic got worse.

I brushed past her, enjoying the warmth from her body and the soft feel of her sweater this close. The scent of her favorite peppermint shampoo—I loved that she hadn't changed brands—lingered on the soft waves of her blonde hair. *Ah. Better.* I sat down and enjoyed my first proper look at her through the small opening in my hood.

She'd stopped blow-drying her blonde bob straight like she used to do, and with her natural waves she looked even more like she'd stepped straight out of a Botticelli painting. I'd seen Primavera at the Uffizi in Florence when we did a concert there, and I knew firsthand just how accurate that comparison was.

My gaze dropped to her lips. Dammit. The need to kiss her was just as strong now as it was then. It had almost happened four years ago, but I'd screwed everything up between us before I got the chance.

"I got to thinking while you were in the bathroom," she announced.

"Oh?" This was good. Lucy was filling all my senses, pushing my anxiety to a small, inconsequential corner.

"Yes." She narrowed her eyes. "I need to say something to you."

From the moment Lucy recognized me, there hadn't been so much as a split second where she'd looked awed or impressed by my fame. I was so used to being surrounded by fans, sycophants, and people who wanted something from me that Lucy's disdain was as refreshing as a glass of ice-cold water after crawl-

12

ing through a desert.

I looked at her chin, with that stubborn dimple that used to drive me crazy. I used to dream about kissing her there too, wondering whether it would make her sigh.

I felt myself harden. This was really not the time or place, but on the bright side at least there was one part of me that wasn't broken.

"Are you paying attention?" She snapped her fingers in my face.

I could *not* be imagining the feel of Lucy's soft body under mine when she was telling me off. "I'm listening."

"I've decided we should just ignore each other for the rest of the flight."

I wasn't sure of much these days, but I knew I could never ignore Lucy Snow. "I don't agree. I'd love to catch up. How old is Alice now?"

She frowned at me. "She's ten. Grade five."

"Wow. She must have changed so much compared to last time I saw her."

"Yes, four years tends to do that."

Her voice was like flint, so why did it sound better to me than a stadium full of screaming fans? "Have you been singing?"

She rolled her eyes. "What do you think?"

Lucy's voice was a miracle, and the thought that she wasn't sharing it with the world killed me as much now as it did back then. "I don't know, Luce. We haven't talked to each other in four years. I hope you have."

"Why do you care?"

"Because your voice is phenomenal." She had more talent in her pinky finger than I had in my entire body, and it made no sense that I was now a famous singer and musician, and she wasn't.

We'd spent countless hours rehearsing for the *Canada's Got Talent!* audition together. For six of the most intense months of my life, Lucy inhabited every thought and dream, day and night.

"You bailed on me half an hour before we were supposed to go on stage."

I exhaled through my nostrils. I'd made the worst mistake of my life signing that exclusivity contract for Northern Junk half an hour before my audition as Lucy's backup guitarist and singer.

Still, her belief she'd needed me to sing was wrong. "Yes, I made a commitment to be your backup guitarist and singer, and I should have honored that, but the truth is you'd grown past the point of needing me. The fact I signed on with Northern Junk was proof I was one thousand percent certain you could get on that stage by yourself and blow the judges away."

Her eyes widened. "Is that actually supposed to make me feel better?"

"It's the truth." Even now I still couldn't understand what was holding her back from believing in herself.

If I'd had so much as a sliver of doubt, I would never have accepted the offer to form a new band under the management of musical kingmaker Gary Simon, ringleader of all the *Got Talent!* shows.

It'd happened so fast. My parents had been so thrilled. They'd made it clear the idea of me turning down Gary's offer was unthinkable. I was their only child, and they'd poured so much love and attention into me. I often found myself wondering if I'd accepted Gary's offer for my parents' sake instead of mine.

"Is that what you tell yourself so you can sleep at night?"

How could I be enjoying myself right now? Yet, I was. God, I'd missed arguing with Lucy—it was like sitting beside a crackling bonfire—fascinating, warm, and a little bit dangerous all at the same time. "Did I just time travel back four years? How are we still having this conversation, Luce?"

"I asked you not to call me Luce." I was struck with that old desire to kiss the ferocity off her face. "And stop looking at me like that." She crossed her arms in front of her glorious cleavage.

"Like what?" I grinned, but a wave of dizziness made me clutch my forehead. God, when was the last time I'd eaten? Or drank water, for that matter? All I'd had was that gallon of black coffee at the airport with a valium chaser.

"Are you okay?" Her forehead puckered.

She leaned toward me and loosened the string around my hood so she could inspect my face. Oh lord, the feel of her warm fingertips against my skin … She still wore that clunky old watch that was her father's. I swallowed hard. "Just a bit dizzy."

"When is the last time you ate?"

Only Lucy could go from wanting to eviscerate me to worrying about me in a split second. I hated that taking care of other people—namely her spoiled mother and her little sister, Alice—had become such an unconscious reflex for Lucy since her father's fishing boat capsized. She took care of everyone except herself.

I shook my head. "I'm fine."

"No, you're not. I've never seen you this pale." She rummaged in the seat pocket in front of her and took out a small red-and-white-striped bag. Glory be to Stephen Hawking and Captain Kirk. Hawkins Cheezies. She thrust it at me. "Eat these."

I clutched the package to my chest. Their unnatural shade of fluorescent orange brought back so many memories of life before stardom. "Wow. Hawkins Cheezies? Do you know how impossible it is to find these outside Canada? I can't believe how much I missed—"

"Stop rhapsodizing and eat them. The salt will help the dizziness."

She was probably right. A bag of Hawkins contained roughly as much sodium as the entire Dead Sea. I opened them and popped the biggest, knobbiest one I could find in my mouth, groaning as a nostalgic explosion of chemicals and cheddar melted on my tongue.

Lucy watched as I ate. "Your color is improving," she observed after I'd almost demolished the bag.

"Thank you. These are perfection."

Her nostrils flared but the corner of her lips tilted up the tiniest bit—barely noticeable to anyone but me. "Fuck you, and you're welcome."

I burst out laughing. If there was ever a sentence that was more Lucy than that, I hadn't heard it. "God, it's good to see you again," I sighed.

"Speak for yourself." She chewed the inside of her cheek, considering me. "You should go back to sleep. You look like a vampire. Anyway, I don't want to talk to you for the rest of this flight."

"But—"

She held up a hand. "I mean it. I'm not interested in rehashing the past."

My head buzzed with frustration. "So, what's your plan?"

"We act like strangers for the rest of the flight. When we land at Heathrow, I'll go my way, and you'll go yours. We'll forget this unfortunate coincidence ever happened."

I knew I should agree, but I needed to make that little crease I loved between her eyebrows appear one last time. "You don't believe things happen for a reason?"

"Not anymore," she said. "You did an excellent job of correcting that delusion."

"Oh, come *on*," I protested. "Yes, I was young. Yes, I was stupid. Yes, I misjudged your readiness to walk out on stage by yourself, but you're making me sound like the devil."

There it was. That crease I longed to smooth out with my finger like I used to.

"I'm not alone in that assessment," she said. "Or haven't you read the tabloids recently?"

My heart sank. Wow. Low blow.

She noticed because her eyes filled almost instantly with regret. She shrugged. "Sorry, but I'm upset."

"Fine," I said, exhaustion rushing over me again. "But I have a limo picking me up, so at least let me offer you a ride wherever you need to go when we get there."

She turned back to her seat-back screen, where *Knives Out* was playing. So she still loved her whodunnits.

She ran her hand through her hair. "I'd rather jump out of this plane without a parachute."

CHAPTER THREE

Lucy

Had I missed the last bus to Oxford?

I dug my hands deeper in the pockets of my light blue peacoat, but they still weren't thawing.

The January night sky over the bus station outside Heathrow was drizzly and black. Not a single star peeped through. I should be used to cold, damp weather, but the shock of Jack must have lowered my resistance.

I was sure I'd read the website correctly. A bus to Oxford was supposed to arrive at the Heathrow bus station every twenty minutes. I'd been here forty-five minutes already.

My feet ached in my new leather ankle boots. Other buses pulled into the parking slots, sluicing through the puddles, then filled up with people and backed out again. Not a single one had "Oxford" on the front. I'd seen buses to Liverpool, Manchester, Bristol, Edinburgh, and a place called Shittington that I wasn't entirely sure was real or just a practical joke, but no Oxford.

I checked my dad's old watch. It was almost ten p.m.

He'd lost it at the pub the night his boat went down, and they'd given it back to us a week after his funeral. It was all I had left of him. I almost never took it off.

Trying but failing to ignore Jack the rest of the flight had sapped me of every last drop of energy. All I wanted to do was get to Oxford, crawl into any available bed, and push him to the far recesses of my mind again.

"Excuse me?" I asked an older man a few feet away. He was neat as a pin, wearing a three-piece suit and reading a newspaper.

It took me three tries, but he finally lifted his eyes from a headline announcing one of the princes of England was officially getting a divorce. So that's what constituted headline news in England—very different from the usual headlines of the St. John's Sentinel—yesterday it had been "Hungry Polar Bear warning in Northern Newfoundland."

"Yes?" he barked.

I'd heard the English could be more aloof than Canadians, but to be faced with this man's impatience when I was emotionally wrung out from my encounter with Jack was more than I could take. I swallowed down a sob of despair. I would not cry. I would *not.* "Sorry, but I'm looking for the bus to Oxford. Do you know when it's due to arrive?"

The man arched a disdainful brow. "It's not." He turned his paper around with a brisk snap and showed me an article on the page he'd been reading. "Oxford Connect Drivers Strike!" read the bold headline.

I sucked in a lungful of air to steady myself, but it was full of exhaust.

If this wasn't the culmination of a truly shit day ... I was stranded in London. I had only Canadian money on me. The exchange places I'd passed in the airport were already closed for the night.

I fought against the urge to sit down on the wet pavement and weep.

Was I going to have to go back to the airport and sleep in there until I could exchange money in the morning? I shivered. The mirage of a warm bed was receding even further.

A shiny black limo whooshed through the puddles in front of me. No matter how much I didn't want to see Jack again, I kicked myself for not taking up his offer to drive me wherever I needed to go. I had a gift for taking stubborn stands at the absolute worst moments.

The idea of him all warm and pampered inside a limo while I stood freezing in the rain was the perfect metaphor for our lives. Everything came easily to Jack. Nothing came easily to me.

Tires squealed, and I looked up to see the limo break hard. The spray drenched the people on the bus platform farther down from me. One man yelled, "Oi! Who do ye think you are?"

The limousine slowly rolled backward to where I was standing. What the—? Surely Jack had left Heathrow already.

A power window hummed down. Jack's face appeared, his hood pushed back, his cinnamon-hued hair a bit wild from the rain. I dropped my shoulders in surrender. I had no fight left in me.

"Hitchhiking again?" Jack's eyes sparkled in the yellow lights of the bus station.

I glanced over my shoulder at the newspaper man, who was now far more interested in me. His stare shifted back and forth between Jack Seary in the limo and me—a random Canadian girl with wet hair plastered across her face and a dripping wool jacket.

"Get in. I promise you can keep ignoring me." Jack's mouth hitched up at the side, flashing one of his famous dimples.

He didn't have to ask me again. At my core I was a pragmatist. I also liked being warm and dry. I grabbed my wheely suitcase and ran with my head low against the deluge, splashing through the puddles to the limo.

A tall, uniformed driver came around the side. He took my suitcase from my numb fingers. "I'll take care of this," he said in a soft British accent. So this was how the 1 percent lived. He opened the rear door and ushered me onto the bench seat opposite Jack.

I climbed in and onto the cream-colored leather. It was a completely different world. My body sank into the plushness.

Rain dripped from my hair into my eyes. Before I could say anything, Jack handed me a huge fluffy towel. "Here. You must be freezing."

I grudgingly took it. "Thank you."

"I turned the heat warmer up on your seat."

That's what that was. How was I supposed to hold my ground with Jack when I was currently enjoying a luxurious bum sauna?

He sniffed. "Why does it smell like a barn since you came in?"

I gingerly took off the culprit—my wet wool coat. I laid it on the heated seat beside me to try and dry it out a bit. "My coat is wool. When wool gets wet, it smells like sheep. Wet sheep."

"That's exactly what it smells like. Have you been to Scotland yet?"

"No." Jack didn't need to know this was my first time in Europe and that in the past four years I'd hardly gone anywhere.

"Whole country smells like wet sheep. Hand to God." He put his hand over the NASA insignia emblazoned across his chest.

"So NASA is still your god?"

His irresistible dimples bracketed a cheeky smile. He'd perked up quite a bit since the plane, surely thanks to the Canadian cure of a bag of Hawkins and a nap. "Some things never change."

I'd read somewhere about a TikTok account called @jacksearysdimples that had over 2 million followers.

In a way I got it. I'd been obsessed with Jack once, too. For six months four years ago, his face lit up my days, and his laugh tapped into a part of my heart that only he'd been able to access.

"Nerd," I breathed.

He grinned. Thank god we hadn't actually kissed or, god forbid, had sex, that night on the roof before the audition. It would've made this moment a thousand times more excruciating. Jack belonged to the whole world now, not to me.

I never thought I'd be grateful for the stench of wet sheep, but at least it helped block Jack from overwhelming my senses.

The limo slid forward into the rainy night as I took a stab at drying my hair with the impossibly fluffy towel. When I was done, I looked up to find Jack watching me. His green eyes were slightly bloodshot but soft, almost in a trance.

I was too intrigued to look away. Heat I couldn't attribute to my seat warmer bloomed through me. *It doesn't mean anything. It didn't when he used to study your face back then, and it doesn't now.* I used to think I knew how Jack's brain worked better than my own, but I'd been proved horribly wrong.

Silence thickened, punctuated only by the muted drips from my clothes and hair onto the seats and floor of the limo. What had it been like for him these past four years? My stomach quivered with nerves. In so many ways he was a stranger, and an intimidating one at that. He was a world-famous rock star who hung out with supermodels and Oscar winners. The Jack I used to know probably didn't even exist anymore.

He was the first to blink. "What happened to your bus?"

Enough thinking about the past. I hadn't come to England for Jack. Soon we would part ways—I would be a law student, and he would go back to touring and recording albums and being fawned over everywhere he went. We'd probably never see each other again.

I cleared my throat. "Evidently the bus drivers between Oxford and London are on strike."

"You're headed to Oxford?" Why was he looking at me like that?

"Yup."

He gnawed his bottom lip, still staring.

"Do I have snot running down my face or something?" It wasn't beyond the realm of possibility.

"What? No! I just ... no." He shook his head. "It's nothing. Where in Oxford do we need to drop you?"

I went back to drying my hair. It was still dripping down my neck. "Beaufort College. I'm a scholarship student there on the Remote Commonwealth Study Program." My voice was muffled by the towel.

A strangled sound came from Jack's side of the limo, but by the time I whipped the towel down, his face was a mask. "What?"

"Nothing."

It was something. "Why are you acting weird?" I demanded.

His eyes darted away from mine and gazed out the window. "Don't mind me. I'm just exhausted. So no buses to Oxford, eh?"

"Nope, but there was a bus to a place called Shittington." It was just the sort of absurd thing I adored and used to share with Jack.

"For real?"

"I saw a bus pull into the station with that name on the sign. Shittington. Do you think it's a real place or just a prank on tourists?"

He chuckled—a warm, generous sound I used to adore. He held up his index finger. "This requires immediate investigation." He tapped a few things into the latest, flashiest model of iPhone. "This is amazing," he murmured. His high cheekbones and finely etched lips glowed in the blue light from his screen.

I gave his shin a little nudge with the toe of my boot. "Don't keep me in suspense."

"There *is* a Shittington. It's located in Bedfordshire."

I settled back into my seat, smiling to myself. "That's one of the best things I've ever heard."

He put down his phone. "Let us not forget there is a place called 'Dildo' in Newfoundland. You know what they say about people in glass houses."

I tilted my chin. "Dildo is good, but Shittington is better. It almost makes up for today."

"Aw, come on, Luce." Jack used that cajoling tone that used to work so well on me. "Is seeing me again that terrible?"

"Yes."

"You must be shittington me."

I swallowed down my giggle. I couldn't let us slip back into our old dynamic. I couldn't let him off the hook and soften toward him again. His betrayal still hurt like barbed wire wrapped around my heart. "I'm serious, Jack."

He rubbed the side of his neck. My heart tripped. That was near the top of the list of soft, secret spots where I'd longed to kiss Jack. "Sorry, but I can't say the same."

I rolled my eyes. He'd always had lethal magnetism. Saying the right thing meant nothing if it didn't go along with doing the right thing.

He grimaced. "Fine. Change of topic. What are you going to study at Oxford?"

That question felt harmless enough. "Law. They call it Jurisprudence at Oxford, though."

"Huh." He rubbed his pinky with his thumb, a habit I knew well but wished I didn't.

"What?" I knew that "huh".

"It's just ..."

"Spit it out."

"I'm surprised about the law thing. What about your singing?"

"Unlike you, I have responsibilities. They inform my choices." Jack never had to look after anyone except himself. No wonder he couldn't understand my life.

I knew being accepted for this exchange and studying law at Oxford should feel like a massive gift from the universe—finally, a reward for all my sacrifice and hard work. What was wrong with me that it felt like a consolation prize?

An Oxford law degree would earn me good money to support my mom and especially Alice. "Oxford is one of the only places I can get a law degree in only two years instead of three. It's efficient, not to mention carries a ton of professional weight."

He frowned. "I always pictured you doing something creative."

I became aware again of that weird cognitive dissonance being here with Jack. In so many ways he looked like the same boy I rehearsed with for all those hours in the high school music room— the NASA hoodie certainly helped the illusion. The same crooked smile. The same lean, muscular frame that moved through the world with an ease everyone wanted a piece of. The same slightly crooked pinky finger.

But it was no longer him, I reminded myself. This person across from me had fame and money parallel to Lizzo and Harry Styles. I used to think we had so much in common, but now the gap between us felt uncrossable. Or maybe it had always been that way, and I'd just been deluding myself in more ways than one. "I'm not you, Jack."

"Maybe I'm not as cut out for this life as everyone thinks," he muttered.

That was ridiculous. Jack had that ineffable *it*. You couldn't be around him without wanting a crumb of his magic. The judges on *Canada's Got Talent!* had seen it immediately.

Besides, if he ever suffered a split second of doubt, he would just have to shift his gaze to his legions of hysterical, slavish fans, one of whom I'd read held an actual wedding with a cardboard cut-out of Jack in a green velvet tux.

"Of course you are."

His nostrils flared as he took a deep breath. "My parents would agree with you. They're enjoying this rock star ride far more than me."

That was a strange thing to say, but I wouldn't see him again—possibly ever—after this limo ride, so there was no point delving deep into it like we would've in the past. I tried to ignore the twinge of regret behind my sternum.

"Do you still watch Star Trek all the time?" I said, changing the topic.

When I'd known him, Jack had been obsessed with astronomy and space. He'd confessed to me that he dreamed of becoming an astrophysicist. I'd always liked that geeky side to him, but I was fairly certain it was now buried deep under the trappings of stardom.

The rain lashed against the windows. "Being a Trekkie is a life-time commitment. You know that."

A spark of relief ignited in me. Maybe there were still parts of him uncorrupted by his stratospheric rise. "Do you still like to watch for shooting stars?"

He sent me a sheepish smile that would have incinerated the panties of Jack Seary fans. I was ashamed it warmed me in places I vowed never to associate with Jack again.

"I don't have much time for that these days." He fiddled with the strings to his hoodie. "But I visit every planetarium possible on tour. Hey, do you remember that night when we went on the roof of the school and saw all those shooting stars?"

Pain lanced through my chest. Of course he'd forgotten what had happened that night. He'd surely been with a thousand girls since then.

That was the night after we'd finally admitted our mutual crushes and had vowed to kiss for the first time once we finished our audition.

But the audition never happened, so neither did the kiss.

He'd come to me with a flushed face and told me fifteen minutes before it was time to go on that he'd signed a contract with Gary Simon—notorious music agent and Svengali—to become part of a boy band called Northern Junk.

The initial shock had paralyzed me. Becoming a famous singer was my dream, not his. He'd robbed me.

"But you want to be an astrologist," I'd said, my voice sounding far away. "Not a rock star."

He'd shrugged. "My parents think I could be both, and that maybe by being a rock star for a few years I could earn enough money to study stars for the rest of my life. They're so excited."

"We'll talk about this later," I said, trying to muster up the bare minimum to be able to go out and perform. "Right now we need to perform. Do you think you should change that D chord to a C?"

"Lucy." He took my arms in his hands. "The contract I just signed means I can't perform with anyone else."

"What?" My brain couldn't compute this.

He'd flushed red. "It's a standard clause, apparently, but it's okay."

"How is it possibly okay?" My voice came out in a shriek.

"The thing is, Lucy, you don't need me on stage with you. Your voice stands on its own. You can do this. I know you can. I'll be cheering you on from the wings."

But I couldn't and I didn't. He'd bailed on both the kiss and the audition I'd pinned my dreams on.

How could Jack have forgotten all that? The idea that he took up infinitely more space in my brain than I did in his prickled like tiny needles under my skin.

I snuck a peek at his face, but we were passing through a tunnel, and it was cast in shadows.

"I ..." he began after at least a minute. "I'm sorry. I forgot for a second—"

"I really don't want to talk about it." I cut him off. "Once you drop me off, I'll probably never see you again. None of that matters anymore."

"But you need to—"

"I'm over it," I lied. In so many ways, I was the exact same girl he'd left high and dry on that soundstage. I was many things, but 'over it' was not one of them.

"I'm not." His voice was a whisper from the other side of the limo.

I cleared my throat. Bringing up the past had thickened the air in the limo, and it pressed down on my lungs. We burst out of the tunnel, and the streetlights lit him in yellow again. His eyes had bags underneath, and his excellent bone structure was leaning toward gaunt instead of chiseled. Even the spray of freckles over his nose and cheekbones seemed faded.

"You look terrible, by the way."

There was a ghost of a smile. "Thanks, Luce."

"Seriously, I've never seen you look so worn out."

He bit his lip and nodded. "That's why I'm in England. I need to figure some things out. Get my head on straight. Do something completely different for a bit."

"You're quitting Northern Junk?" I asked, incredulous. Throwing away such an amazing opportunity was unfathomable.

He shook his head. "I couldn't even if I wanted to. I'm still under contract—a very binding contract. Gary has agreed to let me take eight weeks off to disappear and get my ... stuff ... back under control."

"Stuff?"

He waved his hand. "It's nothing. Like you said, rock star whining. I have a concert commitment soon at Wembley, though. I couldn't get out of that."

"I heard Northern Junk had to cancel a few concerts already." I shouldn't be worrying about him, but I was.

His mouth tightened and he rubbed his torso. "Yeah. It can't happen again."

"But you're clearly not well—"

"Go to sleep," he said, his words a shut door and a caress.

I curled up in my corner. I was too tired to be having this conversation anyway. I closed my eyes, then cracked one open again to find him watching me—The past four years folded in on itself.

"Stop watching me," I said. "It's as creepy as it ever was. Besides, you look like you need to sleep even more than I do."

He pulled his hoodie tight around his face. "You're probably right."

CHAPTER FOUR

Jack

Flashes of light bouncing off my eyelids woke me up with a jerk. I didn't need to be fully conscious to know exactly what that was. Paparazzi.

I wiped drool off the side of my mouth. I hadn't just slept in the limo—I'd slipped into a post-travel coma.

Shit. Lucy.

I looked over to see her curled up across from me, still fast asleep. She'd taken off her sweater. The V-neck on her white T-shirt she wore showed off her phenomenal cleavage. Blood rushed to my groin.

How could Lucy still have the knack of arousing me at the most inconvenient times?

Get a grip. If she woke up and caught me staring at her breasts, she was completely capable of kicking me in the nuts with those pointy leather boots of hers. What was wrong with me that I found her fierceness sexy?

I had to think fast, but my woozy head felt detached from the rest of my body. Who had leaked? Was it the driver? I'd never used him before, but he'd come highly recommended. I racked my brain, trying to figure out how the paparazzi had found out my limo was coming to Beaufort College.

I pressed my palm hard against my sternum, trying but failing to ease the growing pressure there. I should have told Lucy already. If I'd known the media would be here to greet us, I would have. Blood pounded in my ears, making it difficult to think.

Lucy went from sleeping to sitting bolt upright in a millisecond. "Where are we?" She turned a panicked expression on me. "What's happening?"

A glimmer of clarity parted the curtains of my panic. Protecting Lucy came first—my priority was getting her safely into the college. I'd figure out the rest after. "It's okay." I tried to prevent my anxiety from spreading to her. "It's just photographers. The news of our destination must have leaked."

"But how?" she demanded, sharp as always. "You made this detour only to drop me off here."

I opened my mouth to tell her when the window between us and the chauffeur buzzed down.

In the passenger seat him was a man I'd never seen before. He had coal-black eyes and wore a bowler hat. I wondered briefly if he had teleported directly from a Dickens novel.

"Name's Robbie," he said with a curt nod. "I'm the porter of Beaufort College. I've been sent out here to bring you inside."

Lucy swiveled around in her seat. "It's me you want. My name is Lucy Snow. I'm arriving to start the Remote Commonwealth Study Program."

The porter's eyebrows shot up. "Yes. I've been expecting you, but not like this."

"This is not exactly how I envisioned my arrival either," she said with a glance at me. "How am I going to get through this crowd?" She peered out the window where the flashes were still going like machine gunfire and turned back to me, her blue eyes darker than usual. "They look rabid, Jack."

"Sorry. They always are."

"God, really?" Her face was the picture of pity. I wanted many things from Lucy, but pity wasn't one of them.

"Fear not," Robbie said bracingly. "I've got some experience dealing with them." The vice around my chest eased a bit. There was just something reassuring about him, like he'd seen all there was to see in the world and knew exactly how to handle it. "Let's leave the proper introductions for once we're safely inside Beaufort."

The chauffeur and Robbie bent their heads together and devised a plan where they would act as human barriers to give Lucy and me a clear channel to run into the college doors.

"You don't have to come in with me," Lucy said, casting wary eyes at the flashing outside her window. "It's probably better if you don't. I appreciate the ride, but you should just carry on to wherever you were headed."

Should I tell her now? No, better to get her in the college safely and then tell her privately—I had no idea how she was going to react, although I'd bet on a version of *not well*. "I'm coming in with you."

She rolled her eyes. "Why? There's no need."

"I'll tell you when we get inside."

"Fine. Whatever. Suit yourself."

For a little while after that there was no time to think. Robbie and the chauffeur strong-armed me and Lucy through the cameras and the rainy night and somehow managed to get us past the massive, ancient-looking doors.

The chauffeur shut the big wooden doors behind us, leaving all the paps on the other side. Robbie herded us into a small room that reeked of wood polish and was lined with what looked like mail slots on the walls.

"Now." He touched his bowler hat. "We can talk in peace."

"Thank you for your help." I meant it. There was nothing quite as valuable as people who could keep a cool head no matter what. I would never stop feeling guilty I didn't have that skill. I was too sensitive, my parents told me. Too much of a diva, I knew my bandmates whispered behind my back. Ungrateful, according to Gary. "I wasn't expecting them here. I have no idea who leaked."

Robbie shrugged, nonplussed. "Those devils have their ways of finding out. I've seen it before."

I couldn't help but wonder what experience an Oxford porter could have possibly had with the paparazzi in such a serene, academic setting, but come to think about it, my knowledge of Oxford wasn't all that extensive.

He clapped his hands together. "Now! I've been told—or rather, firmly ordered—by the first Remote Commonwealth exchange student to welcome you politely and not to, in her words, 'be a scary grump.'" He was fighting back a smile. "When you meet her, you'll realize disobeying Cedar is not a wise option."

Cedar? I'd never come across that name, and names could get weird in the music world.

William Cavendish-Percy, who spearheaded this exchange program, had told me another one of his Commonwealth Program students was already attending Beaufort. He hadn't mentioned much else about her, except that she came from the other coast of Canada—a good eight-or-nine-hour plane ride away from Newfoundland. That didn't even include connections.

"I'll be on my best behavior with you two, unlike how I welcomed her." Robbie went behind the partitioned-off desk area, where a pegboard full of keys hung on the wall. "Now, rooms!"

My gaze shifted to Lucy.

"There must be some mistake." Lucy blinked, bewildered. "I'm the only one who'll be staying. I need only one room."

Robbie raised an eyebrow at me. I couldn't delay this any longer. She was going to eviscerate me.

I cleared my throat. "Actually, Lucy, you're not."

Her forehead wrinkled. "Not what?"

"Not the only student coming here this term on the Remote Commonwealth Program. There's two of us." I pointed at her. "You." I turned my finger back on myself. "And me."

Her peachy complexion drained of color, and the memory of the last time I'd been the cause of that weighed in my gut. How was I going to make her believe this was all the weirdest coincidence, just as much for me as for her?

"No," she whispered and shook her head. "If this is some sort of joke, stop it, Jack. It's not funny."

I winced, wishing I could spare her this. "It's not a joke. This is what I'm doing for my break. I've arranged to come and study astrophysics here at Oxford for the term. At Beaufort."

"But—but that's impossible." Her knuckles turned white as she clutched the handle of her wheely suitcase. "You're a famous musician, not a student."

I bit my lip. She'd always had a way of making me aware of my own imposter syndrome. "Yes, I'm a musician, but I've always dreamed of being a student."

"But I don't want you here," she burst out.

I knew I deserved that, but it stung all the same.

Robbie sucked in air between his teeth. "Crikey," he muttered.

"I had no idea you'd be here. I swear. I mean, what are the

chances?"

This was answered with stony silence.

"I promise I'll do everything I can to stay out of your way." It was the last thing I wanted to do, but I would do it for her.

"That might be difficult," Robbie interjected. "Beaufort prides itself on being a small, close-knit college."

"Wonderful," Lucy said, with enough flint to let us all know it was anything but. She narrowed her eyes at me. "How did you even get in? The application process was brutal. I had to work so freaking hard for this. Let me guess—this was handed to you on a platter too."

My face burned. She hadn't lost the ability to aim her arrow directly at my vulnerable places. She wasn't wrong. I was friendly with William Canvendish-Percy, who founded and funded the exchange program from his own staggering personal fortune. We ran in the same circles, and I'd always liked him.

The last time we'd met up was at a gala in Sydney, Australia.

I'd just experienced a massive panic attack onstage in the middle of a Northern Junk concert, and the stagehands had had to turn on auto-tune while I struggled to breathe, let alone lip-sync.

Not many people had noticed, but William had, and I'd found myself pouring out my heart to him at the $1,000-a-plate dinner he'd organized in the Sydney Opera House. He was a good listener, and his varied, adventurous life meant he didn't judge.

He'd told me about his exchange program and suggested it might be a way to get a much-needed break from performing. I'd made a hefty donation to his environmental charity, and he hadn't even asked for my grades. Lucy had hit the nail on the head. I'd bought my way in, pure and simple. "I'm friends with William Cavendish-Percy," I admitted.

Her face twisted. "I knew it," she muttered. "Do you even realize the rest of us don't go through life with four-leaf clovers shoved up our arses?"

I'd heard versions of the same thing from my doting parents, my agent, Gary, and everyone attached to the band. *Jack, do you know how many people would love to trade places with you?*

They really didn't need to remind me. Nobody was made more miserable than me by the fact I felt like I was living the wrong life. I'd been desperate to escape. William had offered me an escape hatch and, greedily, it never even occurred to me not to take it.

The bitterness in Lucy's eyes made my stomach churn. If I could only make her understand that I wasn't at Oxford to remind her of the past or get in her way. "I'm sorry. Truly."

Before she could respond, a very damp couple came into the lodge holding hands.

"Thank heavens," Robbie muttered under his breath.

The man combed a hand through his wet, dark hair. "What's going on, Robbie? There were loads of paps outside, but Cedar and I waltzed right by them. They barely even clocked us. And with the princess's divorce and her being shacked up with my father too!"

Now I could see his face properly, this tall, posh guy seemed familiar. Had I seen him before in Capri? Or maybe London?

"They're not here for you, Alfie." Robbie inclined his head toward me. "They've found bigger fish to fry." He waved his hand at us. "Alfie, Cedar, meet our new exchange students, Jack Seary and Lucy Snow."

Lucy stood deadly still. I could tell from the tension in her jaw she was clenching her teeth, something she always did when she was angry.

The girl—Cedar—pushed back the hood of a rain jacket and turned amber eyes on us. "Was Robbie on his best behavior like I made him promise he would be?" She cast him a minatory look.

"He was," I said. Lucy managed a nod.

Robbie let out an affronted gasp. "Have some faith, Cedar!"

Her unusual face lit up with a wide grin. "I do. I'm just teasing." She winked at us. "I'm so glad you're here, Jack and Lucy. Welcome to Beaufort. I'm Cedar, from BC. I was in your position only a few months ago. I'm here to help so you don't have to flounder like I did. Settling into Oxford life was more of an adjustment than I expected." She shook off the droplets that clung to her coat and stepped forward to shake our hands.

Alfie tilted his head, and I could tell from the little nod he gave himself that he recognized me too. He stuck out his hand when we were done shaking Cedar's. "I'm Alfie, Cedar's boyfriend. Pleased to meet you both. Say, Jack, weren't you a guest on Lord Sotherby's yacht in Capri two summers ago?"

"I was."

I didn't even dare look at Lucy's expression for fear it would eviscerate me on the spot.

Alfie snapped his fingers and smiled. "I knew it! Were you still there when Colin Firth drank too much grappa and fell overboard?"

I laughed, remembering. "Not only was I there, but I was the one who jumped into the Mediterranean to fish him out."

Alfie chuckled. "That's right! How could I have forgotten?"

Lucy muttered something undecipherable under her breath.

"Thank you for taking some of the paparazzi heat off me," Alfie said. "I'm in your debt."

That's right. Alfie was being modest, because if memory served correct, he was a high-level aristocrat—a lord or earl or duke or something—and heir to one of the wealthiest families in England. Or was it Scotland?

Cedar, though, was staring at me as though as though she was trying to solve a riddle. "I'm confused," she said. "Why does the paparazzi care about Lucy and Jack?"

"It's not for me," Lucy clarified with a withering look in my direction. "I'm just a nobody from Newfoundland."

"You are not." I reached out to touch her arm reflexively, but she jerked it away. Yeah. That was a dumb thing to attempt.

"I am," she insisted. "They're here for Jack, obviously."

Alfie was looking down at Cedar, his lips curved in amusement. Cedar shrugged. "Okay, but why?"

"Sorry to break this to you, Jack, but Cedar has no idea who you are." Alfie slipped his arm across her shoulders.

"I don't mean it as an insult." Cedar splayed her palms in apology. "Before coming to Oxford I lived my entire life in the woods."

"With bears," Alfie added, his face glowing with pride. My first impression of Alfie when I met him off Capri was that he was just like so many other British aristocrats—impossibly repressed. Now he seemed like a different person altogether.

"Wait a second. You really have no idea who he is?" Lucy pointed at me, an expression of unholy glee on her face now. Fine. I could give her this.

Cedar shook her head. "None. Sorry."

"You're not joking?"

"No."

"You cannot know how happy that makes me."

"Good, I guess?" Cedar said. "Don't worry about it, Jack. Alfie will fill me in. Are you both tired?"

Both Lucy and I nodded. Finally something we could agree on.

"I remember how I was when I arrived. After all that travel, all I wanted to do was find a bed and curl up in it. Are you two feeling like that?"

I'd been feeling like that for the past four years. "Yes."

Lucy's body sort of drooped in on itself. I restrained myself from slipping my arm around her to prop her up.

"I thought so. It's a lot to take in at first, but everything feels easier after a good night's sleep. Let's get you to your rooms. Alfie and I stocked them with some snacks and made up the beds for you."

Alfie eyed me, shifting uneasily from one foot to the other. "Are you sure you're going to be all right?" he asked me.

I understood the subtext, even though I didn't much appreciate it.

Alfie knew I was used to unparalleled luxury and service in my life now, but he didn't know those two things had become precisely what I'd grown to hate. I was never alone since joining Northern Junk. Honestly, right now the idea of a simple college bedroom with a door I could shut and lock felt like the closest thing to heaven on earth. "I'll be fine. I've been famous only for the past four years of my life."

"Do you want to take us up, Robbie?" Cedar waved us back out of the Lodge.

CHAPTER FIVE

Lucy

It felt late, as though the entire college except us had gone to bed a long time ago. I checked my dad's watch. Twelve thirty. What day was it even?

A magical hush blanketed the looming stone buildings surrounding the path Cedar led us along. A few squares of pale light came from the windows above us. Our footsteps echoed on the wet flagstones at our feet.

This moment would totally be living up to my Oxford daydreams if it weren't for the red-haired reminder of my greatest blunder in judgment walking in front of me.

The horrible coincidence created a numbness in my core that was spreading out to my arms and legs as we walked.

It wasn't the same for Jack as it was for me. He was here at Oxford for a kind of rock star vacation—a lark, a whim. I was here to get a degree that would support my family. I ground my molars together. Where was *my* fairy godmother?

Cedar led us up a steep set of stone stairs I would have admired under any other circumstance. Robbie and Alfie had insisted on carrying my suitcase and bag and tried to take Jack's as well except he wouldn't hear of it. He was no doubt trying to make a point of not acting like a spoiled celebrity. It was going to be interesting to see how long that lasted.

I longed to be unconscious. The idea of shutting off the current reality of Jack's tousled cinnamon waves mounting the stairs ahead of me would be a deliverance.

The knee-jerk reaction of hopping on a plane back to Newfoundland occurred to me, but where would that leave me? I'd never get another window of opportunity like this again. I'd be damned if I was going to let Jack Seary ruin another one of my dreams.

Maybe I could just ignore him. That was the thing with Jack, though. Even now, cheesed off at him as I was, I couldn't help noticing his long legs and the perfect butt in front of me.

We reached a small landing with three doors leading off it. "Which one of us is up here?" Jack asked.

Cedar winced. "There's no easy way to say this, but it's both of you."

"What?" I demanded in a voice that sounded dangerously close to a growl. Next she was going to tell us we had to share a bunk bed.

"Sorry. I had no idea you two knew each other. I thought putting you in rooms across the landing from one another meant you wouldn't feel as alone as I did. How could I have known you two have ..." She waved her hand between us, at a loss for words.

"History," Alfie supplied.

Cedar snapped her fingers. "That's it. *History*. I mean, what are the chances?"

She would be surprised. Fate had it in for me. It was as simple as that.

Jack scrubbed his face with his hand. "I don't think Lucy wants me right next door cramping her style."

At least he was right about that.

"I get that now." Cedar shrugged. "What can I say? It seemed like a good idea at the time."

Jack mouthed "sorry" to me. I just shook my head. Was it his fault or fate's? I was too tired to figure it out.

"Let's deal with the room thing tomorrow," Alfie said. "Jack, you are swaying on your feet."

God. He was. This day just needed to end. "Yes," I agreed. "Sleep first."

"All right then." Cedar unlocked one door and then the other. "This is your room, Lucy." She pushed open the door on the right of the landing. Then she did the same with the one on the left. "And Jack." I wondered what was behind the middle door, the one between our two rooms.

Cedar flicked on the light and led me into my room. It smelled faintly of mothballs and tea but in a comforting way. The bed was made up and pushed to the far wall, below one of the two windows. On the bedside table was a tiny vase with a few snowdrops in it. My heart—such a tight, aching thing since seeing Jack on the plane—eased a bit.

"I heard these grow in Newfoundland," Cedar said, waving at the flowers.

"They do. They're beautiful." I reached out and touched her arm. "I swear I'm not normally like this. Seeing Jack again is a shock."

Alfie was hovering by the door jam.

Cedar rested a hand on my arm. "Don't worry. The experience of my arrival here cured me of ever trusting first impressions."

She and Alfie shared a loaded look.

"I'll go and help Robbie show Jack the ropes while you finish up here, Cedar," Alfie said.

Cedar's tour didn't last long. The room was small but perfect. There was a tiny bathroom with an old cast-iron tub and shower. It was scrubbed to within an inch of its life and included a shower curtain. Another tiny vase of snowdrops sat on the sink.

In the main room a big, slightly lopsided antique armoire was positioned against the wall across from the bed. It was full of hangers and shelves for all my things. Beside that was a built-in wooden bookcase and a desk. On the desk was a bunch of maps and brochures.

Cedar had orchestrated all this. Tears pricked at the corners of my eyes. It was such a novelty to have someone look after me for a change.

"So you're going to be studying law here?" She leaned down and smoothed a wrinkle from the duvet on the bed.

I nodded. "I need to graduate with a degree I can start using right away. How about you?"

She chuckled. "Alfie and I both study medieval literature. It's probably one of the most impractical degrees at Oxford, but I love it. Alfie's a few years ahead of me. He was my junior professor when we met, but we're practically the same age."

That was unusual. "I take it that didn't go over well at first?"

She shook her head. "Nope. We didn't even like each other to begin with, but it's amazing what can happen over the eight weeks of a term here at Oxford."

Eight weeks with Jack Seary at the same small Oxford college. Why, life? What had I done to deserve this on top of everything else?

She went to the desk and tapped on a map there. "I made this to show you how to get to the hall. That's where you go for meals. I wrote down the mealtimes here along the side. If you want to set your alarm for tomorrow morning, breakfast starts at nine o'clock because it's Sunday. It starts earlier during the week."

"Perfect."

"After breakfast do you want me to take you to get your academic robe and all that before your tutorials start? You'll need it. I learned that the hard way too." She smiled to herself.

The only time I'd asked for help since my dad died was when I'd asked Jack to accompany me in the *Canada's Got Talent!* audition. That had exploded in my face so spectacularly it cured me of ever depending on anyone again. I didn't want Cedar to feel beholden to guide me around, especially the way I'd been acting. "I'm sure I can figure it out. You must be busy enough."

"Honestly, I'm happy to do it. Alfie can take Jack. Separately," she added.

There was no way I could refuse such a gracious offer without coming across as more churlish than I already had. "That would be great, but after that I'll be fine to figure things out. I promise."

"I'm always here to help. I'll leave you to sleep now. Sweet dreams."

"Thanks, Cedar."

"No problem." She shut the door gently behind her.

I faceplanted on my new bed. Alone. Finally. My phone vibrated in my back pocket. Crap. With the limo ride and Jack, I'd forgotten to call home when I landed. That was so unlike me, but Jack always had a way of making me careless about my responsibilities.

I fished it out and rolled over with my phone pressed to my ear. "Mom," I said. "I'm so sorry. I just got into my room this instant."

"Jesus, Lucy. I've been pacing back and forth across the kitchen for hours." Her voice was even more strained than it usually was.

Pointlessly fretting was my mom's default setting.

"She has! She's worn a groove into the floor." I heard Alice pipe up from somewhere close by, probably sitting at the kitchen table. I was on speakerphone.

"Why didn't you call like you promised?" my mom demanded.

My mom was nothing like Jack's mom, or the parents of the other kids I'd known in school. She didn't make after-school snacks or check Alice's homework or do much besides dream up worst-case scenarios and let me take care of everything. Her parents had spoiled her, and then my dad did the same, and when he died, he passed that baton to me. Of course I'd taken it on, even though I was only eleven. What else was I going to do? Besides, there was my little sister, Alice, to think of.

I considered not telling my mom about Jack, but Alice was a devoted fan of Northern Junk and would no doubt eventually figure out he was at the same college. Better to pre-empt that discovery.

"I'm so sorry. Jack Seary ended up being in the seat beside me on the plane, and ... well, he's taking an eight-week break in England. At Beaufort College. Can you believe that? I'm still in shock."

My mother disliked a lot of people, but she reserved her hate for only a few. Jack Seary was one of them. The day I'd come back from the audition-that-never-was, too devastated by Jack's betrayal to hide that I'd been rehearsing in secret, she got angrier than I'd ever seen her in that unguarded moment and told me a detail about my father's death that I'd wished ever since I could unknow.

She blamed Jack for me going astray and shifting my focus on something other than helping her.

"Did you plan this?"

Disbelief stole my breath for a second. "Are you seriously asking me that?" I demanded.

"It's a sign," she said. "You belong at home, not partway across the world, away from us. Families belong together, Lucy."

I'd accepted I'd have to remind my mother again and again why I was studying at Oxford, but I didn't think I'd have to defend my position this early. "This is the best way I can earn a good living for all of us in the shortest period of time, Mom. Remember? We agreed."

"You bulldozed me," she grumbled.

"It'll go by fast," I said. "I promise the sacrifice will be worth it."

"Something has already come up since you left."

"What?" My heart skipped a beat. It had been only twenty-four hours.

"Alice's teacher recommended she get an educational assessment done."

Nothing life-threatening. Good. "When did this happen?"

"Today!" Alice shouted. She sounded like she was standing right beside my mom. "I see a lot of the letters upside-down and back to front when I'm reading. The teacher told me today most people don't see them like that. Is that true?"

My stomach sank. "It's true."

"Who knows how much that is going to cost," my mom continued, her voice full of doom.

I massaged my temple with my free hand. I should have known that even with the Atlantic between us, my role as caretaker would never cease for a second. The audition had been my one— my only—attempt to reach for a better future. One of the many reasons why I could never forgive Jack was because his betrayal had shown me just how dangerous it was to hope.

"This is actually a good thing, mom." It was a struggle to locate my last remaining shred of positivity. "If Alice has a learning issue, the earlier it's diagnosed and she gets the help she needs, the better. When you find out how much it's going to cost, let me know."

"But where will we get the money from? You'll have to come home," she said again. "I don't think I can manage it."

"I'll figure something out."

"Maybe we shouldn't get her tested."

"We're getting her tested."

"But—"

As usual I wished more than anything that my mother would magically grow a backbone one of these days. "If it's stressing you out, just get Alice to pass on the information directly to me. I'll manage it from here."

"Fine." She made a funny little sound of disappointment.

Five minutes later I managed to hang up. My dad's watch felt heavy on my wrist. The promise I'd made my father just before he died had followed me across the Atlantic.

FIRST WEEK

CHAPTER SIX

—

Jack

The next morning I woke up with the familiar monster of anxiety prowling around the edges of my mind, ready to ambush me the second I let down my guard.

Mornings were the hardest. The thought of having to fight against myself all day was so exhausting that it took everything I had to throw my duvet back and get out of bed.

Maybe if I just stayed on the move, I could outpace it. Robotically, I showered and put on fresh clothes. I grabbed the map Cedar had made and headed out the door to find the cafeteria. What had Alfie called it last night? The hall. That was it.

My stomach rumbled. Eating might keep the panic at bay. I hadn't eaten anything except Lucy's bag of cheezies since before my departure from St. John's. A doctor Gary had set me up with once after a particularly horrendous panic attack in Hong Kong had explained my body was like a thermometer. I needed sleep, rest, food, and a lack of stress to keep my resistance to anxiety high. As soon as the mercury dropped too low, the monster became fucking Godzilla.

The idea my anxiety had any logic or pattern to it was seductive. It would be much easier to manage that way. But the truth was it pounced on me whenever it felt like it, often when I least expected it. It hunted me every waking second of every day. The monster was not just terrifying, but an unrepentant asshole.

I shut and locked my bedroom door behind me with my new key and stole a glance at Lucy's door, hesitating. She'd never been a morning person, so I was fairly certain she was still in her room. I debated knocking on her door to see if she wanted to come with me.

Then, I remembered her look of horror on the plane, then again in the lodge when she'd realized she was going to be in my proximity for the next eight weeks. I would trade a million diehard fans to get Lucy to look at me the way she had four years ago when I'd walked into the high school music room in Newfoundland after answering her Craigslist ad for a backup guitarist and vocalist.

I paced back and forth between her door and mine on the shared landing, trying very hard not to think of her warm body under the duvet or the sweet fullness of her mouth as she slept. My zipper started to cut into me. At least one part of my anatomy was certainly awake.

That decided it. Lucy wanted as much space from me as possible. She hadn't forgiven me. Besides, I obviously couldn't control my physical reaction to her. It would be better for us both if I just let her be.

I headed down the stone staircase, determined to keep my distance.

Following the map, I made my way across a quad and stopped in the middle, stunned at the absolute quiet. My anxiety receded a bit as I took in the morning mist floating above the perfectly manicured rectangles of grass.

The swirling white obscured the bottoms of the golden stone buildings surrounding the quad, making them look as though they were floating in the morning air. They looked as untethered to reality as my anxiety made me feel. Whenever I'd tried to hold on to something solid in the past four years—the music, Gary, my parents, my bandmates, it had a way of evaporating between my fingers.

I filled my lungs with cold, wet January air. Could Oxford be my anchor? It was a desperate last-ditch effort, but something about the calm of the morning here gave me hope that maybe, this time, it could be different. Lucy probably thought this Oxford thing was a whim for me, but the opposite was true. Everything rode on the next eight weeks.

Maybe I could feel safe enough here at Beaufort to get to the root of the lead blanket of unease I dragged everywhere with me these days. My biggest worry was that this one term wasn't going to be nearly enough.

I started walking again. Eventually I found another set of wide stone steps in the next building over. According to the map, the hall was at the top. It was a shame, really, that Lucy and I couldn't discover this new place together. I'd always savored seeing the world through her eyes.

Ah! There were the doors to the hall, huge and wooden the way Alfie had described them. I shoved them open with my shoulder.

They banged shut behind me. This place was no cafeteria—it was straight out of a movie. Huge wooden tables held tidy rows of lamps down the middle under an intricate arched wooden ceiling. A collection of oil paintings featuring scowling old men anchored the far end. This space oozed atmosphere.

It took me a few seconds to register the loud buzz of conversation had dropped to complete silence.

Right. I was famous.

Lucy had treated me with such indifference I'd completely forgotten people would stare. And comment. And probably take furtive photos.

Alfie had explained the night before the entire college body had been briefed about my arrival and given a set of guidelines about interacting with me. There were supposed to be no photos and no demands for autographs.

"Although I can't stop people from trying to come and talk to you," Alfie had added apologetically.

"No need," I'd assured him, eager to put his mind at ease. I'd been naïve.

I concentrated on dragging air in through my windpipe, which now felt no wider than a straw. How was I supposed to breathe again? I reached up and pressed hard against the pressure building under my solar plexus. What I would give to always feel like I did with Lucy yesterday—to be just Jack Seary, the space nerd from St. John's, Newfoundland and not Jack Seary, world-famous guitarist and singer of Northern Junk.

The stares and murmurs were getting louder. Sweat broke out on my temples. I couldn't show my panic. Not here. Not now. These days I couldn't even use a public bathroom without being followed. I'd done enough therapy to know I didn't suffer from social anxiety, but the idea of having a panic attack in front of anyone turned my blood to ice.

The pressure behind my ribs increased and everything became unreal, like the time I saw myself on a movie screen when Gary made me attend the excruciating Northern Junk documentary premiere.

I scanned the hall for other exits. Nothing. I couldn't turn around without everyone speculating over my behavior, but if I continued into the hall, I'd be trapped.

I wished for the thousandth time I could go back in time and not sign that contract with Gary, not join Northern Junk. Unlike Lucy, a music career had never been my dream. It had been my parents' dream. Back then I'd believed making them happy was enough.

People's stares were becoming questions. Why was I acting so strangely? *Move, you idiot.*

I shoved my hands in my pockets and took a step, then another. Just to walk I felt like I had to concentrate or I wouldn't get it right. I made my way into the side room of the cafeteria, where Alfie had explained I would pick up my food.

I should have knocked on the door and asked Lucy to come to breakfast. Even furious with me, the idea of her beside me felt like a safe harbor. I didn't even care if she spent the whole time giving me shit and skewering me with her barbed tongue.

As soon as I stepped into the back room, the chatter from the main hall exploded, ten times louder than it'd been before. It was peppered with shrieks and tiny screams. I coughed, trying to make my windpipe a bit bigger. Were they talking about how weird I was acting?

When I sat at an empty wooden table, I finally considered the meal I'd ordered on automatic pilot while I concentrated on not hyperventilating. Coffee, orange juice, toast and jam, and two fried eggs. Why hadn't I picked up a piece of fruit at least?

Usually, the band's chef or a caterer on the road whipped up a protein, kale, and fruit shake full of antioxidants and healthy things my body needed to perform at the highest level. It was a shame all that nutrition never had the slightest impact on my anxiety.

Within a minute, students—predominantly, but not exclusively, female ones—filled up the benches on either side of my table and the bench opposite me as well. If they only knew how their presence made me want to crawl off to a solitary dark place, where I could suffer alone.

None of them tried to talk to me right away, so I kept my head down and bit off a chunk of toast. My breath was coming in short, staccato bursts, and my head spun. I tensed my muscles, resisting the need to flee the scene, to run and hide in my room while I did my "break the glass in case of emergency" guided meditation. I tried to chew, but the toast was so unappetizing it might as well have been the tuna eyeballs Gary had tricked me into eating one time in Tokyo.

My heart pounded. I hated being watched.

A girl who was being hissed at by her friends while I was failing spectacularly at eating toast like a normal human, cleared her throat.

"You're new here, right?" she asked. "I thought I'd introduce myself. Beaufort College has a reputation of being one of the friendliest colleges, you know."

My stomach churned but I smiled, regardless of the fact it felt like the toast was about to do a U-turn and I was seconds away from throwing up all over her. I knew what would happen if I didn't act polite and gracious. It would be reported to some 'anonymous' news source. The rumors I was a drug addict would spread.

Everyone had a cell phone on them, and the ways people could surreptitiously take photos and videos were as crafty as they were numerous. As bonkers as it was, a blurry video of me forgetting how to eat could net enough for one of my fellow students to retire on.

"Yes, I am," I answered politely, secretly impressed with how relatively normal I sounded "What's your name?"

"Abila. I'm studying Classics. What about you?"

"Astrophysics," I said. Okay. I could do this. This conversation wasn't much, but it was better than the shouted squeals and weeping I normally got. What a relief it was to discuss academics instead of Northern Junk's latest album.

My panic receded a bit. Encouraged, I turned to the girl beside her. "And you?"

Her face went as red as a traffic light. "Philosophy."

"How interesting. Do you enjoy it?"

"Um ... I ... That is to say ... Yes." She stumbled over her words. If only people saw the mess I was inside, their nerves around me would vanish instantly.

"How are you liking things so far?" the first girl asked.

"I only arrived last night," I began, hearing my voice as though it came from someone else and I was just a puppet. "But—"

I heard the hall door bang open. I looked up. Lucy. She could deliver me from these mild questions that nevertheless felt like an inquisition. Relief poured through me.

She was wearing faded jeans and a sweater the same color as her eyes—the blue of the deepest crevices of icebergs that floated past the cliffs back home.

Nobody but me took any notice of her. If they only knew her like I did, they would change their tunes. That was the problem— for reasons I had never understood, Lucy refused to show the world who she was and what she could do. Law? What a waste of her talent.

Her eyes met mine over the heads of the girls clustered around me. Her lips twisted like she'd just tasted mayonnaise. Lucy had almost as much of an aversion to mayonnaise as she did to me.

A spurt of frustration penetrated the low clouds of my anxiety. *It wasn't like I'd asked* these girls to cluster around me. I hoped Lucy realized I couldn't tell them to leave me alone without a brutal backlash.

She disappeared into the serving room when I realized one of the girls was talking to me. "I'm sorry, can you repeat that?"

"When is Northern Junk's next concert?" she asked.

That was all it took for my panic to crest again. I cleared my throat, unable of getting enough air. "Next weekend. At Wembley."

"I've heard the tickets are all sold out," a guy piped up.

"Are they?" I answered vaguely. "I don't know anything about that side of things. The concert promoters take care of all that."

"Pity." He pouted.

"Yes," I answered, distracted as I watched Lucy emerge from the other side of the food service area with a tray of food.

My eyes tracked her until she took a seat at a recently vacated table. Unlike me, nobody rushed over to introduce themselves and show her what a friendly college Beaufort was.

I would trade every single nervous smile around me for one of Lucy's exasperated eye rolls. I nodded toward her to my tablemates. "That's Lucy. She's new here too. She's an exchange student from Newfoundland, like me."

She was staring resolutely at her bowl of oatmeal, banana, and coffee. Lucy was as stubborn as the cat we had when I was little who climbed up on the roof every day even though he could never get down. He'd sit up there and yowl until my dad climbed out the attic window and rescued him.

They all smiled but did not budge. A few chimed in with versions of "that's nice," but few spared her so much as a brief glance.

I shoved the rest of the toast in my mouth. "Excuse me. I have to talk to Lucy about ... Newfoundland things. In private."

Their faces fell.

"Nice meeting you," I said and let myself be drawn towards Lucy. Even after four years of not seeing each other and living completely different lives, I was still the moth to her flame.

CHAPTER SEVEN

Lucy

I had no clue why Jack was headed in my direction. I'd spotted him the moment I walked in the hall, holding court in the middle of a crowded table. Everyone was focused on the rock star in their midst, and I sure as hell wasn't going to add to the adulation.

I tried to ignore him as he wove between tables, carrying his tray of half-eaten food with me directly in his sights. What did he not understand about giving each other space?

I swallowed a spoonful of oatmeal. Great. Now everyone was staring at me too. They didn't pay attention to me when I came in, but they sure were now. I knew they were asking themselves what was special about that curvy, ordinary-looking girl sitting by herself.

I peered a little closer. Their expressions turned to naked envy as Jack closed the distance between us. So this was how it felt to be the center of attention. Something I didn't quite recognize— or *want* to recognize—kindled in my heart. A warm satisfaction flowed through my limbs. Oh shit. I *liked* this feeling. A lot.

It sure beat the anonymity I experienced every other day in my life.

My reaction was *so* not healthy or enlightened but screw it—it wasn't going to last long. Might as well enjoy it.

Jack sat down across from me.

I couldn't let him think any part of me was happy he had come over. I tried to channel my resentment from yesterday, but it wasn't easy with him looking so damn good in a plaid shirt in soft shades of blue and green. If only he didn't have that fallen-angel face and a lean, perfectly proportioned body.

"Bored of your fangirls already?" At least my voice sounded suitably unimpressed.

"Honestly?" He ran his hand through his copper waves, his lips curving at my antagonism. He was still too thin, and the strain around his eyes remained even after a night's sleep. I wondered at that. "Yes, I am. I'd much rather be scorned by you."

I lifted my chin in the direction of the table he'd deserted and the crestfallen expressions of the students there. "Careful," I warned, "or one of your devotees will talk to the paps about how snobby you are."

He rubbed his crooked pinky finger with his thumb. "You think you're joking, but that's probably exactly what would happen if I hadn't cleverly pre-empted it."

My curiosity got the better of me. "How?"

"I told them I needed to come over and talk to you about private Newfoundland things."

Laughter bubbled up in my throat. "There are private Newfoundland things?"

"Of course." He poked at his congealed fried eggs with his fork.

"Jack, if you insist on blighting my morning by making me watch you poke at those nasty fried eggs, you need to tell me more."

That charming, lopsided Jack Seary smile, complete with dimples, hit me like a one-two punch in the stomach. "Ummmm ... cod tongues?" He pushed his eggs to the side.

Despite my best intentions, I couldn't help but be drawn in. "Barf. Figgy duff?"

"Chund. Kitchen parties."

"Icebergs."

"Fog."

I remembered the plane. "Hawkins Cheezies?"

Jack shook his head. "Sorry, you lose. That's a Canadian thing, not just Newfoundland."

"And fog isn't?"

Jack laughed and shook his head. "There's no one like you, Lucy Snow." A sparkle of satisfaction burst in me again. *No.* I could not feed into the basest part of myself. I was angry with him for crashing my Oxford exchange. He was too damn good at using his charm to make me momentarily forget what he'd done.

"Satisfy my curiosity." I wiped the smile off my face. "Why did you come sit here near me?"

He waved his hand in the direction of the table he'd left. "Because I hate that. It's a relief when you give me a hard time instead of acting like sunbeams and rainbows shine directly out of my arse."

"You're telling me they don't?"

He winked at me. "Well ... not every day."

"What about the unicorns?" *Gah. Get a grip Lucy.*

He took a gulp of his coffee. "The unicorns come out only on special occasions."

I crossed my arms and tried to stare him down. Why did he have to be so freaking engaging? "I'm having a hard time believing you don't enjoy the sycophants."

He watched my face intently over the rim of his mug, his breathing faster than normal. My heart picked up pace from the intensity in his eyes. "Do you know what it's like having everyone watch you all the time?"

I shook my head. Of course I didn't.

"It's hell."

I considered this, but it still made no sense. That was one of the secrets I held close to my chest—I was secretly sure I would adore it. "Call me a cynic, but I don't buy it. If it's hell, it's hell with a heck of a lot of great benefits like a crap-ton of money, and seeing the world, and the ability to get anything you want, like eight weeks in Oxford just for the asking."

"I don't need to call you a cynic, Lucy. You *are* a cynic."

I shrugged, not unhappy with the label. My experiences had shown me that it was far safer than being a dreamer.

"Even you have to admit there are some things I can't have now."

I rolled my eyes. "Like what?"

"Anonymity." The strain in his face stopped my flippant retort in its tracks.

"You're serious, aren't you?" It was hard to imagine anyone wanting to go back to obscurity after tasting stardom, but I could tell Jack meant it.

"Why do you sound so surprised?"

"Because I am. How could you not love people thinking you're special? I know what it's like being taken for granted. If you think being famous is unpleasant, try being invisible."

His eyes lowered and rested on my mouth. "I think there's a difference between being invisible and refusing to be seen. I never took you for granted. Not for a second."

This again? My pulse throbbed in my throat. "You took me for granted more than anyone. You abandoned me minutes before our audition."

I flashed back to his expression that horrible day four years ago when he'd come to tell me he couldn't perform with me. The idea of going onstage by myself had been out of the question. It had felt as impossible to me as launching myself into space.

"You keep getting it backward." He pinned me with that green gaze of his, sharp now. "I always thought you were extraordinary enough not to need anyone to bolster you. My mistake was not realizing you didn't see that too."

"Yet you ended up being anointed the golden boy." I gestured toward the hall full of students still staring at us. "Look at them."

Those lines at the corners of his mouth deepened.

Despite everything, I hated being the cause of them. "I'm sorry." I sighed. "I'm being a high-octane shrew. I'm not used to you being here yet. It'll take me some time to create a new vision for this exchange—one with you in the periphery. You might remember I'm not someone who adapts quickly to things."

"I don't need to take up much space."

How he said that with a straight face was a mystery. "Don't be naive. Everyone is watching us right now, and it's sure as hell not because of me. You can't help it."

"Help what?"

How to put it into words? "Being one of those people."

"What people? You mean, one of the sunshine and rainbows and unicorns out of my arsehole people?"

"That's *exactly* what I mean. I don't even know if there's a word for it."

Jack stilled. "Try me."

I rubbed between my eyebrows. "You've got something everyone wants a piece of. Maybe it's charisma? I don't know, but people are powerless against it. It has something to do with confidence, I think. People could watch you for hours and not get bored. If I'm not careful, even I fall into the same trap."

I regretted this confession as soon as it popped out of my mouth.

His mug stopped halfway to his lips. "Wait. What?"

I waved my spoon. "Never mind."

I wasn't stupid enough to think I was the only one who Jack put under his spell. I was no better than the millions of screaming fans or our fellow students watching him now.

His appeal couldn't be explained or bottled, but when you were in Jack's presence, you felt it. Even now, with tired eyed and tousled hair, blinking at me, my fingers itched to reach across the table and touch him.

"It's what made things feel so effortless when we were friends before. I realize now it wasn't just me. You have that effect on everyone."

I'd felt it all those times we'd laughed together at Tim Hortons after rehearsals, trying to prognosticate who we'd be up against and what the judges would be like for real.

He made me feel like he saw beyond the nerdy student, beyond the fact that my father had died, beyond a helpful daughter who took on family responsibilities way beyond her years, beyond the people pleaser and the teacher's pet.

I'd believed Jack was the only person who saw me for who I truly was. Better yet, he seemed to like me. Love me even, at one time. That was why it cut so deep when he'd abandoned me. Deep down I suspected an uncomfortable truth—I'd moved on, but I'd never completely be over Jack.

"It was different with you." He was trying to get me to meet his eyes, but instead I looked down at my plate and shook my head. I'd had plenty of time to see things for how they really were.

"I think that's what that special 'it' is all about," I said, finally. My heart ached. "You have the gift of making everyone feel it's different with them—that it's real. I don't think you even realize it."

He reached out and grabbed my hand with his. His skin was warm and dry, his fingertips rough from strumming his guitar. Electricity tingled up my arm. How could the feel of those callouses still make my insides melt? I fought against the urge to squeeze back.

"You're wrong."

My stupid heart, falling for that Jack magic again. I knew better. I snatched my hand back, shaking it under the table to try and rid myself of the memory of his touch.

CHAPTER EIGHT

Jack

When Lucy finished her breakfast and returned her tray, I followed. When she walked out of the hall and down the stairs, I followed her out to the quad, reviewing every nuance of our conversation.

Had she actually meant it when she said even she could fall into the trap of being attracted to me?

But I'd ruined my only chance of being with her—that much was clear. Lucy's trust was hard won, and I'd lost it. She might put up with me for a while, but I doubted there was anything I could do to gain it back. Like she said, she didn't change her mind easily.

She stopped in the middle of the quad where the two paths that split the grass into four even rectangles intersected. The grass was so weirdly pristine I wondered if it was trimmed with a ruler and nail clippers. She tilted her head up at me. God, that *face*. "Am I your new bodyguard?"

I bit back a smile. "Um ... maybe?"

Her blue sweater looked so soft my fingers itched to reach out and touch it or, more accurately, touch *her* in it. It had to be unhealthy the way my heart flipped every single time I looked at her.

She put her hands on her hips. "Two things. One, I never agreed to that. Two, you promised to give me space. Remember?"

I held up my hands. "I'm sorry. I just like being around you."

She glared at me, beautiful against the backdrop of the golden buildings and silver sky. Pigeons cooed in the distance. This place was such a fairy tale, it almost made me believe I could win Lucy back.

"You'll have to get over it," she said, her voice a reality check. "I'm going to the lodge to check my mail slot."

"Alfie said they call them 'pidges' here, short for 'pigeonhole.'"

"Then I'm going to check my pidge," she corrected herself. "Alone."

I shoved my hands deep in my pockets and scuffed my sneakers on the ground. "Fine." She was right. I'd made her a promise. Besides, I had to stop daydreaming—an unhealthy tendency of mine, according to my parents and Gary.

"Don't act as though I've just put a curse on your firstborn. I'm sure you can find—"

"Lucy!" We turned toward the shout. It was Cedar, jogging over from the farthest building. She bristled with energy. In her Blundstones, jeans, and fleece, she was a refreshing breath of Canadian down-to-earthness in this fantastical setting.

She skidded to a stop in front of us. "You haven't killed each other yet. Nice."

"The day's not over yet," Lucy said with a pointed look at me.

Cedar grinned. "True. Hey, Robbie and me had a chat about your room assignments this morning."

"The porter who helped us last night?" Lucy asked.

"Yes. He's one of my friends here at Beaufort. Anyway, he's going to do his best to move one of you, but ... Well, the college is full for Hilary Term, so it's going to be tricky. Nothing moves fast at Oxford, especially administrative things. A lot of the decision-making will be out of Robbie's hands. I just wanted to let you know it's in the works, but may take a while."

I tried not to show I was secretly thrilled. I would have an excuse to see Lucy almost every day.

"Thanks so much for asking about it." Lucy bit her lower lip. How I would like to catch that between my teeth.

"Yes, thank you for trying," I echoed.

"Anyway, here you are, talking together! That's good, isn't it?" Cedar's eyes moved between the two of us, but I didn't miss the muscle jumping in Lucy's jaw as she gritted her teeth. "Or did I read this wrong? I'm new with all this understanding people stuff. It's much more clear-cut with bears."

"Bears?" Lucy and I echoed, but Cedar just waved away that intriguing segue.

"No time for that right now. Lucy, I'm here to take you to get your academic robe and the rest of your sub fusc whenever you're ready." She eyed me. "Alfie will take you separately, Jack. He thought it might be better that way."

"It is," Lucy answered for both of us without asking if I agreed. "Thanks. What's sub fusc again? I remember reading that somewhere but I'm still not quite clear."

"It's your penguin suit." Cedar's eyes took on a mischievous shine. "The formal black-and-white outfit you have to wear at tons of university events. It's your black academic robe, a mortarboard, a white long-sleeved top, black bottoms and shoes, and a little black silk tie around your neck—the guys get ties. Sounds like torture, I know, but you'll get used to it. I promise."

A man was walking toward us wearing—if I wasn't mistaken—the same Gucci jacket I'd seen on the Paris catwalks in September. I peered a bit closer. Wait. He looked just like—

"Shaun!" Cedar shouted. "Over here! There are people I need you to meet!"

It *was* him.

"Jack!" Shaun threw his arms around me in a massive hug. "Bloody hell! What on earth are you doing here?" He whipped around to Cedar. "Cedar, why is Jack Seary standing in the middle of the quad of our Oxford college?"

"You go here?" I asked Shaun in disbelief.

"Of course I do."

"You never mentioned it."

"You never mentioned you were coming here either," he retorted in his Etonian accent. Shaun's father was one of the wealthiest and most respected businessmen in England—a hard act for any child to live up to.

"How do you two know each other?" Cedar demanded. That crease was back between Lucy's eyebrows.

"All will be revealed, Cedar," Shaun said to her in that arch way of his I remembered. "But first an etiquette lesson. We don't bellow to our friends in the quad at Oxford."

"Why not?" Cedar crossed her arms.

"Most vulgar."

She tapped her foot, the picture of impatience. "Like I care about that."

"I know you don't. But I feel I would be failing you if I didn't at least point it out."

Cedar ignored that and poked his several-thousand-dollar patchwork leather jacket. "You didn't answer my question. How do you know Jack?"

Shaun blinked at her. "How do *you* know Jack?"

"Jack and Lucy here"—Cedar reached out and put a hand on Lucy's arm, making me a little bit envious, to be completely honest—"are the new Remote Commonwealth students from Canada."

Shaun's brown eyes went wide. "You're shitting me."

Cedar snorted. "And you're calling *me* vulgar?"

"It's true," I said to Shaun. "Despite the whole Northern Junk thing, I'm from Newfoundland like Lucy here."

Shaun cocked his head at me and Lucy. "How very odd."

"Not really," Lucy said with asperity.

"Stay on topic." Cedar swatted Shaun's arm. "How do you know Shaun?" she asked me.

"Last year we were part of a big group skiing together at Courchevel," I said, acutely aware of how privileged and obnoxious that sounded.

"And then there was that massive do at Chalet Edelweiss." Shaun grinned at me.

"Right," I continued. "The two of us ended up in a hot tub, sharing our opinions of everyone." I was caught between getting carried away with seeing Shaun here and considering how this all must sound to Lucy. I hated being the cause of her feeling left out in any way.

"We got impressively bitchy. I had ever so much fun." Shaun's eyes danced.

"So did I, until that massive chunk of snow slid off the roof on top of us." I laughed, remembering how shocked we'd been to find ourselves buried under several feet of it. It had been terrifying for the first few seconds, but once the snow quickly melted in the steaming hot tub, we couldn't stop laughing. It had bonded

Shaun and me in some unfathomable way.

"How about you?" I asked him. "I didn't exactly take you for the, uh, studious sort."

"One thing you must understand about me, my dear Jack, is I have *layers*." He winked. "I'm a Medieval English literature nerd, like Alfie and Cedar. We're—What do you call it, Cedar?"

"Friends?"

"No, no. The family of foxes thing."

"A skulk?"

"That's it. We're a skulk. Along with Lachlan and Binita—you probably haven't met them yet, but it's just a matter if time— and my boyfriend, Raphael. I'm a taken man now, you know. He's divine."

"Not to mention unbelievably patient," Cedar added.

"Congratulations. Can I meet him soon?"

"As soon as possible." There was a smile in Shaun's eyes that hadn't been there before. "He's lovely. You're obviously both honorary members of the skulk," Shaun said magnanimously, taking Lucy's hand in his.

A hot flame of envy ignited behind my rib cage, which made zero sense because Shaun never made a secret of the fact he was strictly interested in men. Maybe I was just jealous of anyone who got to touch Lucy when I couldn't. "Lucy, I apologize. My manners have gone begging. I'm thrilled to meet you, much more so than this stroppy sod." He gave me a wink.

Lucy smiled at him. A true Lucy smile—the kind I used to get and missed like oxygen.

Cedar was looking over her shoulder. My heart sank when I saw what she was looking at—a cluster of people that had gathered at the bottom of the staircase to the hall. They hovered there, staring at our little knot in the center of the quad.

Cedar tilted her head. "I'm guessing being a rock star makes the girls like you?"

Shaun guffawed. "That's the understatement of the year, but not exclusively girls, my dear."

"You have to admit, there is a disproportionate percentage of girls over there."

Nobody could argue with that.

"Don't worry," Shaun reassured me. "We can try to get you around incognito. It'll be fun."

"It doesn't sound like fun." I sighed. "But it might be necessary."

"I'll make it fun," Shaun said. "You'll see. I make everything fun, even being hit by a massive wall of snow in a hot tub."

He had a point.

Lucy turned to Cedar. "I'm ready to go now. I just need to grab a coat from my room." Her voice was leaden. "Nice to meet you, Shaun. Have fun catching up with Jack."

"I will. It was wonderful to meet you too. I can guarantee we're going to be the best of friends."

Lucy shot him a skeptical look. Shaun clearly had no idea who he was dealing with.

"Alfie will find you soon." Cedar waved at me and walked off to Lucy's room with her. I didn't take my eyes off them until they disappeared under the stone archway leading to our staircase.

I turned back to Shaun to see him watching me with an odd look on his face.

"It's like that then, is it?" His mouth pulled to the side in thought.

Damn Shaun's ability to read people in a snap. "I don't know what you're talking about."

"It had better be Lucy who puts that expression on your face, because Cedar could not be more taken."

I patted his back. "You've got an overactive imagination, my friend." If Shaun only knew how impossible things were. Four years ago, I'd once and for all ruined my chance to be with her. What I wanted made not one iota of difference.

"In my experience," Shaun said, "you don't stare at someone like you're trying to burn a hole in their back for no reason."

CHAPTER NINE

Lucy

Cedar walked several times faster than any human should be able to walk.

"It's just ahead!" Cedar sped through the crowds on Catte Street. I'd caught a glimpse of the black-and-white enamel street sign as it flashed past.

Even at this speed, Oxford felt like a different world outside the walls of Beaufort College as well as inside them. It was a damp, chilly January day and the sidewalks were clogged with groups of young people, some of them wearing their black academic gowns. Crowds of tourists studied their phones or maps.

Exhaust hung heavy in the air from the honking cars and black taxicabs that weren't, amazingly, something that existed only in movies starring Hugh Grant. There seemed to be far more people per square foot than any other place I'd been, including Toronto.

Cedar kept flinging random bits of information at me as she raced along, reciting the names of the colleges that lined the streets as we passed them, barely giving me any time to admire their beautiful old doors and gates.

In my hand I carried an embossed paper shopping bag from Ede & Ravenscroft, a shop that sold only Oxford academic robes and assorted accoutrements. Walking into that shop had been like time traveling to the Regency era.

I would have been intimidated without Cedar by my side. She seemed to have the gift of showing up in the world exactly as she was, with zero apologies. Except for her passion for Medieval literature and her aristocratic boyfriend, she seemed to me like the most unlikely Oxford student imaginable. Even more unlikely than me, which was saying something.

Jack, on the other hand, already knew Alfie and Shaun. He fit in the world of Beaufort college just like he fit everywhere with an ease that made my jaw clench with resentment. It was impossible to resist comparing my existence with his. Everything about him being here felt like yet another lesson from the universe—a reminder to always keep my expectations low.

We turned onto Broad Street, according to the sign. Cedar pointed out the glorious Sheldonian Theatre and gave me an impressive rundown on its architecture. I retained only fragments—Christopher Wren, 1669, break from Gothic, the emperors, romans …?

She pointed at the shiny facade of a bookstore named Blackwell's. "This place is an institution. You have your book list for your courses this term, right?"

I came back to earth with a thud. "I do." I hoped I was wrong, but studying law sounded about as scintillating as listening to our neighbor Mrs. Quirk explain the rules of duplicate bridge.

"Let's see if they have some in stock to get you started. Oxford profs tend to be sticklers for their students showing up prepared."

"That would be amazing." I was drawn to any bookstore, even

if it was to buy law books.

"Besides," she admitted, "I went most of my life deprived of bookstores, so I never miss a chance to go in."

At least the universe seemed to have given me a potential friend. "I love them too."

As we stepped inside, my phone rang. My home number. Acid rose in my stomach as I braced myself for a new crisis. I gestured for Cedar to go on without me and stepped back out to the sidewalk to take it.

"Lucy!" Alice's little voice came through, excited and a bit strung out. "I just had to tell you."

"Tell me what, sweetie?"

"Mom took me to McDonald's."

McDonald's was off-limits for us. For one thing, it was expensive. Second, I didn't want Alice to get used to food that was bad for her. Alice's desire for McDonald's was a bottomless black hole. If my mom started giving into her, the food budget I'd so carefully saved up before I left would be decimated in no time. Alice would probably develop scurvy to boot.

I tried to give my mom the benefit of the doubt. "Was it a special occasion?"

"No. We just felt like it."

"I see." I didn't succeed at keeping my wariness out of my voice, but Alice was too high on French fries and chicken nuggets to notice. I would love to be carefree like my mom and do things just because I felt like it, knowing someone—me—would shoulder the consequences.

It was just like Jack. He got tired of being a rock star, so he'd come to Oxford for eight weeks to dabble in astronomy. I mean, that wasn't real life. Neither was going to McDonald's just for the hell of it.

"It was good," Alice chided. "We had fun."

"I'm glad about that, but you know it's expensive. It can't become a regular thing." I hated that I had to always be the adult in the household, constantly harping on about sticking to our limited budget.

I'd worked three jobs for four years while studying to save up enough money to provide for my mom and Alice while I was away getting my law degree. I'd never asked for the parental role at age eleven after my dad drowned.

"I know, I know," she grumbled. "I thought you'd be happy we're having a good time."

"I am." I sighed. Alice was good at guilt trips for a ten-year-old. "Is Mom around?" I asked. Burning through our savings too fast meant I might not be able to stay here until the end of my degree. I couldn't let that happen.

"No. She had to fill up the car with gas."

"Tell her I'll call her later."

"Alright. Lucy?"

"Yes?"

"It was fun."

"I know." I hung up. Exhaustion made my knees feel like jelly. This split life between studying law and being the only voice of reason in my household in Newfoundland was going to be even trickier than I'd imagined.

"What's up?" Cedar came back outside.

"Nothing." I tried to muster up a smile.

Her eyes sparkled. "Then let's go book shopping."

We'd both been bookstore-drunk for the past hour.

Blackwell's was pretty much how I imagined heaven. Piles and piles of books filled the two-story store, from the obscure poetry chapbooks to *New York Times* bestsellers. The air was redolent with the smell of paper stock.

Cedar and I had split ways shortly after entering the store, each absorbed with our browsing. She was a keeper—someone who understood bookstores were best enjoyed in silence which allowed the brain to enter into a flow state.

Cedar, clutching five books against her, finally found me reading the back blurb of the latest Lisa Penny novel. "I can afford only one of these, but it's impossible to choose." Her voice was tinged with regret.

I wanted to buy the whole store too. It was bonkers to think Jack probably could. Maybe even Shaun and Alfie too. "You know what one of my recurring fantasies is?"

She was reading the blurb of the top book in her pile. "What?"

"Being locked in a bookstore like this by accident at the end of the day, then having the whole night by myself to poke around and read."

Cedar's eyes widened. "That would be amazing."

"Right? Do you have any idea how long we've been here?" I hadn't looked at my watch once and had completely lost my sense of time.

Cedar frowned. "I think almost an hour or so, but I don't have a watch, and I forgot my phone at the college. I do that all the time—drives Alfie nuts. Maybe we should go downstairs where they keep most of the textbooks and look for some of your law ones?"

My heart sank. If only I could muster up more enthusiasm

about studying law "You're right. Otherwise, you and I could waste the entire day here without even realizing it."

"True," Cedar agreed. "But I definitely wouldn't consider it a waste."

"You know what? Me neither."

She led me down the stairs to the lower floor, where Blackwell's transformed into an academic bookstore. Some of the course texts looked fascinating—history, philosophy, art …

At last we found the section the most devoid of fun—law.

Cedar stood in front of the case books and textbooks, a daunted expression on her face. "Uh. Got your list?"

I took a piece of paper from my backpack and began to go through it. There were so many course books listed, and so many of them had almost identical titles.

Cedar held up a finger. "Hang on. I'm going to get someone."

Numbness spread through my body as I stared at the spines of the law books. Getting into Oxford was my big break. Finally, life had thrown me a bone. I should have been awash with gratitude instead of already discouraged.

Cedar returned with a brisk young man who seemed to know the law section backward and forward. He plucked eight books off the shelves with titles like *Public Law*, *Great Debates in Criminal Law*, and *Torts*. An internal scream echoed off the walls of my mind.

"That should get you started." He transferred the pile of books to my arms. Ugh. They were weirdly heavy. "Which college are you at?"

"Beaufort."

"Tough law tutors there," he said. "Professor Speedman in particular has the reputation of not suffering fools. Brace yourself."

Brace myself? I tried to reason with the sudden geyser of fear inside me. I might not be a brochure-worthy Oxford student like Alfie, and I might not be approaching my studies here as an extended health retreat like Jack, but one thing I knew how to do was work hard.

When we finally popped out on the sidewalk, Cedar sniffed at the drizzly air. "I don't know about you, but all this shopping has made me thirsty. How about we stop at the Turf on our way back to college and I introduce you to our favorite pub?"

Given the law books in my backpack and the fact that courses started the very next day, I figured I'd be wise to grab fun wherever I could. "Lead the way."

She sped off again at her breakneck pace.

CHAPTER TEN

Jack

Alfie, me, Shaun, and his extremely large boyfriend, Raphael, who, incidentally, could have a promising career as a bodyguard, left Ede and Ravenscroft.

Shaun had made good on his promise to disguise me. I wore a toque—which the rest of them kept insisting was properly called a "beanie"—over my distinctive hair. I insisted on calling it a toque, much to their amusement, but regardless, I was thankful for it.

"I can't believe this has worked so far," I said to Shaun once we huddled on the sidewalk, pointing at my toque. It probably didn't hurt that people were walking with their heads bent against the chilly drizzle. I felt deliciously invisible, my panic and anxiety gone for the moment. Christ, I'd be a happy man if I could always live like this.

"I told you I'm good at this," he said. "I was also right that the men working in Ede and Ravenscroft would have no idea who you were, wasn't I?"

"But they would've recognized you if you'd been some obscure Oxford academic from the 1700s," Alfie said. He waved at a Mini with the Scottish flag painted on the roof barreling down the street toward us.

"That's true," Raphael agreed in his deep, rough voice.

"Here's Lachlan," Alfie said. The Mini screeched to a stop, its front tire riding up on the curb.

"I do appreciate the way Lachlan makes an entrance," Shaun quipped.

"Who?" I asked.

"My friend Lachlan," Alfie explained. "He's joining us for a pint at the Turf, our local pub."

"I told you Lachlan was a part of our skulk," Shaun reminded me. "He's a rugby lad but don't hold that against him. He's a surprisingly decent bloke."

"To be fair, Jack has had a lot of new people flung at him." Raphael took Shaun's hand and gazed down at him with an expression of wonder. Spending the past hour with them made it clear Cedar and Alfie weren't the only happy couple at Beaufort.

Alfie motioned us to get in the Mini. Did he really think we could all jam in there? None of us were small, and Shaun hadn't exaggerated about his boyfriend. Raphael was built along the lines of Viking warrior or a WWE star.

"Take the front seat, Jack," Alfie said, ever the well-bred gentleman.

"Nope." Shaun shook his head. "He'll be far more conspicuous in the front. Better bundle him in the back with me and Raphael."

Shaun's logic was unassailable, so Alfie ended up in the front beside Lachlan, with me, the massive Raphael, and Shaun shoehorned in the back. My knees almost touched my ears.

Lachlan peeled away from the curb.

"I never thought I'd complain about being squeezed between two gorgeous men." Shaun squirmed as he tried to find room for his long legs. "But have you ever considered getting a bigger car, Lachlan?" All I could see was the back of Lachlan's large head and thick neck as he drove.

"You always have the option to walk," Lachlan said, his eyes bright blue in the rearview mirror.

"No need to get in a strop about it," Shaun said. "You Scottish are so sensitive."

Raphael fought back a smile.

"Hang tight!" Lachlan instructed. He swung a hard right that landed Shaun and me practically on Raphael's lap, then began to weave through the narrow streets of Oxford at an insane speed.

"Jesus," I muttered, hanging on to the seatback in front of me. A bubble of something I no longer recognized formed in my chest. Wait a second. Was I having fun? My anxiety felt farther away than it had been in a long time.

Alfie turned in his seat and punctiliously performed introductions in his posh voice. "Lachlan, this is Jack Seary, our newest exchange student from Canada. Newfoundland, to be precise."

"And also, you know, world-famous guitarist and singer of Northern Junk." Shaun wore an impish expression on his face.

"Aye. I've heard of ye," Lachlan admitted grudgingly. Not a fan then. He probably didn't know how happy this made me.

"Jack, this mad Scotsman is my best friend, Lachlan." Alfie ignored Shaun. "We grew up on the same estate in Scotland."

"In other words, Alfie's family's sixteenth-century castle in the Scottish Highlands," Shaun added.

"Don't embarrass him," Lachlan defended his friend, something I got the impression came as naturally to him as breathing. I'd thought at the beginning my relationship with my Northern

Junk bandmates would be like that, but in fact the exact opposite was true. It was mostly petty jealousies about who was in front on the album cover and who got the most solo play time at concerts. They had seemed like good enough guys when we were thrown together by Gary, but they'd changed. Maybe we all had.

If only Lucy and I could spend time with this new group of friends—our new skulk—together. I knew she had good reason for wanting to keep her distance from me, but it felt like a damned shame.

Lachlan swerved violently and lay on the horn. "Bloody bikers!" he roared. "Who would be daft enough to try to bike down St. Giles at this time of day and talk on their phone at the same time? Pillocks."

Everyone muttered in agreement. Disagreeing with Lachlan when he was driving didn't seem like a wise idea.

He turned into a tiny cobblestone lane and screeched to a stop underneath a black-and-white no-parking sign. "Here we are."

Shaun turned to me and tucked an errant strand of red hair under my toque. He passed me a pair of chunky eyeglasses with black frames.

"What are these?"

"An addition to your disguise."

"Are these prescription?" I asked, worried. "I've never worn glasses in my life."

"Never fear. They're blank lenses. There's going to be a lot of students at this pub, and everyone is jammed closely together. People will be looking for you now they know you're in Oxford. The beanie might not be enough."

"That reminds me. I brought the scarf Shaun ordered me to." Lachlan rummaged beside his seat and tossed back a navy scarf with a red stripe down the middle.

The wool itched and smelled vaguely like wet sheep, reminding me of Lucy's wet blue peacoat in the limo, which triggered the memory of how luscious she'd looked sleeping in her plain white T-shirt with her overflowing cleavage. Oh God. What was I? Fifteen? Getting an erection every time I thought of her was just not a viable way of existing, because my mind circled back to her constantly.

She'd made it clear she would never forgive me. It had been four years. How could she still be affecting me like this?

Lachlan turned around in his seat. He was as muscular and stocky as a comic-book superhero, with sandy brown hair and humorous eyes under raised brows. Everything about him screamed rugby player. "It's a scarf from my college," Lachlan explained. "Keble."

"Thank you. But why do I need it?"

"It feels a bit traitorous," Alfie said as Shaun wound it around my neck. "But if you walk in there with a Keble scarf and people know you're at Beaufort it will be one more thing that throws them off."

Raphael watched with a sphinx-like expression on his stern face as Shaun knotted the scarf around my neck. Hopefully he wasn't the jealous type, because if he was, I was fairly certain he could snap my neck like a pretzel.

I put the glasses on.

Shaun assessed his handiwork. "This might just work."

The air in my lungs escaped all at once. "Might?"

The anonymity I'd had for a couple of hours only made me hungry for more.

"Without the hair showing, and the Keble scarf, the glasses will throw people off. Trust me."

We climbed out of the Mini extremely ungracefully, except for

Alfie, who managed to make his exit look like a photoshoot from *Town & Country Magazine.*

"Er. This isn't a parking spot, Lachlan." Alfie was reading the street sign with a wrinkled forehead.

Lachlan answered with a dismissive wave of his very large hand.

"You'll get a ticket, or worse yet, you'll get the Mini towed." Alfie was busy buttoning up the tortoiseshell buttons of his wool overcoat.

"I'll argue it's anti-Scots persecution," Lachlan said. "And that I can park anywhere I want seeing as the British robbed us of our sovereignty. *Alba gu bràth!*" He raised his fist and started walking toward a small gap between two brick buildings.

Alfie hesitated a few seconds, his eyes going from Lachlan's Mini to the no-parking sign just above and back.

"I'll pay the ticket or the impound fee," I said in a low voice meant only for him.

"If it comes to that, I will." Alfie grimaced. "I just have a hard time breaking rules. Cedar is helping me with that, but it's very much a work in progress."

This surprised me. "Really? I would have thought you'd be teaching her the rules of being at Oxford. You know, for Canadians—even me—it feels like a different world."

"I tried that initially." Alfie cast me a wry look. "Didn't go well."

Alfie ushered me through the nondescript narrow passageway almost beneath the Bridge of Sighs where the rest of them had disappeared. "It's probably not a bad idea for us to lag behind. We'll attract less attention that way than arriving en masse."

We made our way slowly. of Oxford students had come through here. Wonder tingled through my body. My bandmates had become strangely competitive about who was the most blasé about what we saw and experienced on tour. In my experience, people who had lost the ability to marvel at things were the most tedious people in the world.

The passageway slowly widened enough we could dawdle side by side, then it gave way to a rambling pub with benches surrounding open pit fires. Woodsmoke hung heavy in the air.

Shaun, Raphael, and Lachlan were already sitting on one bench, flanked by Cedar, a girl with purple hair and a nose ring, and Lucy. My eyes settled on her because how could they be anywhere else when she was around? Shit. She was going to think I was stalking her.

She generated her own light—gorgeous and pink-cheeked from the cold—even as she frowned at me. Her blonde waves framed her exquisite face, again like a Botticelli painting come to life, except Botticelli's women didn't look quite so irritated. Here I was, crashing her plans yet again.

"Over here!" Shaun shouted, as if we could have missed them.

As we approached, Cedar was saying to Shaun, "You criticized me this morning for calling out to you in quad, and now you're doing it. Hypocrite."

"It's quite different, my wild thing," he said. "What is perfectly acceptable in a pub is not acceptable in the middle of an Oxford college."

"Aye, it's true," Lachlan agreed, glancing at the purple-haired girl, who had to be Binita, the brilliant mathematician and the only member of our skulk I hadn't met yet. "I tackled one of my rugby mates in the Keble Library once as a joke. Didn't go over well. Here at the Turf though, it'd be nae bother."

I settled myself on the bench across from Lucy and mouthed the word *sorry* at her. She had to know I hadn't planned this, right? She just gave her head a tiny shake, as if to say *whatever*.

Had she decided to tolerate me? I suddenly felt in a much more celebratory mood.

"Jack, this is Binita," Alfie said. "Binita, this is Jack Seary. I'm assuming you already met Lucy?"

"Yes, Lord Invernay, I've already met Lucy," Binita said in a prim accent that was I was fairly certain was affectionately mocking Alfie's posh ways. "Jack, it's lovely to meet you. Welcome to our skulk. I've heard your music. A few of the songs aren't complete shite."

I liked her immediately. The scent of roasting chestnuts over the open firepit in the middle at the center of the benches was like a warm blanket thrown over my shoulders. The only thing that would make this perfect was if I were sitting beside Lucy. Well, that and if I'd never joined Northern Junk.

I couldn't remember the last time I'd felt this cozy. Actually I could—curled up on my parents' couch back in Newfoundland, forcing Lucy to watch old episodes of Carl Sagan's *Cosmos* with me after rehearsals. She'd grumbled at the time, but I saw how relaxed she got too. Sometimes her legs would end up under mine, and we'd stay like that. I would pretend like the casual contact was no big deal, but in fact I couldn't concentrate on anything else when I felt her warm skin against mine—not even Carl's tales of quasars and supernovas.

Alfie dropped a kiss on the tip of Cedar's nose, then wedged himself beside her.

I scanned the crowd around us. Nobody was paying much attention to me.

If anything, Alfie was getting the odd glance. I knew he'd gotten his share of unwanted press attention, mainly because of his notorious father who was currently dating the recently divorced ex-wife of one of the princes. Even so, I didn't think it compared to my situation. *Rolling Stone* recently posted a fake mugshot of me on the cover with the title "Jack Seary: The Most Wanted Man on Earth."

"Apologies, we didn't plan this," Alfie said to Lucy. "Somehow, we just always end up here. We should have thought to take Jack somewhere different." Despite his mea culpa, Alfie, sliding his arm around Cedar's shoulders, didn't look all that sorry.

Lucy's eyes met mine with wry resignation. "I'm realizing I'm just going to have to put up with Jack being here. This is a me problem, not a problem for the rest of you to have to manage."

I was momentarily robbed of speech. What had shifted?

"Did Cedar make you walk to Ede & Ravenscroft?" Shaun asked Lucy, his brows drawn together in concern.

"As a matter of fact we did walk ... she walks very fast," Lucy said with that playful sideways look of hers.

"Fast?" Cedar tugged on one of her French braids.

"You walk the same speed the rest of us run." Alfie looked down at her with affection. "You have my sympathies Lucy. You deserve an Olympic medal for keeping up with her."

"I have to be honest. There were a few times I lost her on the sidewalk."

"Really?" Cedar leaned forward. "I had no idea."

Shaun rolled his eyes toward the gray sky, still thick with clouds. "We adore you, Cedar, but you are the most indefatigable girl. Positively exhausting."

Cedar chucked an unroasted chestnut at him that caught him in the center of his forehead.

"Ow!" Shaun yelped. "That could have blinded me."

Cedar twitched her shoulders. "If I wanted to blind you, you'd be blind."

Everyone laughed, and Lucy and I exchanged a glance. Apparently we had a gang of friends already—the same gang of friends. How was it that I felt more at home with these people, whom I'd just met, than with my bandmates and our manager, whom I'd been traveling with for the past four years.

Lucy was studying my face, chewing her lip in a way that made me think of all the things I could have been doing with her for the past four years rather than strutting around a stage. I squirmed as all my brain cells migrated to my groin. I had to control myself better around her if this truce was going to last, but man, Lucy was my kryptonite.

"Nice glasses," she said finally.

I reached up and touched them, my fingers hitting the unfamiliar bulky frames. I'd been so busy watching her I'd forgotten about them.

"Shaun's idea," I said. "Do I look incognito enough?"

Her mouth twisted a bit as she considered me. "Maybe," she said. "But I'm not the right person to ask. I know your face too well."

We were talking like normal people. I couldn't waste this opportunity. "Did you and Cedar do anything else besides sub fusc shopping?" I asked.

She smiled. A real, unguarded Lucy smile that showed the tiniest dimple on the left edge of her upper lip. "Cedar took me to Blackwell's bookstore."

"You must have loved that." The Lucy I knew had never been able to resist a bookstore, just like I'd never been able to resist an observatory.

"Are you shittington me?" My heart stuttered. Did we actually have a shared joke? "Of course I did."

"I—I ..." With that simple olive branch, she'd left me a babbling idiot.

"I was telling Cedar about how one of my fantasies is being locked in a bookstore overnight," she continued. "Blackwell's would be perfect for it."

How was I unaware of this? "I didn't know that."

"You don't know everything, Jack." She arched an eyebrow.

"I ... I realize that."

She sighed. "It would be amazing. All the hours with nothing to do but linger and read. You really should go in there and have a look. It's magical."

"I will," I promised and tried to think of a way to make Lucy's fantasy a reality. I would make all her dreams come true if she would only let me.

SECOND WEEK

CHAPTER ELEVEN

Lucy

Boredom pressed me deep into the wingback chair I sat in during my second contract law tutorial.

"So, if we understand *Carlill vs Carbolic Smoke Company*, 1893, correctly, offer and acceptance of a contract does not need to be made face-to-face or even person-to-person." My teacher, or "tutor" for this class was the notorious Professor Speedman—the one the bookseller at Blackwell's warned me about.

This was my second contract tutorial with her and I feared I was turning out to be one of those fools that she did not suffer easily.

There were no lectures in amphitheaters like back in St. John's. Tutorials were taught like this—just the professor, me, and two other students in her study. There was nowhere to hide.

Sweat beaded at my hairline. It wasn't that I was shy. I was just the type of person more comfortable in the back row of desks rather than inquisitioned by a brilliant woman whom I was certain was the long-lost twin of Helen Mirren. The same pure white hair. The same piercing eyes. The same disdainful accent. There was no back of the class with her.

"Lucy!" Professor Speedman pointed at me. "Please tell us your definition of a contractual promise based on the ruling of the Carbolic case."

My mind was a freshly wiped chalkboard. I'd read the case but my brain just couldn't seem to make itself care enough to extrapolate conclusions. I'd always been an excellent student due to sheer hard work rather than natural brilliance but I'd never encountered a subject that numbed my brain like law. Why couldn't I love it?

I gave a rambling answer. Professor Speedman sighed. "You missed the salient point, Lucy. You must do better if you wish to remain in this program."

I shriveled inside like a snail left out in the sun. Shaun and the rest of our skulk had warned me that Oxford professors weren't known for their diplomacy. It was viewed as a point of pride amongst them to try and rip to shreds the students' answers.

Shaun swore the harshness of Oxford professors came from a place of mutual intellectual respect, but I wasn't convinced. I couldn't shake the feeling that Professor Speedman took my measure the first time she laid eyes on me—like she had intuited that Law was never my first choice.

The other students were leaning forward, listening to every pearl of wisdom the professor let drop from her mouth. They were younger than me, both only eighteen and fresh out of their A-Levels. They acted as though their whole lives had led to this holy moment when they would be initiated into the mysteries of British contract law.

It didn't matter how I felt. I had to make this work, no matter what I was feeling. Choosing things just because they sounded interesting was something people like Jack got to do, not me.

After this two-year degree and a year of articling, the prestige of an Oxford law degree would be enough to get my foot firmly on a successful job ladder once I got home. I could start earning money, fast.

I could send Alice to more tutors to help with her learning differences, maybe even send her to a private school in St. John's. I could finally get the leaky roof fixed at our house—a rundown fishing cottage near the harbor.

"Joshua, can you please define the concept of consideration?" Professor Speedman asked.

He would and could. Joshua was a keener.

"Consideration is 'something of value' given for a promise. It's required to make the promise enforceable as a contract and is traditionally some detriment to the promise, in that he may give value, or some benefit to the promisor, in that he may receive value."

"Sufficient." Professor Speedman noted something on the clipboard she held in her lap.

Joshua's burning passion for law seemed absolutely sincere. Could he lend me some of that?

My hands moved taking notes, but my mind kept drifting back to Jack, more particularly the sight of him in the heavy black glasses he'd worn at the Turf and every time I'd seen him since. Robbie hadn't been lying about Beaufort being an "intimate" college. It felt like Jack popped up everywhere I went—except my law tutorials—the only places where I would appreciate the distraction.

A trail of Beaufort students tended to follow about ten to twenty feet behind Jack wherever he went, talking loudly or scrolling on their phones in an attempt to appear inconspicuous.

Shaun had been clever enough to spread the word that every member of college was an integral part of an overarching plan to make Jack's experience at Oxford as protected and normal as possible. Still, they all knew who the handsome guy in the beanie and black glasses was.

Avoiding him was impossible. Besides, even though I knew it shouldn't, I was becoming addicted to the thrill of Jack breaking away from his posse of admirers and making a beeline toward me. I didn't want to think too deeply about why it filled me with satisfaction every time he did.

God, he looked good in those glasses—like the intellectual you realized was crazy hot under a buttoned-up exterior. A bit like a space nerd, red-haired version of Clark Kent. And he always sought *me* out. I hated how much I loved it.

I needed to snap out of it. The whole world was in love with Jack. He wasn't my discovery or my secret. I could not let myself become another one of the millions enamoured with him. I had to stay on target, which meant the dreary prospects of the Carbolic Smoke Company.

"Here is your reading list this week." Professor Speedman passed me three pieces of paper stapled together with a smug set to her mouth. "If you had plans for this weekend, you might think about canceling them. I imagine you'll be spending a good chunk of your time at the Bodleian Law Library."

I stared down at the list, horror numbing my fingers.

It contained at least thirty cases to read and assimilate as well as two textbooks on contract. Surely this was the reading list for the entire eight weeks.

"This week's essay question is on the bottom," she said, brisk. "I expect you to arrive at Monday's tutorial prepared to read out your essay *in viva voce* and defend it."

"This is the reading list for just this week?" the young student who wasn't ass-kisser Joshua had the temerity to ask.

"Of course," Professor Speedman said. "This is Oxford, not some online university. The introductory week is over and now the real work begins. I will give you a fresh reading list every week. This one is light to ease you in."

What had I gotten myself into? I slid my backpack on and walked out of Professor Speedman's study like a zombie.

I had no idea how I was going to get all this done in a week and this was only one of my four classes. When would I sleep?

I had to go to a land law tutorial in half an hour. There was only one thing I knew that could ease this cocktail of stress and despair macerating behind my sternum.

I walked toward the college chapel. It probably wouldn't be empty, and I wasn't about to break out in song if anyone was there. I didn't want to answer any awkward questions or, God forbid, be recruited for the college choir. After Jack, I'd vowed not to sing in public anymore. From the looks of my reading list, I wouldn't have time for anything but studying anyway.

Beaufort's chapel was renowned for the massive wall of beautifully preserved stone saints behind the alter that dated back to the 1400s, when Beaufort was established as Oxford's only Catholic college. It had been pulling at me like a persistent undertow since I arrived here—not for the stone saints, but because I'd read it had amazing acoustics.

The gargantuan wooden door creaked as I pushed it open. My footsteps echoed on the flagstones as I made my way up the center aisle—a promise my voice would carry.

I reached the front and stared at the saints as a hush gathered around me. I was alone.

The saints looked troubled and maybe even a bit guilty about something.

They reminded me of how I'd felt about my thwarted *Canada's Got Talent!* audition after Jack left. It had been such a stupid idea.

Singing was always something I'd done with my father, at the kitchen parties of neighbors and at home by the warmth of our cast-iron stove.

He'd had a lovely baritone, and everyone always begged him to sing. I saw the expression on people's faces when they heard him. They either settled back in their chairs or leaned forward, listening intently so they didn't miss a second. His mistake was in reaching for more than kitchen parties, and I'd been foolish and selfish enough to repeat his fatal error. I probably deserved the karmic punishment of Jack taking over my dream and doing a far better job at it than I ever could.

As a child, my father's voice had filled me with incandescent joy. He began teaching me songs and encouraged me to join in with my chirpy soprano. My voice didn't really come into itself until I was around twelve or thirteen, evolving into a rich mezzo-soprano my dad was no longer around to hear.

I did another scan of the chapel. I could smell the slight mustiness of winter humidity settling into the Medieval stone.

I cleared my throat. I hadn't sung in so long, but my confusion and frustration were pushing up my throat. This was the only way I knew how to get those feelings out.

I closed my eyes, and I was instantly back in our kitchen, leaning against the rough denim of my father's knee. That familiar magic I only ever felt when I was singing flowed into me.

"The Ramblin' Rover" popped into my head. He often sang the sea shanty solo and would have everyone laughing through tears by the end.

I'd never had a chance to grieve him, really. Taking care of my mom and my baby sister left no room to process my own feelings.

The memories built up in me until there was no room left for fretting over how I was going to get my contract law essay done, never mind Jack and those glasses that made me melt inside every time I saw him. My voice burst out of me, full of emotion and longing.

When I finished, my face was wet with tears. Silence gathered around me again as the echo of my last note died away, just like it had after my father left that night in his boat and never came back.

We used to be a squad of two, complete with rituals and secret jokes. Every time he left for his boat, he gave me a bear hug and whispered in my ear, "I'm leaving your mom and Alice in your care. Will you promise to look after them until I'm back?"

I would hold up my pinky. "Promise."

That promise still bound me. It bound me for the rest of my life because he hadn't come back, and he never would.

CHAPTER TWELVE

Jack

We'd been given a tour of the astronomy lab in the first week, so this was my first official class in the observatory. There was a lightness in my chest I barely recognized. I couldn't wait to get my hands on the telescopes. I'd been obsessed with looking at the stars since we took a school field trip to Grenfell Observatory when I was in ninth grade and I'd seen Saturn's rings through the telescope.

My research group of four students gathered at the top of Radcliffe Observatory in Templeton Green College. The space was arching and soaked with history and space nerdiness. I was in heaven.

My professor—highly respected astronomer Dr. Viktor Hayden—introduced himself. I knew him by his reputation and had read his papers on Columbae as a pulsating stellar core and magnetic fields in red giant stars. I was an unapologetic fanboy.

"I played a key role and continue to do so," he continued, "in the planning, designing, and building of the Extremely Large

Telescope."

In any other crowd the literal name would have elicited a chuckle from the audience, but to anyone interested in the study of space, the Extremely Large Telescope—the world's largest telescope, being built in the high desert of Northern Chile—was serious business.

It was new and incredible to be in a room full of space-obsessed people like me. Had they also salivated the first time they watched *Star Trek*? I couldn't tell if they recognized me with my beanie and glasses, but even they did, no one was making a fuss.

Professor Hayden clapped his hands together. "To start with today, we'll be going deeper into the astrophysics of how stars are born. I expect all of you know this backward and forward, but there is always value in going back and questioning things we assume to be fact. Who can give me a summary of the dynamics at play in the birth of a star? Um ... Jack, is it?"

I cleared my throat, aware of a prickle of anxiety. Or was that a normal desire to impress Professor Hayden? Hard to tell. I spent my spare time on our tour buses reading space articles and research papers. "A star is born when atoms of light elements are squeezed under enough pressure that their nuclei undergo fusion," I said. "All stars are the result of a balance of forces. The force of gravity compresses atoms in interstellar gas until the fusion reaction begins."

Professor Hayden narrowed his eyes at me. "I suppose that's adequate, thank you."

Adequate? Lucy and I had been warned by our skulk we shouldn't expect any glowing feedback from Oxford professors. Was this what they were talking about? I knew my answer was correct. Had I become so used to the slavish praise I loathed so much as a member of Northern Junk that I expected it as my due in all areas of my life?

If so, I'd just have to get over myself. I wanted to be here in this observatory more than I wanted anything. Well, besides Lucy.

Having a space to talk about things like stars and black holes and quasars gave me more joy that I'd felt playing at Madison Square Garden with a full house of screaming fans.

My musical career had given my parents joy. That was one of the reasons I felt like I couldn't quit. If I had to think only about myself, I would trade it to study astronomy in a heartbeat.

Professor Hayden began to make notes on the pertinent physics equations related to solar combustion on the old-fashioned chalkboard beside the desk.

There was no point in living in a dreamworld—I couldn't quit the band. I was under a punitive contract that I'd been too young and naive—and my parents far too eager—to question signing.

My chest got heavy again with the familiar panic of being trapped. As the only child of parents who considered me their life's work, this life of stardom had never felt like my choice. I pressed my fingers in to ease the pressure and concentrate on the professor's words.

I copied down the equations in my notebook as my breathing steadied.

"Jack, do you mind staying behind?" Professor Hayden asked as he wrote down the last equation.

I tried to get up, but the room tilted like a ship in a storm off the Atlantic. The monster was back. I grabbed the back of my chair. It felt like the only thing that kept me from falling.

What was *wrong* with me? Act normal, goddammit. I couldn't have my professor, whom I was desperate to impress, notice me acting erratically. I pressed my breastbone with my closed palm, something I had gotten in the habit of doing since elementary school to cover up panic symptoms.

My fellow students left, casting cursory glances over their shoulders at me. Shit. Who knew what they would speculate.

When their footsteps faded in the distance, Professor Hayden leaned on his desk and pinned me with his sharp gaze. "I know who you are."

The panic arrived in a whoosh. Everything was wrong. I was missing some crucial skill or knowledge I needed to stay alive, to stay sane. My windpipe shrank. I coughed again in a futile attempt to widen it.

"Are you sick?" Professor Hayden recoiled.

Act normal. I took off my beanie and ran a hand through my hair. "No. I mean ... maybe? I don't know. Probably allergies."

"In January?"

Dammit. As anxiety sped up my adrenaline, it slowed down my brain, so I said stupid things. Had someone cranked up the heat? Sweat pooled between my shoulder blades. "I guess not. Maybe something I picked up on the plane."

He crossed his arms. "Is that disguise working for you?"

I shifted my shoulders uneasily. I didn't know what I'd done, but it was clear Professor Hayden had an issue with me. "The toque and the glasses? More or less. One of my friends came up with it." I attempted a smile, the same one fans swore gave them heart palpitations, but Professor Hayden merely rolled his eyes.

"Don't waste your rock star charm on me. Having you in this class was forced on me. It goes against my principles to support anyone who accesses an Oxford education unethically or takes the place of a worthy student."

"But I'm not taking anyone's place," I protested. "I made sure of that."

I wasn't lying. I'd been scrupulous to clear this point with William Cavendish-Percy before accepting his offer. "A place was made for me, in exchange for supporting—" I stopped, realizing too late the hole I was digging for myself. I had paid for my spot and Professor Hayden knew it.

Why couldn't the anxiety that made me weird and dumb just *go away*? There was absolutely no reason for me to have it. No childhood trauma. No hardship. I'd been coddled and told I was amazing since birth.

Professor Hayden gave me the longest, most loaded blink. "If you think that's going to win me over, Mr. Seary, you are sorely mistaken. I read your application. You don't even have an under-graduate degree."

My skin prickled. I would have loved to have gone to univer-sity like Lucy in St. John's or, better yet, Toronto, but I'd become a famous musician. I'd regretted that choice often enough. "My career consumed everything," I tried to explain.

"You could have attempted an online degree."

I could have, but it felt incompatible with the fractured life of a touring musician living between time zones with no day ever the same. Gary made sure we were almost constantly recording albums and making more money. Plus, there was always my anx-iety to manage.

"I've been reading whenever I can to keep up to date on the latest astrophysics papers and projects like the Extremely Large Telescope and Hubble and—"

He remained unimpressed. "But not in any structured way, and not with any instruction?"

"No," I admitted. The room lurched again, so I grabbed the side of his desk.

He pursed his lips, looking down at my hand, then back up at me with suspicion. Oh shit. He wasn't mistaking my panic for an addiction problem, was he?

"There is nothing I can do about you being here, Mr. Seary," he said. "Believe me, I've tried. However, I think it only fair to warn you—do not think I will go easy on you because of your lack of experience, education, or preparation. And especially not because of your money."

"I don't think that," I sputtered. "I never did."

"Good," he said. "Now, if you please, I need to prepare for my next class."

I understood the dismissal for what it was. Besides, I needed to get back to college for the matriculation ceremony. If I missed it, I couldn't use the Bodleian Library, and from the sounds of Professor Hayden's stern warning, that was going to be essential.

If only I could ask him how to earn his respect—this man was one of my idols. My body throbbed with the knowledge that I was a fraud in the place where I most wanted to belong.

How could a life that looked so glossy from the outside feel so terrible on the inside?

I was so rattled when I got back to my room that I had to listen to an emergency anxiety meditation before I could face anything else. It helped a tiny bit but didn't change the fact that Professor Hayden had made me feel smaller than I'd ever felt.

After that was done, I had to quickly change into my sub fusc. Today was matriculation—the grand Oxford induction ceremony that made new students official members of the University. My lungs thankfully felt like they could take in air by the time I walked out my bedroom door onto the landing and found myself face-to-face with Lucy.

Seeing her brightened everything, like the sun coming out from behind clouds.

She shut her bedroom door behind her, then leaned her back against and pressed her index finger on that spot between her brows. Right. The feeling was not mutual.

"Why are you looking at me like that?" She blinked, dropping her hand. "Don't even think of mocking my outfit. You're wearing the same thing."

Lucy in sub fusc made my hands squeeze so I didn't make the mistake of reaching out and touching her. She wore a flowy black skirt that hit midshin and showed off the shapely curves of her calves, a white silky-looking shirt with sleeves that puffed slightly at the shoulder and cuff, and a black silk tie around her neck. I wondered, not for the first time, what it would feel like to kiss her there.

I couldn't tear my eyes away from her. We lapsed into silence; the air thickening around us. Lust roared back to life in inconvenient parts of my body. I pulled my robe around me to cover it up.

From the wariness in her eyes, it was abundantly clear she had absolutely no idea that standing this close to her on this tiny landing was driving me wild.

"Well?" She raised her brows.

Right. Words. I waved my hand between us. "I was *not* going to mock you. You look perfect."

She rolled her eyes. "Yeah, right."

I couldn't let her believe something so wrong. "You do. I was thinking how clever you look. And beautiful. It's a lethal combination."

Her mouth dropped open slightly. Good god. Had I managed

to leave Lucy Snow speechless? A unique calm stole over me—a feeling I only experienced when I was with her. I couldn't explain why or how, but when everything else in my life felt wrong, Lucy felt right. "How were your first few classes?"

She forced a smile, but her eyes told me something very different. "Fine. How about you?"

I shrugged, unable to reconcile how much I'd loved the class and just how much Professor Hayden resented me being there. "You know me. Anywhere there are telescopes, I'm happy."

She nodded, preoccupied. Something was bothering her.

"Is law how you expected it to be?"

Her lips twisted, confirming my suspicion. She hated it, just like I thought she would. "It seems very useful so far."

Useful? I had an idea—no doubt an incredibly stupid idea—but I was powerless against the compulsion to lift even a small bit of the weight she had to shoulder. "I'll give you money if you want to study something else … something you actually enjoy," I blurted out.

"What?" Her tone could refreeze all the melting polar ice caps.

"Money. Like you said, I have a lot—more than any one person should ever have. I'll give you as much as you need to have the freedom to study whatever you want."

"A loan?" she demanded, her pupils dilating.

"No. A gift." She didn't know it, but she'd be doing me a favor. It tortured me that I had so much money and privilege and luck and yet I was still an anxious mess who couldn't cope with life. I wasn't worthy of my wealth. If I could use some of it to help Lucy, then …

She shook her head. "Are you joking?"

"I wouldn't do that."

She made a sound of disgust. "If you think you can buy me off, you don't know me at all."

Buy her off? "Jesus, is that what you think of me? I see a friend in need, and I have the means to help. That's it, Luce."

She took a deep breath. "This is a stupid conversation, and we're going to be late. I don't need saving by you. I never have."

I couldn't just stand by and let her be miserable. She hated law. I could read her face better than my own heart. Lucy had been put on this earth to sing. "What if I got you an audition so you could earn your own money? I know the right people now. I have pull."

She rubbed her thumb over the face of her dad's watch. "I told you. I've given up on that dream."

My head throbbed. All because I'd been talked into signing that stupid contract.

We stared at each other, both breathing heavily. I wanted to help her. I wanted to make her see herself the way I saw her. I wanted to kiss her. I couldn't do any of those things. Frustration made me clench my hands again. "Truce?" I said finally.

She crossed her arms across her chest. "Fine," she said. She checked her watch. "We need to go."

CHAPTER THIRTEEN

Lucy

By the door to the lodge, Alfie and Robbie were struggling trying to herd the matriculates into a cohesive group to walk over to the Sheldonian Theatre where the centuries-old matriculation ceremony took place.

Robbie waved at us. Alfie charged over, armed with a clipboard.

"Lucy Snow and Jack Seary accounted for." He ticked his sheet. "And they haven't throttled each other."

"Yet," I said, still reeling from my reaction to Jack's offer.

Like most of my fellow Newfoundlanders, I had a visceral dislike of being an object of charity. Besides, the only time I'd accepted help from Jack, it had backfired spectacularly.

"Hey!" Jack protested, looking hurt.

The worst part about his offer was this: for one split second there, I'd been tempted to accept. Not only would it rescue me from studying law, but it would also remove so much of the friction from my life. I never told anyone this, but I'd always secretly longed for ease.

"Smashing." Alfie was clearly too distracted to pay attention to the tension between us. He brandished his clipboard. "No more lollygagging. Join the other matriculates. Cedar, Shaun, Lachlan, Raphael, and Binta are already at the Sheldonian in the audience."

"What? To watch us?" I asked, my anger softening.

"Of course. Matriculation is a significant rite of passage for an Oxford student." Alfie looked the part in his long, flowy doctoral robe and multiple colored silk sashes around his neck. "That's what skulks do—show up for each other to celebrate the good and commiserate the bad. We'll be leaving in a moment."

I took a deep breath as we joined the group, trying to savor this moment. I was being officially inducted in as an Oxford student today. This was monumental. I had to stop letting Jack get in the way of my Oxford experience. I just wished he didn't always make me so conflicted.

I snuck a glance at him beside me. To be fair, he was hard not to notice. Did he have any idea what the sight of him in a black suit and white button-down shirt underneath his academic robe did to us mortals? He wore it with the same ease he did jeans and his favorite Tom Waits T-shirt. The stark black-and-white sub fusc set off his fiery coloring, his copper hair brushing the stiff collar of his dress shirt.

Looking at him made my stomach feel like melting sunlight, and I had no idea how to stop it. I had to constantly remind myself that Jack was used to hanging out with starlets and supermodels and I was just a minor part of this brief eight-week blip in his glamourous existence.

The other matriculates were staring at Jack while trying to look nonchalant about him in their midst. That's who he was now, not the crush from back home I remembered.

I thought about the media lying in wait on the other side of the college door. The list of matriculates was published by the university in advance of the ceremony, so they would be in full formation. These reminders of the differences of my life and Jack's tended to lessen inside Beaufort's walls, so I was grateful for the reminder. "You're going to be mobbed by the media."

His eyes darkened to the shade of a pine forest in the winter. "I know."

My gaze snagged on his hands. They were shaking. My heart clenched. He hadn't been lying about fame rattling him.

I could leave him to the wolves, but it simply wasn't in me to abandon anyone that way. "Maybe we can get you in the middle of the pack?" I suggested.

He reached out, and the calloused pads of his fingers touched my hand. "Thank you."

I tried not to react, but it was impossible to ignore the electrical shock that tingled up my arm. "It's worth a try."

"Do you think I should keep the glasses?" he asked.

I shook my head and slid those nerdy black frames I secretly adored off his face. They were warm in my hands. I folded them carefully to give myself time to recover from the effect the freckles across the bridge of his nose were having on me. "Better not wear them if you want your disguise to work after today." I handed them to him.

He gave one short, sharp nod. "You're right." He slid them from my fingers, his touch filling me with a voracious demand for more.

I had to stop being a fool. I left his side to enlist the other students in protecting Jack by keeping him in the middle of our group. I would help protect him, but I would never let myself fall in love with him a second time.

The media blinded us with flashbulbs and deafened us with shouts of "Jack! Jack! Look over here! Have you gone to rehab for your drug addiction?"

Luckily, Robbie and Alfie had anticipated this and alerted the Oxford police, who had set up metal barricades and were keeping the press behind them.

Our fellow students were delighted to help with my plan. Everyone surrounded Jack, keeping him the nucleus of our penguinlike orbit.

That beautiful smile on Jack's face grew, his dimples deepening to full wattage. I could see it dawning on him that his fellow students, as starstruck as they might be, were putting their awe aside to keep him safe. Was he so unused to feeling protected?

We passed under the Bridge of Sighs when my cell phone vibrated in my pocket.

Shit. Could I ignore it? No. It had to be my mom or Alice. Not answering, even on my way to matriculation, wasn't an option.

I plugged my other ear so I could hear over the rumble of the crowd and the more distant shouts of the paps. "Hello?"

Jack touched my shoulder and raised a brow in question.

"Home," I mouthed at him.

"Lu-Lu-Lucy." Alice's voice shuddered with tears.

"What is it, Alice?" I asked. "Sorry, but can you speak louder, sweetie? I'm on my way to a thing. I won't be able to talk for long."

"What's all that noise?" she asked, sounding more like herself.

"I'm going to an Oxford ceremony." I definitely didn't have time to explain the antiquated traditions of matriculation and sub fusc. "What's wrong?"

She sniffed. "I got all this reading for homework this week, and it took me so long, and the letters kept flipping around, doing somersaults. Some of the other kids called me stupid."

"Screw the other kids. You're brilliant. You just have a different way of learning, and we're going to get you tested to figure out the best way of doing that. I'm working on it, I promise."

"Mom said we won't be able to afford it with you in England."

Ugh. If only my mother could restrain herself from creating problems quicker than I was able to solve them. "That's not true. I promise you I will figure it out."

A shuddering sigh echoed through my phone. "You promise?"

It was stupid to promise. I had no idea how much testing and help would cost and my budget was already tight. But I also knew I wouldn't rest until Alice got every bit of help she needed. It wasn't an option not to figure it out, even if it meant cutting this Oxford plan short and returning home to work three jobs. "I promise."

"Okay," she said. "I'm going to play now." Click. She'd hung up.

I stared at my phone, trying to adjust to this new set of burdens that had been piled on me. Even though I could never accept such a gift from him, a tiny bit of Jack's money would sure come in handy.

I looked up at the Sheldonian Theatre looming ahead of us. We were almost there.

Jack was watching me, a line of worry between his brows. "Everything okay?"

I nodded. They weren't, but I couldn't let him do anything about that.

Filing into the Sheldonian Theatre felt like walking inside a fancy layer cake.

It boasted rows and rows of wooden benches and symmetrical windows, as well as a huge painted fresco on the ceiling. The place echoed with tradition and ceremony.

We were ushered into the benches in alphabetical order, so Jack and I were separated by only a few other students. Everyone was watching him, although Jack kept peeking around the other students in the line and grinning at me. Annoyingly, it was impossible not to smile back.

When the grandiose yet confusing ceremony—big chunks were in Latin—was over and we went back outside, Jack and I were hugged ruthlessly and congratulated by Alfie, Cedar, Shaun, Raphael, and Binita. The police were doing an amazing job of keeping the press outside the tall, black metal gates of the Sheldonian courtyard.

"Lachlan wanted to come, but he had rugger practice," Alfie said, pumping Jack's hand. "He told me to shake your hands and pass on his congratulations." So many other students and dressed-up parents milled around, taking photos, posing with each other, popping champagne.

Grief tugged deep within me. My dad would have eaten this up. He'd always dreamed of a life beyond the shores of Newfoundland.

"Let's go to the Turf and share a celebratory pint—or several," Shaun said.

"Yes," Binita agreed. "You can't matriculate if you don't celebrate."

"We'll join you," Jack said. My head snapped to him. He winked at me. *We'll,* as in him and me?

Cedar gave us a searching look, then tugged Alfie's arm and waved her friends to follow her. "You heard him," she said. "Let's get some benches and a fire. Your places of honor will be ready when you get there."

When they left, I turned to Jack. "What's going on?"

"I want to go back in there when it's empty."

In the Sheldonian? It was a three-hundred-year-old historical monument. I highly doubted they let students just poke around on a whim.

"Yes."

Jack had clearly gotten used to making rock star demands.

"The Sheldonian is a protected architectural treasure. I'm sure it's already locked up. I don't think even your celebrity card could unlock it."

"I saw an open window."

I goggled at him. If he thought I was going to attempt to shimmy my ample body through a small window, he was deluded.

"The acoustics are supposed to be out of this world." He tried and failed to sound nonchalant.

"So?" I demanded, but the memory of the relief flowing through me when I'd sung in the chapel the other day tempted me. I could never resist extraordinary acoustics. Could anyone who sang? "I'm not breaking into the Sheldonian with you. I cannot afford to get expelled."

"Maybe we can just ask, then." Jack's mischievous smile should come with a warning label.

I swallowed down the longing to sing inside that magnificent space. "Go ahead and try Jack," I said. "This might be entertaining."

"I know it's a long shot." He rubbed his crooked pinky with

his thumb, a look of utter determination hardening those angelic features. "But I'm an astrophysicist at heart. I'm all about long shots."

He'd lost me. "How so?"

"It's a long shot that a star's light reaches earth, and yet it does. Every night."

There was no arguing with that. Besides, it might be fun to watch him get shot down.

He'd done it. I was both impressed and appalled.

A custodian was closing up, and Jack had unleashed that trademark Jack Seary charm and convinced him he'd left his watch behind—a family heirloom—and we needed to find it. The custodian agreed he would come back in fifteen minutes to let us out. I didn't think he recognized Jack at all—he was just that persuasive.

Maybe I shouldn't have doubted him. Jack's green eyes were an open invitation to everyone to join in his world. Few could resist. God knew I hadn't been able to at one time. Even now I was going along with him, wasn't I?

I could never quite figure out how things like getting back into the Sheldonian came to him for the mere asking. My life had been so very different. We'd clearly been born under different stars and I'd never been given any reason to hope that could change.

Jack led the way up the center alley. The space felt completely different empty than when it was filled with robed academics.

I could tell from the echo of our footsteps that he hadn't been exaggerating about the acoustics. They sounded even more promising than the Beaufort chapel. My throat ached with the need to sing.

In front of the dais, where Oxford's vice-chancellor had led the matriculation ceremony with gravitas, I turned to Jack. "This is pretty cool," I admitted.

He looked around, his face full of wonder. It said something about him—something good—that after the past four years he still held on to the capacity to be impressed.

"You brought me back in here to sing, didn't you?" I called his bluff. The thing I couldn't let him know was that as much as he might want me to sing, I yearned to sing a hundred times more.

He shrugged. "I always want to hear you sing." I couldn't be in a building with these acoustics and not sing. It just didn't feel physically possible.

"Fine," I said, trying not to show the enthusiasm bubbling up in me.

"Really?" His eyes went wide.

"Really. What's your request? Keep in mind this might not happen again anytime soon, so choose carefully." How had he convinced me to do this?

"'The Banks of Newfoundland.'" It was a sea shanty we had grown up hearing and singing, and we'd sung it together almost every time we rehearsed as a vocal warmup back in the high school music room in St. John's.

"Are you trying to make me feel nostalgic for home?"

He gave his head a tiny shake. "I'm trying to make you feel nostalgic for me."

Unfortunately, despite my best attempts to forget him, I didn't need to sing to feel that. I had to turn away then, because the soft look on his face made me feel as though four years and his abandonment of me had never happened.

I tried to clear the emotion in my throat. "No. I'm going to sing something else." I couldn't sing "The Banks of Newfoundland" for him. I might want to burst into tears like I had when I'd seen who I was sitting beside on the plane.

I turned away and climbed a few rows of seats behind the dais to best take advantage of the acoustics.

I checked Dad's watch. Our fifteen minutes had already dwindled to seven. No time to waste.

I took a deep breath and started Northern Junk's first hit single, a rollicking little ballad about falling in love with a best friend, kind of the flip side to Taylor Swift's "You Belong with Me."

I closed my eyes to block out Jack. It wasn't the most soaring song, but I let my voice rip, and I felt a familiar sensation of flying above all the troubles of my life.

In the second to last stanza, Jack's lyrical tenor mixed with my alto. His voice had never been as powerful as mine, but it had a wistful, gritty beauty all its own.

I was snapped right back to those heady six months when we were inseparable—rehearsing together in the music room and after at his house, with his mom preparing snacks while we watched old episodes of *Cosmos*, or when I'd have a restaurant shift and he'd hang out and do homework and buy a coffee every hour to justify staying there while I worked.

After the last note, it took a few moments for the echo of our voices to dwindle to silence. Jack was right—the acoustics were out of this world. Maybe the best I'd ever sung in.

I opened my eyes and turned to Jack after my voice faded away.

He was looking at me with ... What was that? Reverence? It rekindled a bonfire in my soul I hadn't realized I'd been missing.

"So?" I asked finally.

His throat worked as he swallowed. "You've still got the power to render me speechless, Lucy Snow."

I had to steel myself against how he was making me feel all mushy and hopeful. "You were right. The acoustics are phenomenal."

"Not just the acoustics. You."

Jack's compliments flustered me. It would be so much easier if he ignored me and acted like a jerk. It felt too scary to accept his praise, but at the same time it had been sincere so I couldn't throw it back in his face either.

Silence settled over us I checked my watch again. Only two minutes left. "We should head out. We can't make that poor custodian come looking for us. What excuse are you going to make for your missing watch when—"

"Will you come to my concert this weekend?" Jack burst out.

"What are you talking about?"

"I just ... I needed this break at Beaufort for a reason, Luce." He stared down at his expensive-looking shoes and tapped his foot on the marble floor. "I've been struggling with anxiety when I perform."

Anxiety? Was that what his trembling hand was all about? Jack seemed so confident, so out of my league he was in a different galaxy, that the idea of him having anxiety seemed absurd.

"Stage fright?" I asked, softly. The expression on his face was proof enough he was truly struggling, even though he always seemed so assured on the stage—an absolute natural.

"Something like that." He ducked his head. "Look, it's embarrassing, but I know to you I'll always be just Jack. I would be so grateful of that anchor at Wembley. You tether me."

That was me. Salt of the earth, even though I longed for so much more. "Me?" I confirmed.

"Yes. You. I know it's a lot to ask, and you have no reason to say yes."

He was right. I didn't, except there was something in Jack's eyes that made me consider it anyway. I pressed that spot between my eyebrows. "Fine, but I don't want to be in some kind of mosh pit with a bunch of screaming fifteen-year-olds."

He did a double take. "Does that mean you're considering it?"

"I guess."

"You'll be backstage with me. I will make sure you're treated like royalty. I promise."

"I don't know how I can miss that much study time," I said. "I'll have to figure that out."

"You can work backstage and in the limo on the way there and back." His words were measured, but his face was eager and vulnerable.

I chewed my lip. "Okay," I finally agreed. "When do we leave?"

"Saturday midafternoon," he said. "The limo will pick us up and take us to Wembley."

Since when had my life transformed into a reality TV show? Take the humble girl from Newfoundland, stick her across the hall with a famous musician who she shares a past with, and ...

The worst part was I could barely wait to watch the next episode.

CHAPTER FOURTEEN

Jack

Backstage at Wembley, I grimaced at my reflection in the mirror. The familiar scent of sour sweat and stale pot made my stomach churn and my ears ring. If it wasn't for Lucy curled up on the couch behind me, I'd be deep in a full-blown panic attack by now.

"I don't care how much they pay the band's stylist." Lucy was staring directly at my crotch with intriguingly flushed cheeks. "Those pants are too tight. Aren't you worried about splitting a seam mid-guitar riff?"

I was. The leather pants were too tight, or maybe I'd gotten too used to the English fry-up breakfasts in the hall at Beaufort. The waistband cut into my hips, and my genitals felt like they were stuffed into a too-small duffel bag.

"Maybe too much bacon and eggs?" I turned sideways in the mirror and sucked in my stomach.

Was that admiration I saw in Lucy's reflection in the mirror? It was gone too quickly to be certain.

"No. You're still long and lean. Blame the pants."

"One of the things I signed away in that contract with Gary was any choice in what I wear onstage."

"Seriously?"

"Seriously. Do you really think I want to be shirtless that often?"

She laughed. "I did, actually."

"No way. It gets really fucking cold. That's not even the worst part of the contract."

"Really?"

I nodded, trying to ignore that crawly feeling under my skin.

Why hadn't I read that contract through? I would never again sign something blindly, but that didn't help me out of my current dilemma. Gary had all three of band members by the nuts and never failed to remind us there was nothing we could do about it.

My heart started beating faster—too fast. It was taking up too much room. leaving no space for oxygen.

"What will happen if you fart in those pants? I have concerns— where would it even go?"

She was trying, and failing, not to appear amused. If my only accomplishment was to make Lucy smile several times a day, that would be enough. She was maybe the only person who could get me out of my head. "I have no idea and don't particularly want to find out."

"You might explode. Maybe that's what the urban myth of spontaneous combustion is really all about—overly tight jeans."

"I wouldn't rule it out."

I wished I could take her onstage with me. She felt like the only tangible thing that stood between me and the panic sinking its claws into me in front of a Wembley audience.

"I apologize again for how my bandmates acted when I intro-duced you." They hadn't even bothered to give Lucy a smile or ask her a polite question or two about who she was. They just stared at her quizzically, and Oliver had rolled his eyes and grunted, "Yeah, whatever."

I watched in the mirror as Lucy shrugged but didn't miss how her eyes darkened. "I'm not the kind of girl famous musicians generally take much interest in."

I turned around so I faced her. I wouldn't put up with anyone belittling Lucy, so I sure as hell wasn't going to stand by while she belittled herself. "What are you talking about?"

Her left shoulder moved up and down quickly under her soft-looking sweater, this time it was a pale lilac. "I don't have that groupie look. Tall. Skinny. French braids. Wearing a crocheted halter top and vintage cut-offs."

No, that wasn't Lucy. She was a million times better. Lucy had no idea how much I wanted to grip that pouty lower lip between my teeth, how much I wanted to slip my hands underneath that sweater of hers. I'd never been able to pay attention to anyone else when she was in the vicinity. "You're a million times more interesting than any groupie."

Her eyes flew to mine with a question in them, then lowered again almost as fast. "You always knew how to charm me, Jack Seary, but I'm a wiser now."

I leaned against the counter, my face itching under the heavy stage makeup. "That still won't stop me from trying to get you to see yourself the way I see you."

"Stop it, Jack," she ordered. I loved fierce, pissed-off Lucy best of all.

"I will not. Even if you won't admit it to yourself, you have more to offer an audience than any of the band members in Northern Junk could ever dream of."

"Jack," she warned, her voice as frigid as those icebergs that drifted into the bay.

"Okay, okay." I waved my hands and flopped beside her on the couch. What I really wanted to do was reach over and pull all of her warmth and realness and guardedness into my arms.

There was a knock on the door. "Fifteen minutes!" a stagehand hollered. For a moment Lucy had made me forget I had to go on-stage, but now my panic roared back. A sickening certainty that everything was wrong, that I wouldn't survive this concert, infiltrated every cell. My hands started to shake.

How was I going to spend the next three hours pretending I was a normal person on stage? Every one of my expressions and movements would be photographed and videoed. They would notice I was barely holding it together.

Yes, my fans would be there too, but I'd seen fans turn on their heroes in a split second. Besides them, there would be thousands of people who wanted a story about me or the group to sell for as much money as they could get. It didn't matter if it was true.

I knotted my hands together so Lucy wouldn't notice, but the shaking was getting worse. My heart galloped so fast my ribs didn't feel big enough to hold it.

Lucy narrowed her eyes at my hands. "Your hands are shaking."

"Yeah." I should have known better. She missed nothing.

She inspected my face. "And under all that pancake makeup ... Wow. You look green."

"I know." Having someone spot the signs of my panic, even Lucy, ramped it up. My ears burned. I should be stronger than this. I should be less sensitive. Why did just being normal feel so impossible? I was going to pass out onstage or throw up. It would be all over the newspapers. Everyone would say it was an overdose.

Everything was spinning out of my control. Certainty something terrible was going to happen pressed down on me, squeezing my lungs so my breath was ragged.

"Oh my god." She searched my face. "This is the anxiety you were talking about in the Sheldonian?"

I dropped my head in my hands and tried to take slow, even, "square" breaths, like I'd learned from online anxiety forums, where I'd gone by the anonymous name "PanickedGinger." Even the air felt threatening. I couldn't get enough. Come to think of it, this technique had never fucking helped one bit.

"Jack." Lucy's hand was warm on my shoulder. If she could just keep it there for the whole concert, maybe I would survive. "Are you going to be able to perform?"

"Not really," I managed. Every performance felt like going to war. I'd struggled with these horrible attacks for as long as I could remember and had never understood them. I'd hoped that by signing on to Northern Junk they would magically vanish—my younger, more naïve brain had reasoned that rock stars didn't have panic attacks.

I would jettison this defective glitch in me in an instant if I knew how.

"This is more than just stage fright." I felt Lucy's fingers knead into my back.

"I have panic and anxiety disorder. This is a panic attack."

"*That's* why you're taking a break?"

I nodded.

"And I made the assumption ... Jack, I'm so sorry."

I waved away her apology. *She* didn't need to apologize to *me*.

"I'm assuming you've tried therapy and everything?"

"Yeah," I said ruefully, thinking of all the times I'd been full of hope at the beginning of a new book or course about mastering my panic and anxiety, only to end up in the same state—or worse—than when I started. It was devastating. It was exhausting. And it made me feel defective. "I can't talk about it in this environment." I waved my hand around the room. "As you can imagine, Gary and my bandmates don't have much patience with it."

"Arseholes," she muttered, using the Newfoundland slang for the more common word. Now she knew and she wasn't blaming me—it was a beam of light shining through the dark.

"My parents and Gary think my bandmates are marvelous guys and should be my best friends. They think I should confide in them about it, but I can't trust them. They'd throw me under the bus in a heartbeat if it got them ahead."

"Seriously?"

"Seriously. I've never said this out loud before, but I suspect one or both of them being the source of the drug rumors."

She slid her hand from my shoulder to my back and started rubbing in firm soothing circles that in any other circumstance would have been a massive turn-on. Why did her touch feel so much better than anyone else's? "For all the celebrity and fandom and everything, the way you live isolates you from normal people, doesn't it?"

I nodded, digging my fingers into my forehead as another wave of panic grew speed. "It's like living in a cage and I don't like the people I'm trapped with."

"I may not understand a lot of your life—" Lucy kept rubbing. I had to hold back a groan of relief. "But I do know how it feels to be trapped." She had to be referring to her caretaking role.

"I should be stronger than this," I muttered, conscious of the familiar grip of shame around me.

"If anyone has ever made you feel like the anxiety and panic you're feeling is your fault, Jack, they're wrong." Her voice was steely.

I let out a bitter laugh. "You don't think it's just another example of how I don't appreciate everything I've been handed?"

"If there was a switch to turn off your anxiety, I know you would flip it."

I exhaled loudly. She got it. "That's true. Lately I think it's been trying to tell me something."

"Like what?" she asked, genuinely curious.

There was a knock on the door. I gave my head a shake and cleared my throat. "Yes?"

"Five minutes!" the stagehand shouted.

I turned to Lucy. "There's no time to go into all that now. I have to prepare myself." I cupped my hands over my mouth and breathed into them, trying to counteract the spinning of my head.

"I'll sneak you out of here if you need me to." Her voice was urgent.

She would too, barreling past anyone who tried to stop us. I shook my head without looking up.

"Are you sure? Sneaking you out of here under your manager's nose sounds way more fun than listening to some godawful boy-band."

I laughed. How did Lucy know exactly how to get me out of my own head? My heart slowed a bit, just enough for me to pretend to be normal for the next few minutes. "You don't know just how badly I want to take you up on that. Having you here helps a lot."

"This is better than you usually are?" Her voice was ripe with horrified disbelief.

"Yes," I admitted.

"I never thought I could feel sorry for you, yet here we are."

I'd wanted Lucy Snow to feel many things for me since we'd met, but sorry was never one of them.

Lucy flinched. Without warning, the door to the dressing room flew open, and Gary Simon—music impresario and my manager—burst into my dressing room. As always, he looked like a pickled version of a human—skin so tanned it resembled oiled leather, veneered teeth, and a Botoxed face.

Gary pointed at Lucy. "Is this your girlfriend?"

"Christ no," Lucy answered in an instant.

Ouch. The speed of her response didn't feel good.

Gary tried but failed—because of the Botox—to lift a questioning brow at me.

"This is Lucy Snow," I said, hearing my own voice as through it was underwater. "You can talk to her directly. We knew each other in Newfoundland. She's studying at the same college as me in Oxford."

"Isn't that nice," he said in a way that made it clear he didn't think it was nice at all. "So, Jack, have you gotten your ... issues straightened out since last time I saw you?"

I frowned at him. *Issues.* Gary handled my anxiety and panic like it was plutonium. "What you are really asking is am I okay to perform tonight, right?"

"Not asking," Gary said with false patience. "You're still under contract. It's your job to perform—not a choice."

"I couldn't forget my contract even if I tried. You remind me about it every time we talk."

He played with the heavy gold signet ring on his finger. "I wish I didn't have to."

"Yeah, well. That makes two of us."

Lucy had stopped her back rubbing when Gary burst in. I missed her touch.

"I suppose you've seen the press?" he said.

And there it was. The anxiety was back, choking me. "I haven't been looking. I've been on a break, remember?"

"You'd better catch the hell up," he snapped. "Don't forget there's a 'cleanliness' clause in your contract. The tabloids are full of rumors that you're in rehab and the whole Oxford arrival was just a coverup. If you still insist on not making a public statement, you'd better come up with an alternative story, and quick."

"You can't enact that clause if the rumors aren't true."

Gary tilted his head and pursed his lips. "I can make anything happen. You should know that by now. I can even make rumors true. My patience is not without limits."

He wasn't going to back out of our deal, was he? "You promised me eight weeks, Gary."

"Not if the press continues to be this damaging."

Darkness collected in the edges of my vision. I was in no state to battle with Gary right now.

"I'm studying law," Lucy broke in. "And I doubt clinical anxiety fits the definition of unbefitting behavior."

Gary sniffed. "There's a mental instability clause too."

"A legal one?" Lucy demanded. Lucy shouldn't be fighting my battles, but how wonderful it felt to have someone I could trust on my side.

"I can pay for lawyers that make anything fit anything." As much as I hated to admit it, I knew he was right.

"Go away," I groaned, trying to still my hands. God, how was I going to play guitar with them shaking like this? "I'm going to go out and perform, and your harassment is not helpful."

"Look, I'm not your enemy." He went from threatening to wheedling in a heartbeat—a tactic I knew all too well. "I'm on your side. I've even arranged a surprise for you at the end of the show."

Oh god. Whatever it was, I was sure I was going to hate it.

"What have you done?"

"You'll love it," he said. "You'll see."

The headset-wearing stagehand arrived behind Gary. "Showtime," he said. I had no choice but to stand up on my Jell-O legs and take my panicked self to perform like a circus monkey.

"You'll be in the wings, right?" I asked Lucy, trying to sound like I wasn't begging. Judging from her soft expression and Gary's disgusted one, I wasn't fooling anyone.

"I'll be there. The stagehand is going to take me in a few minutes like you arranged, remember?"

Right. Anxiety made me forgetful too.

She stood up on tiptoe and kissed my cheek. *More.* Her lips felt like silk. "You can do this," she whispered in my ear, then glowered at Gary. "If for no other reason, because you're not going to give your fucking ghoul of a manager an excuse to screw you over."

Lucy's fierceness felt solid—something I could hold onto. Defiance filled my chest, pushing the anxiety to the side just enough to play my part.

I nodded once. "You're right. I'll look for you in the wings."

"I'll be there. I brought my earplugs."

And somehow, just like that, Lucy left me smiling as the stagehand escorted me to the stage.

CHAPTER FIFTEEN

Lucy

I was still trying to absorb this whole new side to Jack when a different stagehand came to get me a few minutes after Jack was escorted away. To think his ease had been hiding panic all this time … his confession turned so many of my assumptions on their head, and I still hadn't made sense of it all.

As I was led through the backstage maze, I was amazed at how many people it took to pull off a show of this magnitude. Literally hundreds. Stagehands, prop people, sound engineers, costume designers, and handlers of all kinds. Finally, the stagehand stationed me at a spot in the wings where I could watch.

Almost immediately, Jack and his bandmates made their entrance onstage. The roar of the crowd was loud enough to make my eardrums bleed.

Jack was trembling, but it could easily be interpreted as excitement by people who hadn't seen him in the dressing room beforehand. I'd never realized how brave Jack was, or how much it cost him to go out and perform when every second was torture.

He strummed the first lick on his guitar. The audience screamed louder for more of him.

He was so fucking beautiful. Just like everyone else in Wembley, I couldn't tear my eyes off him as he played his guitar and sang in harmony with his bandmates like he was born to do this. His hair was burnished under the stage lights, and every time his dimples flashed the audience lost it.

Those pants might be way too tight, but maybe the stylist was onto something—goddamn did they do him justice. He looked every inch the rock god. My mouth kept dropping open as I watched, and liquid heat swirled between my thighs.

It was clear he had done this performance hundreds of times, and he went through the motions like a well-oiled machine. He was so good that nobody except me would suspect how much he was struggling. For the first time, I saw through his act.

It wasn't actually the real Jack out there. He was just brilliantly playing a role he hated. Nothing could dim his charisma, but I noticed the strain across his shoulders. His back muscles had felt like poured concrete under my hands.

Every time he turned away from the audience his concert-ready expression dropped and his eyes searched wildly for mine.

I gave him a thumbs-up or the round "okay" symbol with my thumb and forefinger, my heart aching for what he was going through. He didn't need to explain how difficult he was finding performing. I could see it in every nuance of his body and his face. He was hanging by a thread.

It must be difficult to be so insanely good at something he hated. The world just assumed that desire followed talent, but that wasn't the case with him. That envy I'd always felt around Jack was softening into something else, although it was too soon to know what.

That disconnect I'd felt was back too. Even as I worried about him in the wings, the screaming audience drove home that Jack Seary—my old crush, my greatest disappointment, my fellow Oxford student—was a massive global superstar. Not only that ... I, plain old Lucy Snow, martyr of St. John's and dutiful daughter—was the one he was getting reassurance from now.

It wasn't just tonight. I'd been trying to avoid thinking about it, but Jack was making me feel like the VIP of his life ever since we'd arrived at Oxford. I hated how much I loved being the chosen one for once in my life—Jack's chosen one.

The roar of the audience rippled like waves after Jack and his bandmates played one of their first-ever hits, "Stars in Your Eyes." Jack was rumoured to have written it. Despite the fact it had been sound engineered to sound like a Northern Junk song, its bare bones were a beautiful love ballad. I often wondered which one of Northern Junk's many groupies over the years had inspired it.

A ball of hard, heavy jealousy formed inside me. I couldn't imagine a more terrifying destiny than falling in love with a man the whole world was already obsessed with.

What would it be like to have all these people running around to amplify my voice? The sets, the costumes, the musicians, the sound engineers ... it all tugged on me like a powerful undertow. I wanted the life that Jack didn't. It was reckless and irresponsible, but here at Wembley it was impossible to lie to myself any longer.

There were three encores. Panic or no, the public people couldn't get enough of the magic of Northern Junk or Jack.

When he finally came offstage, his shiny shirt clung to his chest muscles with sweat. He made a beeline to where I stood among the stagehands and technicians, his expression like a starving man. Sparks shot up my spine.

"Lucy." His voice was hoarse. "You stayed."

He handed a stagehand his guitar. As if I would have left. "I don't break promises."

He blinked at me as though he wasn't sure if I was real, then in one swift movement gathered me against him. What was happening?

His body sagged in relief, but his grip was tight and possessive. My nose stung with unshed tears as I teetered on a cliff between joy and terror.

His sweat was damp against my cheek, and a drop trickled down my cleavage. He ran his palm, hot and calloused from playing guitar, up the back of my neck. I shivered at how perfect it felt.

The love I had for him roared back from where I'd shoved it away, deep inside me. Damn. It hadn't gone anywhere. I should step away. I couldn't be feeling like this about him. Instead, I examined his face. "Are you all right?"

He looked down at me with the ghost of a smile. "Better now."

His eyes were bloodshot like the first time I'd seen him again on the plane, making his irises glow an otherworldly jade. "Let's go back to my dressing room." His hands traced between my shoulder blades.

I didn't miss the edge of desperation in his voice. "You're one thread away from breaking, aren't you?"

His eyes widened and he swore under his breath. "How do you do that?"

"Do what?"

"See me."

God, that look on his face. Everyone bustling around us faded away, and all I could think about was how badly I wanted him to pull my sweater off and run his hand up and down my spine, then move to twist into my hair and pull my head back to better reach my neck. Any coherent words I might have had fled the scene. "I—I don't know."

It was the truth. This inexplicable connection between me and Jack had been there from the first time we met. It was even there, I realized now, in those four years we'd been apart, when his sudden disappearance ached like a phantom limb. Another reason I'd hated him was because I was never able to stop missing him.

I didn't have a name or an explanation for this thing either.

As we made our way through the backstage labyrinth, Jack took my hand. Our fingers slotted effortlessly together, unleashing a cocktail of fear and excitement in my veins. The yearning I had kept locked away for so long were now as undeniable as Jack's grip on me.

The raised brows and expressions of curiosity from the people we passed weren't lost on me. As we neared his dressing room door, he squeezed my hand in a little pulse that made my heart flip over. "I'm going to make this quick. Dressing room, shower, then limo back to Oxford. I can't wait to get out of here."

Why was I letting Jack in, even though I'd promised myself I wouldn't? He opened the door. The only reason I could think of was my hand just felt like it belonged in his.

I shut the door behind us and slammed into Jack's back, then I peered around him to see what made him freeze in his tracks.

There was the reason. Two of them, actually.

Jack's parents sat along the couch I'd curled up on before the concert. They had aged a bit in four years, and Jack's mother's hair was dyed a bit lighter. I recognized them both immediately.

"You're not supposed to come in here," Jack's mom said. It took a second to register she was frowning at me. Wait. Did she think I was some kind of stalker? Jack gripped my hand even tighter.

Maybe their son had become a rock star, but I hadn't changed that much. "It's me, Lucy Snow. From Newfoundland. Do you remember me? Believe it or not, I'm studying at the same college at Oxford as Jack."

Their faces puckered at the word 'Oxford' like they'd eaten a rotten squid. Jack dropped my hand. The energy in the room became stifling all of a sudden.

"Ah, yes. Now I remember you," his mother said, devoid of warmth.

"Hi, Mom," Jack said and sat in the chair in front of the mirror instead of going to hug them, which surprised me. I remembered them being close. "You two must be the surprise Gary mentioned." His voice was guarded.

His mother let out a tinkly laugh. "Gary couldn't resist giving you a hint, could he? He's so naughty, I swear."

Ew.

"We swore him to secrecy." Jack's father grinned, flashing the dimples Jack had inherited and employed to a far more devastating effect. Genetics was a bonkers thing. Two quite ordinary-looking people had given birth to Jack, who looked like a demigod.

I darted a glance at Jack, who I could tell was trying to look pleased but instead ended up looking like he was suffering from a bad case of the stomach flu.

I was puzzled by this dynamic. From what I remembered, Jack's parents were devoted to him, and vice versa. He was their golden child. Jack had told me once his parents had struggled for over a decade to have a baby before he'd arrived. He'd confessed their single-minded attention felt like a burden as much as a gift.

He was their only shot, and they wanted the world for him. They were prepared to give it to him, too, as long as his dreams coincided with theirs.

Jack didn't seem to know what to say, so I leaped into the breech. "How have you been, Mr. and Mrs. Seary?" Jack sent a grateful look at me and got up to pull me over a chair.

"Wonderful, as you can imagine." Jack's father's face glowed as he waved his hand around his son's dressing room. "We're so proud of Jack and everything he's achieved." He winked at Jack. "You know how proud of you we are, don't you, son?"

The lines of strain deepened around Jack's eyes. He didn't answer and the silence stretched uncomfortably long.

"He's extremely talented," I said.

"Didn't you used to sing?" his mother asked me. Was her tone condescending or was I just imaging things?

"I did, but I'm studying law at Oxford now, except they call it jurisprudence there. We're discovering Oxford has a different name for *everything*." I forced a laugh to keep things light for Jack while he recovered his wits.

Jack's mom clicked her tongue. "What a shame you stopped, although perhaps it's for the best. Not everyone can have the kind of trajectory Jack did. His kind of talent is few and far between."

Jack jerked out of his trance. "Lucy is far more talented than I could ever hope to be in a million years."

Both his parents stared at him, incredulous. "Is that so?" his father said finally, faking a smile, trying to jolly the tension along.

"It's a fact." I'd never seen Jack's face, usually so open, look so forbidding.

"You've always been so generous with your praise," Jack's mom said to him, ignoring me.

"It's not generosity Mom." Jack's face was stony. "It's the truth."

"Whatever you say, son." His father cut off another retort I was certain was going to fly out of his wife's mouth. "In any case, incredible show."

"But you're so pale." His mother reached out to him and then, thinking the better of it, dropped her hand. "You look exhausted, sweetie. I've said it before, and I'll say it again. This whole Oxford insanity is far too much to take on in addition to your music career. It's like Gary said. Your music needs to be your number-one priority. You made a commitment to Gary and to Northern Junk."

"Did I?" Jack's eyes glittered. "Or did you make it for me?"

"You agreed," his father reminded him.

All the fight went out of him like air from a punctured balloon. His body sagged against the chair. "I did. It was a moment of naïveté, but you're right."

I hated seeing the effect they were having on him, especially when I knew he was already so drained. "I should leave you guys to catch up." I started to get up from my chair. I had no idea where I would go, but I'd manage to find a quiet corner somewhere backstage to read the law books I had in my backpack.

Jack's arm flew out, stopping me. "Stay," he croaked. There was a plea in the crooked set of his mouth I couldn't refuse.

I sat again.

"You're stretching yourself too thin, honey." His mother twisted the big round-cut diamond on a chain around her neck.

"Yes, son." His father clasped his hands in front of him, clearly readying himself for a Hallmark-style father-son chat. "I've been thinking about this whole stage-fright business, and I believe you're just burned out. I agree taking a short break like you're doing is good, but you should spend it resting, not studying, so when you start Northern Junk's North American tour, you can even be stronger."

Jack shook his head, his cheekbones too sharp against his pale skin. "I love what I'm studying at Oxford. I'm so much better when I'm there and don't have to be 'on' all the time. That *has* to mean something."

His mother waved a hand. "No, it doesn't. Right, Lucy?"

Sure, I'd resented how quickly Jack's star had shot up in the sky, but if his mom thought she was going to rope me into encouraging Jack to continue doing something any idiot could see was destroying him, she had another think coming.

"I think Jack is the only judge of what's best for him," I said.

His mother's eyes narrowed. "I see. Are you two going out?"

"Mom!" Jack gasped. "Stop it."

But the way she was examining me with distaste made me feel conniving and pathetic.

"You don't need to worry," I said, my voice like flint, probably to convince myself as much as Jack's parents. "Jack and I would never go out in a million years."

"There! I knew it." Jack's dad looked inordinately pleased with himself. "He's never mentioned you, after all, and he's talked about a few of his other girlfriends."

Girlfriends? Oof. The word knocked the wind out of me, but maybe it was a timely reminder to double up on the walls around my heart.

Jack's features held a strange combination of horror, anxiety, and hurt.

"But what about his money?" his mother said.

"Christ, Mom! Stop," Jack hissed.

He stood up so quickly his chair rattled across the floor. "Will you please refrain from talking about me like I'm not even in the room? My anxiety does not make me stupid or deaf. Mom, how dare you suspect Lucy of ulterior motives?" His words were like lashes of a whip. "Lucy's right. I *do* know what's best for me. For the next six weeks, that's studying astronomy at Oxford."

"Don't shout at me," she said, her voice trembling now. "We just want what's best for you."

I was getting the impression that Jack's parents wouldn't know what was best for him if it smacked them across the face.

"It's true," his father said. "We tried to give you everything—all those music lessons and sports camps and everything else."

Jack crossed his arms over his chest. "Mom, Dad, I know what you've sacrificed to give me a good life, and believe me, I never forget it."

I bet they never let you forget it.

"But I think you do," his father said. "When we see you taking a wrong turn, can you blame us for trying to help?"

"Astronomy is not a wrong turn." Jack shook his head. "I always loved studying space more than music, but no matter how many times I tell you that, you don't believe me."

His father splayed his hands. "I believe this is a grass-is-al-ways-greener situation—"

"I give up," Jack said as he pinched the bridge of his nose. His shoulders drooped, and under his freckles his face started to take on a worrisome gray undertone.

His father cleared his throat and squirmed on the couch. "I should also mention Gary has warned us of something in your contract. About unprofessional behavior and a cleanliness clause."

"Dad," Jack said in a warning voice. "That is none—"

"You can't blame us for worrying," he continued talking. "We co-signed that contract for you because you were underage. We're liable too if you break it."

Jack's face went from exhausted to a mask of horror. For a few seconds I didn't think he even breathed. "You what?" He wheezed.

"We co-signed the contract. There was a separate codicil."

Oh shit. Professor Speedman had covered codicils in our last contract tutorial. I had understood enough to know that they could be used very sneakily.

"I've read the contract over a thousand times," Jack said, his face pale as cod flesh. "I never saw a codicil."

"It was an addendum," Jack's father said. "But it was referred to in a footnote."

"But ..." Jack trailed off, then dropped his head and clawed at his hair. "How could I not have known that before now?"

"We didn't want to bother you with it, but we figured now might be a good time to remind you that your decisions affect us too, son."

Jack blinked at his parents, but his gaze looked very far away. "I just need this term at Oxford, like we discussed, okay?"

"Only six weeks now!" his mother said in a way that made me think she had a calendar where was secretly crossing off the days.

CHAPTER SIXTEEN

Jack

After saying a stilted goodbye to my parents, my single focus was getting us out of Wembley and into the limo as fast as possible.

A fucking codicil? How was it possible no one had mentioned its existence in the past four years? Oxford had given me the mental space to seriously consider the ramifications of leaving Northern Junk and facing up to my parents' inevitable disappointment. But now ... another iron chain connected me to this life I didn't want anymore and this was the thickest, heaviest one yet. I didn't care about financial consequences for me, but I couldn't ruin my parents.

I put my arm around Lucy as we rushed through the crew who were dismantling our set and the sound and lighting techs sharing cigarettes backstage. I told myself it was to keep her safe, but really it just felt like such a relief to feel her body tight against mine.

Her lightning-fast response to my mom about never going out with me in a million years still stung, but I could mull over that later.

I spotted the door where I'd arranged to meet my limo driver, and my heartbeat slowed a bit. "Almost there," I said to Lucy.

She nodded, preoccupied.

The driver was standing beside the exit and hadn't noticed us yet.

"Jack."

My heart dropped to my feet. Gary. He stepped out from the shadows on the other side of the door, with Northern Junk's PR person and all-around mother hen, Cathy, by his side.

Gary was like a spider, always crawling out of dark corners. "I need a word before you leave." He gave me a smarmy smile. "Did you like your surprise?"

My head spun, and the muscles in my arms were screaming for a hot bath. Gary always had the gift of sensing the exact moment when I could not take one more thing. That's when he attacked.

I reflexively pulled Lucy even tighter against me. "What do you want, Gary?"

"Now, now," he tutted. "There's no reason for that tone of voice."

"I'm exhausted. Out with it."

"You poor boy." Cathy reached out and squeezed my free hand. Her palm was unpleasantly moist. She was a strange choice for Gary's sidekick. She worshipped him even though he treated her like dog shit on the bottom of his shoe, and followed him around like a shadow with her garishly floral polyester tops and brown bob that was styled like Darth Vader's helmet. "You need to be tucked into a bed."

Lucy's chin wrinkled as she took in this clucking middle-aged woman.

"Cathy and I have been talking," he said.

That was never good. I took a deep breath through my nose. "And?"

"We think this whole attempt to be low-profile at Oxford is the wrong path. It's just fueling stories of your addiction."

"Yes," Cathy chimed in. "You know I've always considered myself the mother of Northern Junk. I stay awake worrying about you at night, Jack. I've done my best to scotch the drug rumors, but the media are saying such horrible things."

Lucy made a little sound of anger under her breath.

"I don't *have* an addiction," I said. "I have anxiety."

Gary shrugged.

"Jack, dear, you know better than anyone that reality is never as important as optics." Cathy fluttered her hands around like demented butterfly wings.

That was wrong on so many levels, but in the bizarro world of being a rock star, it was also true. "We think this little stint at Oxford could add to your mystique if it's handled properly." Gary said.

I was intrigued despite myself. This was the first time he mentioned my stay at Oxford with any sort of equanimity.

"Yes," I said. "I've been thinking about this actually. We need to tell the media about my love for space and my research idea—"

"Don't be daft," Gary scoffed. "No one is ever going to buy you as a space nerd."

"You're far too handsome." Cathy batted her eyelashes, but I was immune to her odd behaviour. She wasn't the one I had to worry about.

"Don't interrupt, Cathy," Gary snapped.

She giggled and made a zipping motion across her lips.

Gary's gaze shifted from me to Lucy. "But if you're at Oxford because you're in love with a girl going there ..." He pursed his lips and nodded. "Now that could play well with our fans. Maybe you could stay for the whole term, in that case."

I was way too frazzled to make much sense of the nonsense coming out of Gary's mouth. He'd already promised me the full term, but then again, I should know by now that Gary's promises were worthless. "But there is no girl." That wasn't entirely true, but I sure as hell wasn't going to talk to Gary about Lucy.

He dug his hands in his pockets and rocked back on his heels. "Very minor problem. Cathy agrees with my idea that we need to make it look like you're madly in love. That way, when she dumps you, all the fans will fight for the privilege of supporting you."

Nausea rose in my throat. "You and Cathy should never be left in a room together."

Gary pointed at Lucy. "This would work especially well if the girl you're with is an … unconventional choice. You know, somebody who would make all your fans feel like they have a chance."

"Yes. Somebody completely different from your previous girlfriends." Cathy smiled.

I felt rather than saw Lucy flinch. Wait … they weren't talking about her, were they? My fist closed in readiness. I stepped in front of Lucy to shield her from their vile words and even viler insinuations. "No. Absolutely not. How could you ever think for a second I would agree to that?"

"I would think about it if I were you." Gary sneered. "I can invoke that cleanliness clause quite easily. I made sure it was drafted rather *large*, if you get my meaning. And I had a brief chat with your parents before they left. We discussed that codicil—"

I felt like the astronauts must have felt in the *Apollo 1* capsule, hearing each of the complex hatch locks clicking shut, one by one, before it caught on fire and killed them all.

"You bastard," I breathed. He had me over a barrel. I needed to *think.*

He shrugged and winked at me. "Think about it. By the way, I've decided the band will stay here in Britain until you've gotten this Oxford lark out of your system." He slithered away, dragging a waving Cathy in his wake.

I stormed out, holding on to Lucy even tighter.

"I can't believe that happened." Lucy was the first to break the silence.

My finger traced the path of a raindrop down the limo window as I tried to find a way out of Gary's latest trap. We'd been in the here over half an hour, driving through the night back to Oxford.

I leaned back in my seat with a groan. Exhaustion went deep in my bones and pressed down on my soul. I dreaded to guess what Lucy was thinking. I hadn't planned to expose her to so much— my panic, my parents' ambitions for me, Gary's toxicity … I hoped she didn't think Gary and Cathy were referencing her, but then again I'd felt her flinch.

If only she could see herself the way I saw her. Lucy was the last thing from an "unconventional choice." I couldn't pinpoint just one reason—maybe it was the brave way she carried responsibilities way beyond her years, maybe it was her trustworthiness, maybe it was that exquisite face or her transcendent voice. I knew it also had something to do with the passion and sensuality I sensed behind those tall walls around her heart. For that and a million other little things, she was the only choice for me.

"I'm so sorry," I said. "For all of it. I should have known tonight would turn into a nightmare."

Lucy rubbed that spot between her eyebrows. "What are you going to do?"

I gnawed my lip. "I honestly don't know. I can't think straight."

She shifted in her seat and tucked her legs underneath her. I caught a whiff of peppermint and sea salt. She fiddled a bit with her dad's huge watch around on her wrist. "I've been trying to figure out this dynamic with Gary, not to mention with your parents."

I took a breath through my nose. "Have you made any sense of it yet? I sure as shit haven't."

Her lips twisted. "Have you really sat your parents down and explained what this career is costing you in terms of anxiety and panic?"

My stomach knotted with frustration. "I've tried to explain the anxiety piece to them, but no matter how I approach it, they don't understand how something they can't see or feel—something happening only in my mind—is real. They say I've been oversensitive since I was a child and I just have to toughen up. Sometimes I agree."

"What do you mean?"

I chewed on my thumb, thinking. "How can something that in a way is a figment of my imagination be a valid reason to leave a career? I'm not sure I can really blame them for not understanding."

"Well, I can." Lucy's phone rang, and she pulled it from her jeans pocket and checked the number. "Crap. It's my mom. I have to take this."

I nodded and shifted my gaze out the window at a big blue Tesco sign whipping by.

"Hi, Mom," she said, then she listened for a long time. I could hear sobs and sniffling coming from the other end of the line.

"Mom, dyslexia is not the end of the world—" Lucy stopped talking and listened again. "It says nothing at all about Alice's intelligence. She's just as smart as she always was. She just needs to adapt to some different learning methods. I've been researching it. There are so many tools, and—"

She listened for several minutes more. If only she'd let me help.

"Six thousand dollars?" Out of the corner of my eyes I watched as Lucy's lovely creamy complexion drained of color. "Can't the school help with that? There must be public funding of some kind we can access."

She listened some more.

"But, Mom—"

"Yes, of course she needs it, but surely—"

A huge sigh seemed to come from the depths of Lucy's soul. "I can't come home now. Can't you see? If we can make this work, after these two years and a law degree, we will never have to have conversations about money again. I can start saving for you and Alice, so—"

Money was so strange. Even before Northern Junk, my parents had been comfortable. They'd had me later in life and, unlike Lucy, I'd never felt a lack of anything. After the money started pouring in from the band, and the novelty of being able to buy whatever I desired waned, it dawned on me that my wants hadn't changed that much.

I still dreamed of being left alone to geek out over astronomy and space. After I'd bought my parents their dream home in St. John's and donated to charities and all that, my money still couldn't buy me freedom to do what I wanted for longer than eight weeks and that didn't feel like nearly enough.

"I'm exhausted," Lucy said, bringing me back to the present. "Can I call you first thing tomorrow morning? I need to think."

Her forehead puckered.

"Mom, I have to go. Give Alice a hug for me. I'll figure this out. I promise. I'll call you first thing tomorrow, England time. Yes. I promise. Yes. You too. For the love of God, do not let Alice think she's stupid. Not for a second."

She hit the button on her phone and dropped her head in her hands with a groan. "You heard all that, didn't you?" Her voice came out muffled behind her palms.

"Yes." I would give her all the money and all the help, but I'd already seen how she reacted when I offered. Besides, Gary had managed to inject his poison into it now too. "Would it help to talk it over?"

She looked up, her eyes bleary. "I don't know. Maybe."

I leaned forward, exercising every last shred of self-control not to take her hands in mine. I couldn't be this close to her and not want to touch her. It was just beyond the laws of physics. "Tell me."

She launched into an explanation of Alice's need for a full psych ed assessment. "We're fairly certain it's dyslexia and affects both numbers and letters. I can't bear the idea of her not getting the help she needs to thrive. There are only two people in Newfoundland who do the government-recognized testing, so they charge through the nose for it."

"How much?"

"Five thousand dollars. Elsewhere in Canada, it's half that. Then there are the extra tools she will probably need. A scanner thing for reading, a new iPad and an Apple pencil, dictation software, etcetera, etcetera. I have no idea how much all that is going to be. Can you believe it?"

I could.

"I'm guessing you don't have that amount?" I asked delicately, aware anything I said about money could be easily construed the wrong way. Every cell in my body wanted Lucy to experience ease. She nodded. Her blue eyes clouded over. "It might as well be a million. I can't think of how I could lay my hands on either amount."

Screw Gary and Cathy. I had to at least try. "Don't get mad, but let me help you, Lucy. Let me give you the money. It's nothing to me. Honestly. This is going to sound crass, but I don't even keep track of how much money I've got anymore."

She hesitated, then shook her head. "I believe your offer is sincere, but I can't take charity from you, or anyone for that matter."

But she'd paused. I'd seen it. If there was a slight splinter of possibility she would let me help her, dammit, I was going to try. I opened up the console near my armrest and took out a package of Hawkins Cheezies I'd had my assistant stock the limo with and passed it to her.

She took it. Her eyes remained guarded, but her lips twitched. "Hawkins Cheezies? That's not playing fair."

I waited until she popped one in her mouth and a blissful expression stole over her features before I groveled.

"Lucy," I began. "I made the biggest mistake of my life four years ago. Not only did it trap me in the wrong life, but it broke your heart. I will never, ever forgive myself for hurting you. It was stupid and selfish and if I need to spend the rest of my life making it up to you, I will. I completely understand why you don't trust me anymore, but please give me this chance to show you that you can."

Her eyes were huge, but she still didn't say anything. Time to bring out the big guns. "Anyway, this isn't really about us," I said.

"It isn't?" Her voice was faint.

"No. This is about Alice." If Lucy cared about Alice getting help, then so did I.

She exhaled. "I just ... I don't know when I could repay you—or if I could repay you."

Was she ...? "Consider it a gift then."

She recoiled. Uh oh. Definitely the wrong tack to take. I'd been avoiding it, but the solution was staring us both in the face—a way for me to give her the money that would square with her conscience. It was a gross thing to ask of her, especially after Gary's disgusting—not to mention untrue—insinuations.

On the other hand, if it meant she would finally agree to accept my help, maybe this was an instance of doing the wrong thing for the right reasons. Did that make it okay? I had no clue. My stomach lurched. It didn't know either.

"I might have an idea," I ventured.

Lucy's hand clamped around her ankle, bracing herself. "From the look on your face, I can already tell I'm not going to like this."

"Maybe not right away, but it would be a way for you to accept the five thousand without feeling like it's charity. On second thought, let's make it ten thousand. Alice would do better with some tutors and all the devices and tools she needs."

Lucy's hand moved from her ankle to her throat.

"You would be helping me. I think this is the only way I'll be allowed to stay at Beaufort the entire term." I said. "I can't think of anyone else I can ask."

I could see the exact moment the coin dropped and she stopped chewing her cheezie. "This is about the fake-girlfriend thing Gary was blathering on about?"

I swallowed past the lump that had formed in my throat. "Yes."

She froze, a mask sliding over her face. At least she hadn't booted me in the groin yet. I chose to take that as a good sign. "Are you asking what I think you're asking?"

"Yes. I will transfer ten thousand dollars into your account right now if you agree to be my girlfriend until the end of term." There was no way of making that proposal without it sounding grimy, but if it meant I could take some of the financial burden off Lucy, it was worth it.

Lucy counted on her fingers.

"What are you doing?"

"Counting how many days that is."

Oh my lord. This woman. "It's six weeks, Luce. Forty-two days."

I could practically see the smoke coming out of her ears as her brain worked overtime. "And this would get you out of the cleanliness clause thing he was threatening you with and would mean you could finish Hilary Term at Beaufort?"

She was so bloody noble, even now, making sure I would get what I needed out of the bargain. "Yes. It would give me a reprieve from Gary's threat to pull me out early as well as from the codicil my parents signed, which he wouldn't hesitate to use as leverage either. It would allow me to at least enjoy my six weeks in peace. It's priceless to me."

Her forehead puckered. "But surely you have saved up so much money that even with the codicil, Gary can't really hurt you or your parents."

My breath came faster as I considered how trapped I was. "He has teams of lawyers and way more money than me. I don't know exactly how he would go about it, but I have every confidence he would. I cannot underestimate him. If it was just me, I wouldn't care. In fact, that was what I was considering doing before tonight, but I couldn't in all good conscience let him persecute my parents."

Lucy was nodding slowly. Her eyes lifted to mine. "Why me?" she asked. "Did Gary's reasons make sense to you?"

A knife to the heart. How could she possibly think that? "Everything he said was complete bullshit." My voice was shaking. "I would be the luckiest bastard on earth if you wanted to be with me."

Her brows pulled together as she took this in. I ached to reach out and show her how much I wanted this, and all the things she made me want to do to her.

"But there's so many other girls who would jump at the chance."

"I would never consider this with anyone else. It's you or no one."

Lucy's gaze flew to my face, then down to the knotted fingers in her lap. My eyes fell to her soft, creamy curves above the V-neck of her sweater. The problem with being her fake boyfriend was I probably wouldn't be able to kiss her there like I wanted to.

You're what I need, I wanted to shout, but of course I couldn't say that. Nothing could be better calculated to make her run in the other direction.

She cleared her throat. "What would my girlfriendly obligations be?"

I should have thought this through before asking her. "Be seen with me," I began. "Be physically affectionate in public." My stomach lurched at how much I looked forward to this part. I would rather take Lucy's crumbs over anyone else's feast.

She twisted her bulky watch around her wrist. "Lack of time is a problem. Coming with you tonight was already a stretch. I'm already behind, and I'm stressed about that all the time. I haven't even figured out how its humanly possible to keep up with the reading for my classes."

"We can work with that."

"How?"

Come on, brain. Think fast. "I can't help you with your law essays, but I'll feed you and keep you supplied with good coffee."

From the softening of her expression, I could tell something I'd said had resonated with her heart. Probably the coffee part. "You can take the lead, and I'll do everything I can to make it work. I promise."

Her eyes darted up in question. Ugh. Right. She didn't trust my promises anymore, with good reason.

"Give me the opportunity to show you a promise from me can mean something." I was begging now, but I wanted this so much, I wasn't even ashamed.

"Okay," she said finally.

My breath caught. "Is that a yes?"

She lifted her shoulder a smidge. "I guess."

A storm of gratitude rose in my throat, but I sensed I had to keep the exchange as transactional and businesslike as possible. If Lucy felt I was getting emotional, she would call time before it even began. "What's the best email to use?" I picked up my phone. "I'll transfer the money now."

"Thank you," she said and spelled the address connected to her bank account.

After a few taps I looked up again. "Done."

She gave a small nod. "All right. We have an agreement. Now, I need to read a case about a squatter who claimed he had rights over a garden shed he was living in." She unzipped her backpack beside her on the limo bench.

"Really? Did he win?"

She gave me an arch look. "I don't know yet. I have to read it to find out. You should try and get some sleep. You look like you've been dragged through a knothole backward."

"Yes, babe." I couldn't resist.

She grimaced. "No."

"No what?"

"Just no. You're going to have to come up with a better term of affection."

"I'll sleep on it."

THIRD WEEK

CHAPTER SEVENTEEN

Lucy

I was deep in the judgments of *Todrick vs Western National Omnibus Co Ltd* (1934) and trying my best not to fall asleep when there was a knock at my door.

I did my best to squash the anticipation fizzing in my chest and got out of my chair to open it.

Please let it be him—my fake boyfriend of four days. My heart pounded, and energy zipped through my veins. I shouldn't be feeling this excited, but who wouldn't look forward to seeing that lean, muscular frame and those flashing dimples lounging in their doorway? I was a human being after all.

I flung open the door so forcefully it banged against the bedroom wall. A little shower of white plaster fell to the floor. Way to play it cool, Lucy.

There he was. He had such a visceral effect on me—like my whole body was plugged into a light socket when he was near. I saw him so much these days, but it still didn't feel like enough. He wore a different nerdy NASA hoodie and jeans with his black glasses. His copper waves had grown a bit, curling under his right earlobe.

He held two brown-paper bags that were giving off whiffs of turmeric, ginger, and curry. Why did he have to be so much more tempting than the interpretation of land easements?

"Good evening, my sweet."

I mock gagged. "Nope. Keep trying." Jack was hellbent on finding a term of affection for me, but so far his ideas were going from cringey to cringier.

"I didn't have high hopes for that one." He held up the bags. "I brought you some dinner."

This was the third night in a row Jack had brought me food—and not just any food. Rock-star food.

As promised, he was keeping me exceptionally well fed. Because Jack was, well, *Jack Seary*, lead guitarist of Northern Junk, this meant extravagant treats like morning pain aux chocolats fresh from La Poilane in Paris, La Duree macarons, and one molecular dinner from a three-star Michelin restaurant we both agreed would have been better if it wasn't served in test tubes.

I didn't want to think too hard about the people who were running around getting all this stuff for Jack or the environmental impact of all the travel involved. The appalling truth was I loved being pampered.

This temporary arrangement was going to end in a little over five weeks, and I hated how that deadline made my heart ache a little more every day. I was going to miss the perfect food, but I knew I would feel the absence of his soft green eyes and devastating smile more.

"Do I smell curry?" I asked.

I stepped aside. He walked into my room, completely at ease. "You do indeed."

"Where is it from? Let me guess. Direct from Mumbai and still hot?" I was learning the reach and breadth of what a rock star could get his hands on was truly mind-boggling.

He shook his head, put the food on my chair, and started rearranging my case books into neat piles on my desk. "That would be a feat even I'm not capable of. It's from one of the best curry places in East London."

"I'm disappointed," I joked, "but nevertheless relieved to hear there is something fame and money can't buy."

"Trust me, Luce, piping hot curry from Mumbai isn't the only thing fame and money can't buy." His sage gaze focused on my face, then dropped to my desk again.

The room tilted around me. There had been other little moments like this, where I was left wondering if Jack Seary could possibly be interested in me like that.

Much to my shock, our friends had bought our story that we were now a couple with a complete lack of surprise. I was still trying, and failing, to make sense of their lack of reaction.

I had to constantly remind myself that Jack had the gift of making everyone feel singled out and special. That's what charisma was, after all. I had to stop searching for something that wasn't there. It was terrible for my mental stability. This was a fake relationship. He'd been crystal clear about the transaction, and I could not forget it. "Will you eat it with me?" I was a weak, weak woman.

"I thought you'd never ask." He reached up under his hoodie and rubbed his flat washboard abs. That wasn't playing fair.

He transferred the food bags to the cleared desk surface and began to unpack them. I didn't think I'd ever get tired of watching him make these little unconscious gestures to care for me.

"You don't need to keep indulging me every single day Jack."

Because I'm too weak to not fall in love with it.

He waved my suggestion away and hissed as he took out the final carton from the biggest bag. "It's a good thing my fingertips are so calloused from playing the guitar. That motherfucker was piping hot."

With Jack, I could sense the part of me that had iced over the day they'd called off the search for my father was in danger of melting. Instead of relief though, I felt fear. I needed my cold center. It was what gave me the ability to power through so much tedium and unpleasantness to fulfill the promise I made to him before he drowned. It shook me to my core to realize just how fast I could get used to being cared for—and just how much I craved it.

He opened a carton, and I was almost knocked over by the delicious scents of freshly buttered naan bread and cumin. "Nothing is too good for my girlfriend."

"Pretend girlfriend." I had to keep reminding us of this, for my sake as much as his.

His mouth tightened as he ignored that. "It's high time you got spoiled a little, Luce."

Jack opened the top desk drawer, which he'd filled with plates, glasses, cutlery, and a little bottle of dishwashing liquid and a sponge, then plated out the most heavenly smelling chicken curry over rice with steaming buttered naan bread on the side. He served himself and sat at the top of my bed, patting the spot beside him for me to join.

I stood there for a moment, tempted to pinch myself. Jack Seary had just brought me a delicious curry dinner and was sitting on my bed, signaling me to join him. How on earth was this happening?

My phone rang. Hardly anybody called except my mom or Alice. There it was—the reality check my swoony self needed.

I put the plate down on the desk.

"It's going to get cold!" Jack protested from the bed. "Can you call them back later?"

"No," I said. "It's home." I picked up.

It was my mom checking the dates and times I'd sent her for Alice's assessment the next week. The $10,000 Jack had transferred allowed me to get Alice to the front of the line, but it was essential my mother remember to take her to all the scheduled appointments. There were six in total, which I feared was too much for her to deal with.

I flipped open the page in my notebook where I'd written them all down.

"So," I said, "this Monday to Thursday is every day for three hours, from one o'clock until four o'clock. You need to take Alice to the educational psychologist's office at 28 Peet Street, okay? That's not far."

Jack hadn't started eating. Instead, he was watching me from the bed.

"I'll Google it," my mom said, making me do a double take. She wasn't in the habit of taking initiatives like that.

"Make sure you get there on the early side and give yourself time to park," I reminded her.

"I figured I'd give myself half an hour leeway," she said. Her voice sounded more capable than usual.

I mouthed "eat" to Jack while miming the motion. He shook his head.

"The final two appointments are the week after, on Wednesday and Thursday, from nine o'clock to eleven o'clock. Same place. After that they will do up the report and recommendations. I've arranged a Zoom call with you and me and Dr. Robertson's team on February 16. Does that work?"

"Perfect," my mom said in a crisp voice that sounded nothing like her. My mom always found a way to complicate things, but this was turning out to be—dare I think it?—straightforward.

"I put it all in an email last night and sent you calendar invites, so everything is in one place."

"Great. I think I have everything I need. Lucy?"

Here it was. The inevitable problem. "Yeah?"

"Thank you. I don't know how you managed to arrange all this from there and get the money. You probably don't even want to tell me—"

I glanced at my dazzling fake boyfriend, waiting for me on the bed. I definitely didn't want to tell her how I'd managed this. All she needed to know was I had.

"But I just want you to know how much I appreciate it," she continued. "With you gone, I've been doing some reading, and a lot of thinking, and ... well, thank you."

"It's no problem, Mom." It was, of course, in the sense it had taken a huge chunk of time and mental bandwidth from my work, but Dad had left them in my care. I'd been making them the priority for so long doing so was hardwired into my brain.

"Good night honey," my mom said.

"Good night." I hung up the phone, took the plate and fork, and went to sit beside Jack without meeting his eyes.

Why did that conversation make me so uneasy? I took a forkful of curry to distract myself. The sauce was creamy and perfectly spicy, with warm cumin and turmeric hitting every tastebud. "This is so delicious. You should eat," I said without looking at Jack. "You don't want yours to get cold."

After a few more forkfuls, I ventured a glance at him. He still hadn't moved.

I ripped off a bite of naan with my teeth. It was soft as a cloud and lightly sprinkled with cumin seeds. I groaned as it melted in my mouth.

Jack's mouth dropped open.

"Sorry," I said through the mouthful of naan. "This is amazing."

"No apologies necessary." His voice was strained. It reminded me that I'd been so wrapped up in Jack taking care of me I hadn't properly been reciprocating.

"How has your anxiety been since the concert?"

He started eating. "Better once I got back here and away from all that," he said finally. "I mean it's still there—it's always there more or less—but it's quieter most of the time when I'm here at Beaufort, if that makes any sense."

"It makes total sense."

"I can't tell you what a relief it was that you believed me."

I'd seen Jack's face at that concert—he had the same expression I imagined someone would have if they were stuck on a track with a train barreling toward them. Not even an Oscar-winning actor could manufacture that level of terror. "People don't believe you?"

"Most don't. They think I'm making it up for attention—or just to be difficult and spoiled. I stopped talking about it unless absolutely necessary."

The inhumanity of that took my breath away. "It's obvious you can't control it. Are they blind?"

He took a bite of naan. "You're right. This is fucking glorious naan."

"Right? You'll excuse me for moaning about it."

"I didn't mind. In fact, I was considering begging you to do it again."

My face caught on fire. I knew for Jack this was just the light-hearted flirting he did with his fans and girlfriends, and even the occasional reporter, but I couldn't playfully flirt. I cared too damn much.

We ate for a while in charged silence. "So what have you been up to in the astronomy observatory?" It was a feeble attempt to change the conversation, and Jack would see through it.

But instead of calling me out, his whole face transformed. Those lines of strain around his eyes softened, and his mouth tilted up in a grin. "The main part of my term here is an independent research project as part of my astronomy class. I chose a star I've been intrigued by for a few years. That interest has expanded into full-blown obsession. Professor Hayden resents my presence, but I'm hoping I may be able to show rather than tell him I'm not just some dilettante."

"Which star?"

"BPM 37093."

Jack said it so reverentially I nearly choked on my rice. "How poetic. Let me guess, it's named after a Greek god."

His dimples deepened and he chuckled into his curry. "Most stars are given designations like that. This one does happen to have a few different names, though."

"Don't keep me in suspense."

"V886 Centauri."

I snorted. "Oh yeah, that's way better."

Jack's smile was adorably crooked.

"Why that star?"

He stretched his long legs negligently in front of him and crossed one ankle over the other.

"The thing with BPM 37093 is it pulsates, and there's this crystalline theory I'd like to apply to that phenomenon." His green eyes sparkled with enthusiasm, and he waved his fork around. "You see, no one has thought of doing that before. I've been researching it since I got here, but I've found no trace of any studies. It astounds me. I mean, it's just so unique."

I adored seeing him light up like this. It was night and day from how he'd been at the concert.

He cast me a sheepish glance. "I'm boring you."

"Absolutely not." I was just envious I didn't feel the same way about studying law. "That does sound cool." Far cooler than learning the difference between types of easements.

His cheekbones went red under the scattering of freckles. "Did you see we have a black-tie dinner next Friday?"

Aw. He was trying to change the topic. Eager, nerdy Jack was adorable. A perfect little red wave dropped over his left eye just then. Also devastating.

I nodded. "I got an invitation in my pidge. I don't think I'll be able to go."

"Why?"

I sighed. "Too much work and not enough ballgowns in my armoire."

The reading lists for my other classes were just as horrific as for contract. I'd had to stay up two nights in the past week just to get the reading done and my essay written. Unfortunately no amount of being well-fed changed that. I'd been hoping if I just worked incredibly hard and stuck at it, I would begin to like it as well. So far that wasn't happening. The opposite was true. The more exhausted I became, the more boring and hopeless it felt.

"I'm afraid I can't accept that." Jack took my empty plate and put it with his on the bedside table.

I shrugged. "Sorry."

He scratched his ear. "Maybe your tutors would give you a bit of a break for the black-tie dinner? It's a centuries-old Oxford tradition, after all. I get the impression they're big on things like that here."

I snorted. "Not in the law faculty. The tutors delight in telling us at every tutorial that nobody gets a break in an Oxford law degree. It's survival of the fittest. They're proud of failing students."

His bent one of his legs and held on to his knee. "Can't you drop a class? Five seems like too much."

Jack Seary was fretting over me. There was something surreal about that it. Even though I was enjoying—far too much for my own good—being worried about, he didn't need to. "Nope. If I did, then I wouldn't be finished in the accelerated two years."

His sigh sounded like it came from the depths of his soul.

"I hope that wasn't for me," I said. "I'll be fine."

He reached across and took my hand in his like he did at Wembley. It was warm and rough. That hollowness at my core roared to feel more of him. "Help me understand why as a child you felt this responsibility to take on your father's role at home. I hate feeling like I don't have the missing puzzle piece to understand you."

He squeezed my hand, signaling how much he truly wanted to know me.

He had a point. I'd never told Jack why—not specifically, anyway.

I shouldn't tell him now, but the thoughtful curry and his nerdy excitement had softened me somehow.

Not even my mother or Alice knew about the promise I'd made my dad. I'd just acted on it. My mother had been so lost and deep in grief I didn't think it ever crossed her mind to question why I'd assumed leadership of the household. She just followed my lead.

But now, I could sense the truth—or almost the whole truth—ready and waiting on my tongue.

"I made my father a promise," I began.

Jack stilled. I don't know what he saw in my face, but he clearly understood this was not something I talked about easily. "What promise, Luce?"

I rubbed between my eyebrows, where that spot of tension always ached. "Every time he left for fishing we had a little ritual. He would tell me to look after Mom and Alice when he was at sea. I would promise, and he would give me a kiss on the forehead to seal it."

The silence stretched out. Part of me couldn't believe I'd shared what had defined the last decade of my life—and shared it with Jack Seary, of all people.

"In your heart your dad is still at sea, isn't he?" Jack's voice was full of sympathy.

That was it exactly. I hadn't anticipated he would understand without me having to explain. My promise became unbreakable the moment my father slipped under the surface of the Atlantic.

My chin quivered, and I rubbed the face of my dad's watch. "Yeah."

Suddenly he was everywhere, crushing me in a hug so complete and perfect I couldn't help but tighten my arms around the muscular lines of his torso and hug him back. His breath was warm against my ear, so soothing a sob clawed up from that melting ice inside me, burning my throat like only the coldest things can.

They were the unshed tears of eleven-year-old me who had never had the time or space to grieve my father properly. Who, in some deep part of myself, held hope that one day he would walk through the door as if no time had passed, and I would be able to tell him I had kept my promise.

Jack cleared off the bed and pulled my duvet over us. We fell back like that, intertwined, tears pouring down my face.

"My poor Luce," he murmured in my ear. "I see now." He

smoothed back my hair and planted soft little kisses on my fore-head, and I let him. His solid, firm warmth flowed around me. Maybe melting didn't have to feel scary after all.

CHAPTER EIGHTEEN

Jack

I woke up with my arms around Lucy. Her breasts were pressed up against my chest, and her head rested on the crook of my shoulder. Her turmeric-scented breath puffed against my shoulder. Waking up with an opulent five-foot-three inches of blue eyes, blunt words, and layers of defenses felt like the best-ever dream.

How was it we fit so well together when our bodies were so utterly different?

Her leg was thrown over mine, and her full lips were relaxed in sleep. A dried trickle of mascara on her cheekbone was the only evidence of her tears the night before. My heart clenched when I remembered how she had let down her guard with me.

I concentrated on staying absolutely still, trying to orient myself in what felt like a changed world. So Lucy still felt bound by a promise to her father—a promise no parent should extract of their child.

To give Lucy's father the benefit of the doubt, I imagined he'd hadn't planned on his boat capsizing that night. I doubted he would have gone through their usual routine if he'd been able to see into the future.

Lucy shifted in her sleep, but I stayed perfectly still, not wanting this moment to end.

I'd been with other women, but not one of them cracked my heart open with tenderness like Lucy, or made me want to lie in bed and watch the expressions cross her faces like clouds in the sky, or make love to her for hours—make that days—on end. Desire roared to life within me. Oh no.

Feeling Lucy's silkiness against me made my blood flow to my groin. To be fair, it was morning, after all. My heart pounded in my ears but from lust this time, not anxiety.

We hadn't had sex that night, or even kissed.

Would she ever give me another chance? My erection, now rock hard against her pillowy hip, was not going to help my case.

I started to draw back, but, sighing softly in her sleep, she shimmied forward, pressing the apex of her thighs squarely against the ridge of my hard cock. My heart skipped a beat, then another. Was I having a stroke? So much softness to sink into ... If there was a heaven, I was certain it felt like this.

I should pull away, but good God, she felt even better than I remembered. My cock twitched and pulsed as hot jolts of desire coursed through me. She pressed harder against me, and I almost came in my jeans. Her arm flopped over my back and she started to trace my vertebrae with her magical fingers.

Who was I kidding? I wasn't going to pull back from her—from this exquisite torture. Maybe some men had that much self-restraint, but not me—not when it came to her.

She slid her leg up higher, struggling to get even closer, to ride me in her sleep. Sparks exploded through my blood. Her hand moved down and traced my right butt cheek, and she jutted her hips sharply against mine. Lucy Snow was the match to my phosphorous.

Jesus fucking Christ, I was going to—

I rolled away so violently I almost fell off the narrow bed, stopping just in time. I clung to the edge of her mattress and tried to conjure up the least appealing things I could think of—Gary's bleached teeth, Cathy's helmet haircut and stretchy polyester pants, the smell of sweat backstage, seal flipper pie … Okay. Better. I escaped to the bathroom.

The idea of relieving myself ran through my brain, but there was no lock on the door, and if Lucy walked in on me … I refused to be that gross guy and ruin any infinitesimal chance I had with her.

It took me about five minutes to splash water on my face and calm myself down. There was a sound on the other side of the door. Lucy was waking up.

Making as much noise as possible, I left the bathroom. Lucy sat on the bed, holding a pillow against her stomach, blinking owlishly at me.

Beaufort's chapel bell chimed in the distance. I cleared my throat. "Good morning, sunshine."

"What happened between us?" Her eyes were huge and blue as a summer sky.

"Nothing. Well, almost nothing. You were dreaming and you got a little carried away."

Lucy swore and rubbed her eyes. "I thought so. That dream …". A scarlet flush rose up her neck. I wanted to be the one bringing that stain of pink to her cheekbones "It's coming back to me. Did I take advantage of you?"

I grinned. "No, temptress. I think maybe you were dreaming about it, though."

She buried her face in her hands. "I'm so embarrassed."

I was sorely tempted to ask if she wanted to follow through on what she'd started in her sleep now she was conscious, but there was no way to phrase that question without potentially scaring her off. "No need."

She finally gave a chuckle and looked back at me. She cocked her head. "Do you hear that?"

I strained my ears, but all I could hear was the faint chime of another church or college bell somewhere. "What?"

"It's the sound of all your groupies' heads exploding at the same time."

I grinned. "You think?"

She rolled her eyes. "I know."

We laughed, but something in the room shifted. It was as if the atoms in the air between us started spinning faster. Our eyes locked. If I went to her right now, how would she react? I had to try. I took a step toward her, then another.

Her lips snapped shut and she gave a short, sharp nod. "I should hop in the shower. Thank you for staying with me last night." There was fear in her eyes. Her message was crystal clear. I swallowed back my longing as best I could. "Thank you for telling me about your dad and that promise."

She hopped off the bed and started taking clothes out of her armoire—a clear sign she wanted to be left alone now to over-think all this, not to mention get her schoolwork done.

"I'll let you get to work." Disappointment clogged my throat.

She spun around. "This boyfriend–girlfriend thing. You do remember it's just for show, right?"

But it wasn't—not for me. Holding her all night long had felt like the most honest thing in the world.

She held her fresh clothes in front of her like a shield.

"That's up to you," I said, softly.

She froze. A pigeon cooed outside her window. Somebody shouted out in the quad. My blood slowed in my veins as I waited for her reaction. "Lucy?"

She shook her head. "We made a bargain. We need to stick to it. I don't want to wreck our friendship or ... whatever this is. Not again. There won't be a third chance."

"But—"

"Stop." Her eyes flashed in warning. "I know you're used to getting what you want, but that doesn't include me."

How could I get her to understand nothing else mattered if I couldn't have her? I couldn't think of anything besides continuing what I was doing. Caring for her. Feeding her. Spending time with her. Showing her she could trust me. Making her realize she was so much more than she believed herself to be. What I needed to do was create another opportunity for it to happen.

"Understood," I said. "But can you come to the black-tie dinner with me?" I couldn't explain why this felt so imperative, but it did.

"I told you. I can't."

I needed to make her feel like a bloody princess for a night, if for no other reason that she deserved to see herself that way. If I had to bend the truth to convince her, so be it. "I know what you told me, but it's the perfect opportunity to be seen in public as a couple. This won't work if people think it's a scam."

Her lips twisted to the side. I hated using her overdeveloped sense of duty to sway her, but I was quickly discovering how ruthless I was when it came to Lucy's greater good.

"I guess you have a point." Her forehead puckered. "Everyone will have cameras to take photos of themselves and their friends."

"Exactly." I nodded. I wouldn't let slip I wanted to escort her because I was proud to have her on my arm and wanted to spend every possible waking moment with her.

Her eyes traveled over the piles of casebooks on her desk. "I wasn't lying about my workload. It's a real problem."

"I know." I started tidying up last night's containers of curry. I would take all this back to my room. The last thing I wanted to do was leave her with extra chores.

She gnawed on her thumbnail. "I can't remember ever being this stressed about school. All this pressure is building up in me and I can't release any of it."

I was certain I could help by driving into her again and again with my hands on the bedframe and her writhing body beneath me, her ivory skin flushed all over. Shit. I was getting hard again.

"What about your work?" she demanded. "Aren't you stressed by the CMP 400067 or whatever?"

I winced. "It's BPM 37093, and my research term isn't structured anything like a law degree. Also, I like the stuff I'm studying." In fact, every moment I couldn't be with Lucy I wanted to be studying the stars.

She waved me out of her room. "Go away and don't rub it in. So black-tie dinner next Saturday?"

Thank God. "Please."

She stomped to her bathroom door and turned around. "I don't have a dress."

"I'll pay for one."

"Normally I would refuse, but seeing as I wouldn't be going except to help you, I'll accept it."

She looked so thwarted I couldn't help but smile. "I refuse to have fun," she added with lowered brows.

"Understood."

Her phone started ringing again. She slipped it out of her back pocket. "It's Alice. You need to go."

"I'd better hurry," I said. "I have a lot of work ahead of me if I'm going to pull off the most miserable black-tie dinner in Oxford history."

"You certainly do," she shouted as I closed her door behind me.

CHAPTER NINETEEN

Lucy

Two days later I was heading to hall for lunch, but Jack had asked me to stop by his room and get him on the way.

I'd been doing my best to avoid him since our night together, using my overwhelming workload as an excuse. It was the truth, but I knew—and I knew he knew—that I was running scared after my confession and the night spent in his arms.

I was late and flustered at the idea of having to spend so much time with Jack when I felt so vulnerable. Still, I'd found myself humming and singing to myself more in the past two days than I had in the past four years. I worried it was a sign that I was becoming careless.

Instead of knocking, I just opened his door which was already slightly ajar. He was expecting me, after all.

"Sorry I'm late. I ..." My words dribbled away.

Jack was standing in front of his armoire wearing only his jeans. The scent of lemon was thick in the room and was working on me like a chloroform-soaked cloth. His guitar case was

175

open in the corner—ah, that's why it was so strong. Or maybe my light-headedness was caused by Jack's bare chest, sharply cut muscles, and tattoos.

I never thought I had a thing for tattoos, but I was rapidly revising that opinion. I'd bet good money that there was a TikTok account for those too.

He had a Gibson guitar on his shoulder, and a traced outline of Newfoundland above his right bicep and—

"You're not wearing a shirt," I managed.

He turned to me, and a look of mischief flared in his eyes. "No. I'm not."

I tried to unstick my tongue from the roof of my mouth. "Why?"

His dimples flashed. "I'm just looking at my options. I need to do laundry."

His pecs were perfectly carved, and his biceps had just the right amount of swell. And those abdominal muscles that cut down into a 'V' above his belt—I wanted to *lick* them.

I swallowed hard. "Your assistant doesn't do your laundry?"

He shook his head. "Nope."

Instead of law, I wanted to take a degree in mapping the tattoos hidden under his tops. Was there one on his hip bone? And was that a star or something on his shoulder? His sheer beauty woke something insatiable in me. It also made me want to shelve my fear and distrust and walk—no, run—towards pleasure.

"Sorry for the partial nudity." His eyes glinted with something that made me think he wasn't sorry at all.

Jack awoke a greediness in me I'd pushed down so far I'd forgotten it had existed in the first place.

I wanted that gorgeous chest sculpted by performing. I wanted those ever-changing sage-green eyes. I wanted to slowly slide down those worn jeans that hung around his hips perfectly. I didn't want to share him with anyone. But who was I to demand such a thing?

My tongue was a sand dune in the Sahara. "I didn't realize you had so many tattoos."

He shrugged. "Rock star. I kind of had no choice."

How was it possible all this had been underneath his clothes when he'd held me all night.

Jack had said whether we were a real couple or not was up to me and I'd been running scared since then. Had he meant it, or was he just flirting?

People always praised me for being strong, but I wasn't. If Jack and I got together, and he left me a second time, I honestly didn't know if I would survive. Playing it safe was the only way to stay safe.

He plucked a white T-shirt from the armoire and pulled it over is head. My heart sank to my toes in disappointment.

I wanted him to kiss me, drive all the doubts out of my mind. "Have you been outside yet?" he asked nonchalantly, as though his chest wasn't a big deal. It was a fucking huge deal! Michelangelo would've had a field day sculpting him if Jack had been alive back then. "Do you know how cold it is?"

I shook my head, mouth still full of cotton. "Sorry."

His T-shirt had a drawing of what looked like the Hubble on the front.

"I need to see something," I said and walked over to where he was standing by his armoire. Now it was his turn to look shocked and ... was that eagerness? My heart pounded and every hair on my body stood on end being this close to him, but I tried to ignore it and looked past him into his armoire.

It was full of space-related T-shirts and hoodies—all variations of NASA, different telescopes and satellites. My heart lurched. It was adorable. His stylist filled his wardrobe with Gucci and Prada, but he chose Nasa gear.

"I guess I've sort of been collecting them while I've been touring," he admitted, sheepish. "I never got the chance to wear them until now."

The love for Jack I'd been holding at bay started to push so hard against the walls I'd built. Cracks and leaks were forming faster than I could plug them up. Nerdy Jack was dangerous because he made me forget that he was also Jack Seary, world-famous rock star.

"It's an amazing collection," I managed, my heart in my throat.

I needed to escape out of his room before I caved. My fortifications were crumbling with every second I stood close to him like this. "Let's go," I said. "I need coffee."

We left his room and almost bumped into a harassed-looking FedEx person on the landing.

"Lucy Snow?" the man asked.

"That's me," I answered, making round eyes at Jack. Did he know something about this?

"I have some pastries from Paris for you here." He handed me a glossy white box beautifully wrapped with pink ribbon and an ornamental sheaf of straw on top. It was *heavy*.

"I forgot about those," Jack said. "This boulangerie in the Marais was just voted the best pain au chocolat in Paris. There's enough in there for our friends. Let's bring them to hall to share." The delivery man marked something off on his electronic pad.

"You have to stop doing this." Even though I hated to admit it, I loved Jack spoiling me. I never wanted it to stop, but it would stop. It had to.

"That grumpy man manning the entrance almost didn't let me up. Bloody bulldog, he was," the deliveryman huffed.

Jack and I exchanged a smile. Robbie.

"Hey," the delivery man focused in on Jack's face. "Are you—?"

"I'm sorry for the trouble," Jack cut him off. "Thank you." Jack reached into his back pocket, took out his wallet, and crammed a hundred-pound bill in the man's hand. "I hope this goes some way in compensating for the hassle." The man's eyes went round. "Anytime," he breathed. "I mean that."

And with that, he raced down the stairs like he was worried someone would find him and divest him of his windfall.

In the quad, it was snowing for the first time since the beginning of Hilary term. Snow was nothing new for us as Newfoundlanders, but the quad was crowded with students running around trying—and failing—to scrape up enough snow to make snowballs and taking selfies with their tongues sticking out.

"You'd think they'd never seen snow before," I muttered, trying not to let the fairy tale romanticism of the white flakes falling on golden, ancient stone rob me of all my common sense.

He took the pastry box from me and stopped me in the middle of the quad. He lifted my chin, his warm hand molding around the curved bone. "You have snowflakes in your hair," he said, softly. "And in your eyelashes."

Jack did too, the white stark and beautiful against his copper hair.

"You look like a snow princess," he said, his lips softly curved.

My entire body yearned for more of his touch.

If only he didn't have this effect on me, but he did. Oh, did he ever.

A few students glanced our way. Most smiled, one girl scowled, but most importantly they were seeing us together as a couple. "Is it just me, or are people calming down about you being here?" I asked.

"It's not just you. They definitely are."

"Does that feel good or bad?"

"So good." His fingers lingered along my cheekbone. "I didn't realize how much I craved feeling normal. For the first time in so long I feel safe. I don't know how I'm going to make myself leave."

Right. He was leaving in five weeks. I could not let myself forget that, even though the feel of his hand cradling my face was giving me temporary amnesia.

It was so ironic that Jack had the life I dreamed of and didn't want it. I tried to imagine loathing it like he did, but I just couldn't fathom the idea. I yearned to sing where everyone could hear me, where I could connect with people all over the world and make them feel something. We each longed for the thing the other had.

We were lucky. Our skulk was sitting at a hall table when we arrived except for Lachlan, who was probably playing rugby somewhere or eating at his own college.

They quickly descended on the box of Parisian pastries like they hadn't eaten for four days. "Bunch of animals," I observed.

Jack cleared his throat. "Ahem. These *were* for Lucy." He plucked out a pain au chocolat and passed it to me. "Goddamn. I think my fingers almost got bitten."

I took a bite and closed my eyes to savor the delicate pastry as it melted in my mouth along with the decadent gush of melted chocolate.

Jack's arm slid around my waist. I fought against the heat rushing through me and the temptation to lean into him. This was just a necessary part of the fake-dating show, surely.

I finished the pain au chocolate and opened my eyes. "That was beyond delicious. Thank you." I brushed the crumbs off my hands.

"Wait," he said. "Look at me." His fingertips rested along my hairline.

"What is it?" My voice came out faint.

He traced my bottom lip with the pad of his thumb. His calloused touch was so impossibly gentle and his eyes so intent on my mouth that his closeness reverberated through every atom of my body. If this was all part of the act, the next five weeks might just kill me.

"Jack?" I asked, my voice as hollow as the emptiness inside me.

"Crumbs," he said, his eyes not leaving mine.

"Are they gone?" His thumb still pressed against the corner of my lips, and that little patch of real estate was fast becoming the epicenter of my world. The echoed chatter around us and the conversation of our friends receded into the background.

He shook his head. "Afraid not." His eyes moved up to mine. My breath caught at his dilated pupils and heavy eyelids.

His hand slid behind my neck.

"Jack?" I asked.

He huffed softly. "I can't ..." he muttered. He leaned down and kissed me.

Everything stopped then. Every thought. Every noise. Every fear. His lips explored mine with a perfect reverence that made me feel like I was already everything I dreamed of being. Our mouths fit together as perfectly as the rest of us.

It started as a gentle exploration, but then Jack's tongue darted out and tenderly brushed my lower lip. All that lust I had been trying to hold back burst through and I deepened the kiss. Jack let out a squeak of surprise and pleasure that instantly became my new favorite sound.

I must have moved closer because I could feel his heartbeat against my chest.

"Just look at Jack and Lucy," I vaguely heard Binita say. "French pastries are so an aphrodisiac, Shaun. Why else do you think the French are having sex all the time?"

We pulled away at the same time. I stared at him, blinking. His eyes were fathomless emerald pools.

"Ah! I see you two have come up for air," Shaun said.

"Do you think that deserved the best pain au chocolat award, Luce?" Jack asked me, his gaze still locked on my lips.

I was still trying to recover from finally getting the kiss I'd dreamed about for so long, not to mention discovering that it was even more delicious than I'd ever imagined. All I could manage was an enthusiastic nod. That's when I spotted Professor Speedman, staring at me from the High Table. Oh God. Had she seen the whole thing?

Jack pulled me closer. "I'll make you a hedonist yet," he whispered in my ear. I shivered. If the kiss was any indication, that wouldn't be difficult. I'd never wanted anything more.

Surely a kiss like that wasn't just to play a role, was it? It had felt so real, so right … I needed certainty, now more than ever.

I let the conversation roll over me as I marshalled my senses. Jack's arm stayed tight around me. Finally, Jack said, "So where should I take Lucy to look for a dress for the black-tie dinner?"

I really didn't want to go dress-shopping with Jack, even though I'd agreed to attend the dinner. "The whole thing is going to be such a hassle," I grumbled. It was easier to act disgruntled than feel so acutely exposed after kissing Jack.

Besides, I was still traumatized from my high school graduation. I didn't get asked by anyone, and the dress I ordered was an inexpensive concoction without much going for it but a beautiful shade of pink—or so I'd thought. When it arrived, it was the lurid color of bubblegum. In all the grad photos, I'm trying to hide as much as possible behind my fellow students.

"Help," he said to our friends. "Lucy is dreading the shopping part."

"Can you blame me?" I asked. Sure, some things had changed in my life since high school—here I was in an Oxford hall, the arm of a world-famous rock star squeezing tight around my waist, with an eclectic and impressive new group of friends, but some things never changed. "I don't want to have a bunch of haughty fashion people try to squeeze my size-sixteen body into size-two samples, then cluck their tongues and make me feel like crap. I'm not a masochist."

"You're perfect the way you are, Luce," Jack said, his voice hard-edged.

The sentiment was so lovely, but clearly Jack had no idea what it was like for a plus sized woman. "Tell that to designers."

"Cedar?" Alfie asked his girlfriend. "Could you help Lucy?"

Shaun, Binita, and Cedar burst into gales of laughter.

"What?" I asked after a while.

"Sorry." Cedar wiped tears of mirth from her eyes. "Alfie, your vote of confidence is as sweet as it's misguided. You know very well that as far as clothes, especially black-tie clothes, I have absolutely no clue what I'm doing."

"Like, *none*," Shaun confirmed.

"But," Alfie stuttered.

"Don't you remember the dress store?" Cedar opened her eyes wide at her boyfriend, and Alfie's face went an interesting shade of scarlet.

"Oh, right." He shared a look with Cedar. "I could never forget *that.*" He leaned down to whisper something else in her ear. She nodded, her eyes dancing with mischief. To be able to have that complicity with Jack, and to know for sure it was real, and wouldn't end up breaking my heart again ....

"Then what should we do?" Jack pressed on, unwilling to let this go.

"The man you need is sitting right across from you," Cedar said. "Shaun helped me find my dress. He's the best stylist you could ever hope to have."

Shaun held up his hands and gave me a wink. "Guilty."

"Can you help her, then?" Jack asked.

"I have no doubt Shaun is an incredible stylist," I said. "But even he can't change the fact that, if England is anything like Canada, the stores that have clothes my size are all for the mother of the bride or attending funerals."

Shaun reached over and covered my hand with his. "Shhhh, child. I have resources. So many resources you wouldn't believe it. How about I arrange for some dresses to be brought to my room next Saturday. All you need to do is come and pick what you like. You'll be my Cinderella."

Cinderella? Me? The ways this could backfire were numerous and terrifying. I imagined Shaun giving up on trying to make me the belle of the ball in despair. "But what about jewelry and shoes and all that?"

"Trust me," Cedar said. "If you put yourself in Shaun's hands, he will take care of every last detail. You won't regret it."

"She speaks the truth," Raphael said.

"Lucy?" Jack squeezed my arm a little tighter in question.

I sighed. "Okay. You win."

Despite my grudging agreement, a flame of hope ignited in me. Maybe the back-tie dinner with Jack would be magic, or had Jack's kiss just made me reckless? If I let that carefree side of myself out to play—even for one night—I worried I might not be able to stuff it back down again. After all, it had almost destroyed me only four years before.

FOURTH WEEK

CHAPTER TWENTY

Jack

At 2:50 on Saturday afternoon I knocked on Lucy's door.

I'd just returned from the astronomy lab, where Dr. Hayden had been enthusiastic about the idea of employing radio waves to analyze BPM 37093's frequency spectrum. He had the brilliant idea of using asteroseismology to determine its composition. It was a massive open door to proving what was special about this star.

I was vibrating with excitement of that and the prospect of spending the evening with Lucy. She'd been avoiding me again after our kiss. I knew she was deluged by her coursework, but it was far more than that—it was a sign her doubts about me and about life still had the upper hand.

I probably didn't need to remind her to go to Shaun's room so he could dress her for the dinner, but she had a habit of losing track of time when she was caught up in her cases.

I'd had to work hard this past week at creating opportunities to see her face. Our kiss was never far from my mind, even when

I was wrapped up with telescopes and calculations. It was like BPM 37093 and Lucy had become intertwined in my head—both sparkling fantasies that felt just out of reach.

I heard a muffled groan of protest and then something crash to the floor. Had she been sleeping?

"Are you OK, Luce?" I asked through the door, my heart in my throat. I'd tried every term of endearment I could think of, but she hated all of them so I'd reverted back to 'Luce'.

"Fine." I heard her faint reply, then more noise before she unlocked the door. Her blonde waves looked like they'd been blown around by gale-force winds, and she was blinking like a mole emerging from underground.

I stared beyond her into her room. Piles of books covered almost every available surface. She'd knocked a glass of water to the floor; broken glass was everywhere.

She looked over her shoulder. "I was doing my contract reading in bed and promised myself I wasn't going to fall asleep." Her eyes dropped to the shattered glass. "Crap. That really broke. I didn't just dream it."

She looked so adorably disoriented all I wanted to do was snatch her in my arms and kiss her again, but I knew I had to wait until she made a move. Biding my time was fucking torture, especially because I didn't know if she'd ever be ready to initiate anything further, but if it meant I might have a chance with her …

"It's time to go to Shaun's room to get ready. He's waiting. I'll clean this up."

She pressed that spot between her eyebrows. I hated that this event was an added source of stress for her, but at the same time she needed a break from the law books she loathed so much. "Are you sure?"

She stared up at me, and that lower lip looked so full, so delectable … God, I had to stop getting distracted. "Positive."

"Do you own a broom?" she asked, gesturing down at the broken glass.

"Yes, Ms. Skeptical. I own a broom. I haven't forgotten all the life skills I had before I joined Northern Junk, you know."

She shrugged. "Just checking."

"Did you have a good sleep, at least?"

"I slept like the dead, but I drifted off reading about a case where a woman found a decomposed snail in a bottle of ginger beer, so my dreams were definitely weird." She frowned down at her wooden floor.

I noticed her face had new creases, surely from the hard cover of the case book she'd fallen asleep on. "That actually sounds entertaining."

"For a bit, but the judge's exegesis about the duty of care was not. I'm starting to wonder if all law stuff gives me narcolepsy."

I wanted to remind her yet again that she should be singing, not studying law, but I needed to stay on target. "Hm. That's a problem."

"If you hadn't knocked, I don't think I would have woken up for three days."

I held out the fresh coffee I'd picked up on the way back from the observatory from the best coffee place in Oxford. "Here you go. This will help."

She stared at me like I'd passed her a bar of gold. "Thank you. And thank you for your patience and all the food in the past few days."

It had been a week—the longest seven days of my life.

"I know I haven't been keeping up my end of our arrangement," she continued. "But—"

"Stop Luce," I said. Of all the things I wanted from Lucy, an apology certainly wasn't one of them. "I knew you would be studying. You warned me before we struck our deal, remember? Besides, we have tonight."

She raked a hand through her hair. "I did warn you, didn't I? Yay, past Lucy."

"You did, but now it's time to be spoiled. Don't forget to have fun."

She sighed and took a sip of coffee. "In my experience, trying on clothes is never fun."

"That's because you probably look best without them." Whoops. Way to play it slow. I hadn't meant to say that out loud. I held my breath, waiting for the hammer to fall.

Her face flushed crimson. "What did you just say?"

I couldn't take it back, so the only thing left to do was brazen it out. "I stand by it."

"How would you know?"

"I don't. Tragically."

Our gazes locked. The air between us pulsated with questions and unsaid things.

Finally, she shook her head, breaking the spell. "I'm not awake enough to know what to do with that."

"Just remember it. I'll wait for you tonight at the doors to the hall. Have a blast."

"Your optimism is adorable but misplaced." She grabbed her phone from the desk.

I stepped forward and eased it out of her hand. "Leave this here. Tonight is about you and no one else. Everything else can wait."

"But—"

"How long has it been since you were carefree? You deserve a break for one night."

She finally let go of the phone.

Her dad's heavy wristwatch caught my eye. I undid the metal clasp and slid it off her wrist, not missing the goosebumps that appeared everywhere I touched her. "I'll safeguard this too. Let's forget about time for one night."

She slowly, purposely removed her arm from my hold. Clutching her coffee and glaring at me, she slipped past and made her way out her door, her feet dragging as though she were headed to the guillotine.

Time was going too slowly, so I went downstairs to do laundry—always a humbling experience in the ratty, clunky old machines in the bowels of this beautiful but ancient building.

I came up an hour or so later, wondering what was happening in Shaun's room. I hoped he would use his reputed magic to make Lucy feel as beautiful as she was. Maybe it would lessen her need for certainty for a few hours and loosen the grip fear had on her. Most of all, I hoped that it would open her soul just enough so she would believe me when I showed her how I felt about her.

I could use some magic too. My life with Northern Junk was feeling more and more like a curse and that fucking codicil bound me to it. As I climbed up the stairs holding the laundry basket, I noticed my door was ajar. I was sure I'd closed it.

I pushed it open with my shoulder.

Cathy was standing in my room, fussing with a tuxedo hanging on the slightly ajar door of my armoire.

"Cathy?" I said.

"Jack." She turned and smiled, her eyes shining with affection. I had always been her favorite in the band. I knew she liked to think of herself as my de facto mother, even though I'd tried to make it clear without hurting her feelings I already had a mother who was far too interested in my life. The last thing I needed or wanted was another. "I was wondering where you were."

"What are you doing here?" My anxiety had been quiet since the concert, but now that crawly sensation between my ribs returned. Oxford, Beaufort, and this room were all my safe places, refuges from my life with Northern Junk. Cathy was invariably a tentacle of Gary, and having her here, standing in a place I'd never given her permission to enter, felt like a violation. "I arranged for my assistant to drop off my tuxedo," I tried to keep my voice neutral.

"I've been worried about you," she said. "I thought this would be a good opportunity to check up on you, so I intercepted your assistant. I always do the job of looking after you better than him, anyway."

I took a deep breath. I wanted to enjoy these last few weeks in peace. The last thing I needed was to upset Cathy, which by extension meant starting a fight with Gary. I needed to stay calm and polite if I wanted to enjoy tonight, figure out the mysteries of my star, and convince Lucy to be mine forever. That wasn't too much to ask, was it?

"Does Gary know you're here?" I tried not to sound as panicked as I felt.

She shook her head. Her hair didn't move. "No, I came for you. Gary doesn't know anything about it."

My shoulders dropped. All right. I could handle this. I put down the laundry basket on my bed. "How did you get into my room?"

Her expression was smug. "I have my ways. You shouldn't leave your door unlocked. You're an extremely precious and coveted commodity. We can't have people sneaking in here, you know."

People like you. But that was probably too cold-hearted of me. I knew for all her awkwardness and oddness Cathy was more than anything an object of pity.

"Thanks for the reminder." How was I going to get rid of her?

She came beside the bed and started digging through my laundry basket. She plucked out a T-shirt the washing machine had snagged on the shoulder, making a small hole on the neckline.

"Jack! Don't tell me you're doing your own laundry!"

"Why wouldn't I?"

She shook her head in dismay. "It's just as I thought. You need me around to take care of you. You are far too talented to be doing menial chores."

"Cathy, I'm an adult. An adult who can't take care of their basic needs is pretty pathetic, if you ask me."

She shook her head at the ripped T-shirt. "And look what it's doing to your lovely clothes."

"It's fine. I appreciate your worry, but I don't like being fussed over. You know that."

She patted my cheek with a moist palm. "I do, but I know what's best for you."

You have no idea what's best for me. You have no idea who I really am, or what I really feel.

"Are you taking that girl to the dinner tonight?"

"That girl!?" It almost came out in a snarl. "And how did you know about the black-tie dinner?" I hadn't mentioned it to anyone in Northern Junk.

She shrugged. "I looked at the college calendar and knew you were having your tux delivered. I put two and two together."

It was creepy she was keeping tabs on the college calendar, but then again Cathy had never been good with boundaries. "Yes. I'm taking Lucy."

Her lips thinned. "She must have had a hard time finding a dress, poor thing."

My body filled with disgust. I did not want Cathy talking about Lucy, or even thinking about her. "Lucy always looks gorgeous, no matter what." Hopefully my forbidding tone of voice would put an end to this line of conversation."

"You must admit, she's not like your past girlfriends."

"Thank God she isn't." She was different in the best possible ways.

She gave a little shrug. "Hm. Well, I do hope she finds something, poor dear."

I had to get her out of my room or I was going to lose it. "I should start getting ready," I lied. I didn't need to get ready for a few hours yet.

"Of course." She fluttered her hands. "I'll be on my way."

I closed the door behind her, then leaned against it. I telescoped in on myself, like I was watching myself from far away—'dissociation' as it was called on the anxiety forums. My four weeks left at Oxford had never felt so short.

CHAPTER TWENTY-ONE

Lucy

As I stood there on Shaun's landing I marveled at the weird twists of fate that had me running in the same circle of friends as Alfred, Lord Inverrnay, Shaun Webb—son of a famous and beloved entrepreneur—and Jack Seary, international rock celebrity.

Would Shaun forget I was just a normal girl from Newfoundland and not one of their jet-set posse who always wore clothes straight from the Paris runway?

He must have sensed my hesitation through the door, because suddenly it flung open, revealing racks of clothes and two people dressed head-to-toe in black setting up a rack of shoes. I almost turned on my heel and ran. The assistants looked far more cutting-edge chic than I could ever hope to be in a million years.

Jack had said I probably looked better without clothes. I clutched on to that tightly to get through this.

After that had popped out of Jack's mouth, I should have said or done something to reinforce the boundaries between us I'd been desperately trying to rebuild after our kiss. I didn't take risks, after all, especially not with the only person who had ever captured my heart.

The problem was the memory of our kiss lived under my skin now. Nothing was working to silence that voice inside me shouting for more.

"Here she is!" Shaun cried. "Our belle of the ball."

"Might want to lower your expectations."

"Nope." Shaun took a firm grasp of my arm. "You're not escaping my clutches until you're the *belle*. I'm *so* excited."

Fear clogged my mind. I was going to disappoint him, and his two impossibly chic assistants, the rest of the skulk—and, worst of all, Jack.

If I just stayed small, I didn't risk failing and being shattered by the fallout. Yet Jack and the rest of our friends had a knack for trying to drag me kicking and screaming into a life made for a bigger, better, more glamourous person than me. The same type of life my dad had reached for, and which killed him.

With a glint in his eye, Shaun took a key from his jeans pocket and locked the door behind me.

I was officially trapped. "Are you the fairy godmother or the evil witch?"

He winked. "A little bit of both, of course."

I had never felt so out of place. Everything was shiny and sparkly on the racks. I didn't know where to look until my eyes landed on Raphael sitting on the couch with an amused smile. How had I missed him before? He was the answer to the riddle of "which one of these things doesn't belong in this room?" Come to think of it, we both were.

"I'm here for moral support." He answered my unspoken question.

"I think I'll need it." My breath was unsteady.

"Possible," he admitted.

"Nonsense." Shaun pulled me briskly to the center of the room, and the two assistants descended on me, buzzing around and conferring with Shaun.

I cast a panicked look at Raphael.

"Just go with it," he said, his deep voice soothing. "You can trust Shaun, even though it may not seem like it."

"Hey!" Shaun protested. "I'm not deaf, my love."

"It's just to people like Lucy and me, these sorts of things can be a lot." Was Raphael a mind reader?

Shaun sighed. "Don't you think I know that? But sometimes baptism by fire is the most humane approach."

Shaun's agreement stung, even if it underlined what I'd been trying to convey to Jack this whole time about me pursuing singing. Every time I reached for more in my life, my hand was slapped away like a child with her fingers in the candy bowl.

"Just put yourself in his hands." Raphael smiled. "You won't regret it."

It wasn't like I had a choice. Already the expensive vanilla smell of a flickering candle on the marble coffee table was weaving past my nose, casting a spell.

What would it be like if I *could* be someone different—the person Jack seemed to see?

Here I'd thought I was made of stern enough stuff to resist the Cinderella fairy tale.

Shaun was going to coerce me into a dress and makeup either way. I could do this kicking and screaming, or I could go with it and try not be completely miserable. It wasn't every day I got the opportunity to attend a black-tie event at Oxford University. Dammit. I deserved a night of escape after this past decade. A thread of anticipation weaved up my spine.

I concentrated very hard on surrendering to Shaun as his people held up my hair, then stood around, hands under their chins, contemplating what to do with me.

After much consultation, they plucked five or six dresses from the stuffed racks and took them into a makeshift dressing room in the corner.

"What kind of music do you like?" the assistant with three piercings in her nose and an accent like one of the royal princesses asked.

I was about to answer when Shaun interrupted. "Don't bother answering. This requires Abba."

Within seconds, "Dancing Queen" was blaring out of a speaker.

I shot another panicked look at Raphael. He was settled in Shaun's couch, which looked both extremely stylish and extremely expensive, with an arm slung over the back and a bemused expression on his usually serious face. He gestured me to keep going.

"Just go with it," he mouthed.

Shaun stuck a glass of champagne in my hand. "Drink this first."

"Why?"

"It's Dom Perignon, love. Trust me. It makes everything *magique*."

I took a sip and completely rethought my opinion of champagne.

The ones I'd tasted back home at weddings and baptisms were invariably biting and acidic. They hurt my throat and gave me an instant headache. This one tasted like the tiniest, most delicate stars exploding on my tongue.

"This can't be champagne." I frowned at the flute.

"Of course not, darling," Shaun said. "It's Dom Perignon. They are two entirely different things. Pay attention, because this is a life lesson. Champagne and Dom Perignon must never be confused."

Between the Abba and the exquisite bubbles and the manicure and pedicure they gave me, I went from surrendering to having fun for real. But I hadn't started to try on dresses yet. That would sober me up fast. Even if they were horrible, I could remember Jack said I looked better naked, so maybe I could hold that as a talisman against humiliation.

I slipped on the first one—a dark aubergine silky affair with a handkerchief hem that made my legs look curvy instead of stout. To my utter amazement it fit me perfectly, even my ample chest, which usually never fit into dresses. No cheap fabric or bursting seams here. I swung my arms forward and back. I could *move* them.

I came out of the dressing room in bare feet and took a hesitant look at my reflection in the full-length mirror.

Somebody else stared back at me. A woman who demanded notice. Somebody who liked to wear deep-red lipstick and could stand on a stage with a microphone and command an entire room.

It was a glimpse at who Jack was always telling me I could be— who I might have been if I'd gone through with my audition. This dress was smothering that lurking suspicion that the bad things that had happened to me in my life were because I was not worthy or deserving enough.

This dress connected my wildest dreams and my current reality. Maybe I could command a room, after all.

Shaun pursed his lips, inspecting me. "You look gorgeous. That goes without saying. You *are* gorgeous Lucy, like some Renoir painting of a snow princess, but that dress is not quite it."

"It's not?" This dress was the most perfect thing I'd ever worn.

He gave his head one final, definitive shake. "No. The color is too dark. You need something more ethereal. What do you think, Raphael?" he called to his boyfriend, who had just downed his second flute of Dom Perignon.

Ethereal? Me? I felt like I was waking up. My whole life I'd thought I was one thing, and now Shaun was making me think I could be something completely different. All it took was a good dress. Well, and Dom Perignon. And Abba.

"I think she looks lovely," Raphael said.

I felt a surge of love for my new friend. Such a dark horse, that one, with the exterior of a Viking and a heart of mush.

Shaun cast him a pointed look.

"But I suppose it's always a good idea to try on a few more," Raphael added, ever the diplomat.

After that came a mint-green one that I particularly liked, then a light gray one that was striking but which we all deemed not to have enough oomph.

For the fifth or sixth dress—with the Dom Perignon and laughter, I'd started to lose count—I pulled on a sparkling gold one with a flirty, loose hem that struck just below my knees. It had a gathered waist and draped in a way that made my cleavage look extravagant.

I emerged from the dressing room to the tune of "Take a Chance on Me". Everyone in the room gasped, even Raphael.

"That's it." Shaun clapped his hands together. "We've found the dress."

I couldn't take my eyes off myself in the mirror. Even with my regular hair and usual lick of mascara, I looked like I belonged on a red carpet.

Tomorrow reality would surely come crashing down, but for tonight ... Maybe just for tonight I could be this girl in the mirror and live the alternate life that always felt just out of my reach.

"I love it," I murmured.

"Of course you do, and you should love me too. I have the most amazing taste," Shaun said.

This dress transformed me into the kind of person who got noticed, who got picked the way Jack was picked by Gary. It broadcast to the world that I had that elusive "it" I'd always believed I could never embody.

I'd been waiting for that—some person or thing to tell me I was worthy of being celebrated. When Jack was invited to join Northern Junk, it made me question everything and give in to all my doubts and fears about not being good enough.

After it had all blown up in my face, I started to dismiss that special thing I felt inside. Demanding more just felt futile and reckless—like I was willingly playing an active role in the family curse.

Staring at my reflection now, I wondered if for tonight I could reclaim a tiny part of that dream. I wouldn't be greedy—a few hours were enough.

I could take a breather from my mother's and Alice's care, from Professor Speedman's all-seeing stare, and from the sheer tedium of reading law cases until I felt like my eyeballs were going to bleed. It probably wasn't wise to snatch this escape from reality, but I was too weak to resist.

Shaun thrust another flute of Dom Perignon at me. "Take a seat, Cinderella. Now that we've found The Dress, it's time for hair and makeup."

Shaun insisted he and Raphael escort me to hall, where Jack had promised to meet me in front of the doors.

As we crossed the deserted quad in the cold, sharp air, Raphael checked his watch. My stomach filled with nerves as the North Star twinkled bright in the inky black sky.

Both he and Raphael had taken turns to sneak away and get changed during my transformation. They looked dashing in their tuxedos.

Shaun wore his with the same ease he wore pajamas, whereas Raphael looked like a Viking who was confused about how he'd shoehorned himself into his. In completely different ways, they both made the formalwear work for them.

Shaun had thought to provide a warm cashmere shawl to throw over my shoulders, a rich ivory shot with glittery gold strands to go with my dress. It was February after all, but I was so overheated with nerves I just carried it in hand.

Shaun had dismissed the wizards after they'd finished my hair and makeup, as well as chosen the perfect shoes and jewelry for my dress. They turned out to be lovely and kind and heaped me with praise.

For once, I believed it.

This sparkly gold dress made me feel like a goddess. That was a feat not even Jack had been able to manage. Either Shaun or the dress was enchanted, that was for sure. Maybe both.

Star-shaped crystals dangled in my ears and a matching bracelet hung from my wrist. I would never be an ectomorph, but this dress made my hips, curvy legs, and ample cleavage look sumptuous.

"We're going to be late." Raphael frowned.

Shaun clucked. "No, *mon amour*. We're going to be just on time. Lucy deserves an entrance, and I intend to give her one. We'll be just late enough that everyone will be seated, then she and Jack can appear and bowl everyone over."

Right ... to ensure there were photos of my fake relationship with Jack. That brought me down to earth with a thud. Shockingly, nobody took photos or video of our unexpected kiss in the hall, so tonight was to be our big, public photo op as a couple deeply in love. Well, so be it. I didn't know what reality was and what was pretend anymore, and—fuck it—looking this amazing I didn't care.

At the bottom of the stairs to the hall, I turned to Shaun. Gratitude for him filled me up. He'd brought out a version of me I'd never been convinced existed outside my wildest fantasies.

"Cedar was right." I tried to blink away my emotion before it spilled over. "You really are a fairy godmother."

"That's me. Everything but the pumpkin." He handed me a tissue plucked from his tuxedo pocket. "But for the love of god, Lucy Snow, if you start crying and wreck that amazing winged eyeliner, I will throttle you."

We all started laughing, but right when I least expected it, fear seized me again. Would people see right through me, as a stupid girl acting out some sort of teenage fantasy? "Maybe we should go in now before everyone sits down," I said. "I mean, do I really want to draw that much attention to myself?"

Shaun stared me down. "Yes, Lucy. You do."

"Okay." I gulped, trying my best to push down my doubts.

Raphael gave me a little nod as a reminder to trust Shaun.

My hands trembled. We reached the bottom of the staircase up to hall. "So Jack is waiting up there?" I looked up the stairs, questions stampeding over one another in my brain.

"Yes. I have coordinated everything down to the second. I can't wait to see his face." Shaun chuckled.

My heart somersaulted.

"You two go ahead," I said. Shyness slowed me down, as well as my Grecian-style gold heels.

Shaun straightened Raphael's bowtie, then leaned over and gave my cheek a kiss. "My mission is complete. Now it's up to you to decide what you want to do with it."

I nodded, not trusting my voice.

Raphael took Shaun's hand, and they walked side by side up the stairs. I followed half a staircase behind.

"Jack!" Shaun's voice echoed above from the stone landing. He'd reached the top.

"Where's Lucy?" I heard Jack demand, his voice carrying a desperate note through the February air.

Was I really doing this?

"Wait for it," Shaun said, and I heard the hall door open and then bang close again.

I stepped up the last few steps, until I could see Jack's feet, pacing back and forth. The swoosh of my heartbeat filled my ears. I wasn't brave enough to meet his eyes quite yet ...

I stopped at the top. God, even my legs were shaking. It felt like I was teetering on the top of something very high, but damned if I was going to take a step back now. I was going to get my fairy tale tonight, even if I needed to tackle it to the ground.

I raised my head slowly until my eyes met Jack's green ones. His gaze devoured me from head to toe while the air between us snapped and hummed. He swallowed hard, then opened his mouth. No sound came out.

One of us had to say something.

"It's official," I said, my voice shaky. "Shaun wasn't just boasting. He is a bonafide genius."

Seconds ticked by, but Jack just stared at me, blinking. I

couldn't stand this empty space between us that felt so full.

"Jack," I begged. "Say something,"

"I'm going to die if I can't kiss you right this instant." His words came out in a burst.

Of all the things I imagined he'd say, I hadn't expected that. "What?"

"Please." His hands balled into fists. "Can I kiss you?"

The kiss with the pain au chocolat crumbs was still burning in me, demanding more. "Yes." I answered quickly.

Jack shook his head slightly, as though he couldn't quite believe I'd agreed. "Really?"

"Now," I added, my voice firm and steady.

He moved so fast that he was standing inches from me in what felt like a split second, his tuxedoed chest so close to my cleavage, rising and falling rapidly with his ragged breathing.

"You are the most beautiful thing I've ever seen," he whispered. His hand landed on the small of my back. Every one of my cells crackled with the warm contact.

Heat inched up my neck. Was he going to kiss me or just stand there staring? I ducked my head, suddenly shy. "Shaun is so talented—"

"No, Lucy." His hand on my back traced up my spine until it reached between my shoulder blades. "Not just tonight. You've always been the most beautiful thing I've ever seen."

His eyes glowed. This kiss—this night—might destroy me, but the memory I would gain would make the annihilation worth it.

He tilted my face to his. With his other hand, he cupped my jaw. His palm fit there perfectly, as if it were designed with the exact contours of my face in mind. He swayed toward me, and my eyes drifted closed in surrender.

"I meant it when I said now," I reminded him.

He chuckled as his lips met mine. There was no gentle, hesitant prelude like in the hall. His mouth was firm and desperate. He kissed like he was suffocating and only I could give him oxygen.

My lips opened and our tongues tangled, making me sparkle as bright as BPM 37093.

I nipped and sucked his full lower lip. Jack groaned, and it sounded ripped from his very soul. Us, finally together, consumed everything else.

My breasts felt full and heavy. Pressed against his broad chest, they were almost spilling over the draped front of my dress. My hands went lower, and I claimed his firm rear with my palms. He tilted sharply toward me, so I could feel exactly how this kiss, and me in this dress, was affecting him. He invaded every part of me, making me glimmer from within.

I vaguely registered the hall door opening. "What are you two waiting for?" I heard Shaun's voice, then a delighted cackle. "Ah! Excellent. Fairy godmother, signing off." The hall door banged shut.

I staggered backward, and Jack tightened his grip on me. "I'm not letting you go," he said. "And I'm definitely not letting you fall backward down the stairs. We need to talk—"

I held up a hand. "Not tonight. Tonight is my Cinderella night."

His brows shot up. "Your what?"

"It's decided. I don't want to think. I just want to live in a fairy tale for a few hours."

He gave me a funny smile. "Your wish is my command. May I take your arm?"

CHAPTER TWENTY-TWO

Jack

If it was *my* wish being granted, it certainly wouldn't be escorting Lucy into the hall. I would throw her over my shoulder and take her to my bed, where I could sink into that glorious body and make all my fantasies real.

Lucy looked like a shooting star. Those quick and perceptive blue eyes that sparkled when she laughed, her full bottom lip, and those opulent curves were finally highlighted for all to see.

I took her hand in mine and she gave me a tremulous smile. The lust and tenderness that whirled inside me like a tornado made me want to get her somewhere private, but this was Lucy's night. I needed to make it so perfect she would realize what I had known from the first time we met—she was spectacular.

I opened the hall door and led her through.

She turned over on her ankle a little bit, but I steadied her smoothly. She squeezed my hand in thanks. Didn't she realize by now I would do anything for her?

The entire room fell silent and turned to stare at us, then started taking photos and videos, not even caring about being conspicuous. For once I didn't feel the familiar thrum of panic gain speed within me. The stares weren't for me this time; they were for her.

A few phones were surreptitiously snuck out.

"Kiss me again," Lucy said so low I couldn't be sure I'd heard properly.

"Luce?"

"Kiss me. On the lips. Now. Unless you don't want—"

I didn't give her the time to finish. I tilted her head with my hand at the back of her neck. My lips touched hers and I felt the warm silk of her arms as they wound around my shoulders.

A response vibrated through her body—I'd always known somehow that Lucy was a closet sensualist, but to actually have proof in my arms ... she let out a tiny sound—meant just for me—that landed somewhere between a groan and a purr. *More.*

Somebody cleared their throat.

We broke apart, breathing heavy and looking at each other with wild eyes. Whatever we'd unleashed wasn't going to be easily stuffed back into a box and I couldn't be happier about it.

"Clearly Cedar isn't the only one I need to lecture about proper behavior," Shaun said.

"Oh, be quiet, Shaun," Cedar rolled her eyes. She must have come to greet us when we were kissing. "Love is beautiful, and so are you, Lucy. Absolutely stunning."

"Same. I love your dress," Lucy said, still flushed. I loved that I had something to do with that.

Cedar did look nice in a dress of ... who was I kidding? I was incapable of paying attention to what anyone looked like except Lucy.

We followed Shaun and Cedar back to the table the rest of our skulk had taken over.

"You look gorgeous, Lucy," Binita said.

"Aye, you look lovely lass," Lachlan added with a smile and a nod.

I put my arm around Lucy's waist and pulled her against me. "Mine."

I had no idea where that caveman possessiveness came from, but from the flare in Lucy's eyes I didn't think she minded it as much as she knew she should.

"Don't worry," Alfie said. "Nobody is planning on stealing Lucy from you."

I'd like to see them try.

Lucy found a spot on the bench. I slid in beside her.

Throughout the lively meal, full of pomp and circumstance on college china, she and I were pressed tight against each other. I had to hold a white-knuckled rein on my desire, but it was fraying by the second as I snuck tantalizing glimpses down the draped front of her dress.

This evening should have felt like enough, but it didn't. The more Lucy gave me of herself, the more I wanted. If only I knew exactly where I stood with her. I couldn't believe we could go back to pretending we were just friends after tonight. The mere idea throbbed like a physical ache.

It felt like I would die if I didn't have her. I'd never felt this desperate about any other woman before—only Lucy.

The main meal included a salad I whisked away from Lucy before she could even take a bite because the dressing contained mayonnaise. If she let me be her prince for the evening, I was going to do it perfectly.

Everyone lingered over the dessert of trifle, then platters of cheese, chocolate, and dried fruit, all copiously paired with red wine, which everyone except Lucy, Cedar, and I referred to as "claret."

It was as magical as Lucy wanted in the atmospheric and dimly lit hall with its high ceilings, long oak tables, and uniformed waiting staff.

I couldn't wait for it to be over.

All I could think of was how my fingers ached to trace the curves of Lucy's body in that dress, and then out of it, and of all the ways I wanted to make her flush pink. So, I died a little inside when Lachlan suggested going to the Turf for a last pint.

My heart sank when Lucy agreed enthusiastically, but I knew I had no choice but resign myself to the plan. If the Turf was part of her fantasy, then that's where we would go.

Our skulk snuck there via a back lane, cleverly evading the sleepy paps, and drank pints in a corner booth in the low-ceilinged pub.

Lucy continued to dazzle, verbally sparring with Shaun, her cheeks rosy with happiness and an easy gurgle of laughter ready at her lips. She didn't want this evening to end any more than I did.

We were squeezed so tightly together in the booth she was almost on my lap, and my head kept getting woozy from lust. Lower down, everything remained rock hard. Just before last call, an idea struck me. An exhilarating feeling in my gut told me it was a good one.

I slipped out of the booth and made a call to my assistant, and another one to Robbie. An hour or so later, the bartender started the task of kicking everyone out, and we gathered our jackets and wallets.

Lucy turned to me, that divot back between her brows. "Every fairy tale has to end, I guess."

I hoped she liked my crazy idea, because by now it was probably all set up, waiting for us. "I don't think it does," I said. "At least, not yet."

She scanned the pub, which was quickly emptying of patrons. "They won't let us stay here, or were you planning to use your star power for that? Anyway, my daydream was spending the night in a bookstore, not a pub."

"I didn't forget." Little did she know that fact was carefully filed away. "I think we should head back to college. There may be something waiting for us there."

"What are you up to?" God, I adored how her look of suspicion contrasted with her ethereal appearance.

"A surprise."

Her eyes filled with panic. "Please God, not a surprise party."

I chuckled. "As if I don't know you better than that. I would never do that to you."

"Then what? Am I going to hate it?"

Oh, the sweet distrust of Lucy Snow. "I hope not, but you know I would never force you to do anything, right?"

She snorted, belligerent, as she shifted against me. "As if you could."

I swear to God, I almost passed out from desire.

It was the perfect night—cold and crystal clear—and I was going to gamble everything to show this glorious conundrum of a woman how I felt about her.

FIFTH WEEK

CHAPTER TWENTY-THREE

Lucy

It was past midnight by the time we tumbled out of the Turf. I knew one thing for certain—even if I hated whatever surprise Jack had in mind, I didn't want my fairy tale to end.

I was having the time of my life and was mentally kicking myself for taking so long to just let myself enjoy being the girl on the rock star's arm.

My honesty forced me to admit it was more than that as we made our way through the skinny brick alleyway toward the Bridge of Sighs. Jack's fame didn't explain why it felt so right when he held me close.

It had everything to do with that invisible cord of connection I'd felt between us ever since I'd laid eyes on him four years ago, when he waltzed into my high school music room in response to the covert ad I'd posted on St. John's Craigslist looking for a backup guitarist and singer for my *Canada's Got Talent!* audition. My entire body had breathed a sigh of relief. *There you are. Took you long enough to find me.*

I couldn't explain it now any more than I could then, but for tonight at least I wasn't going to deny it.

When our skulk reached the wooden door of Beaufort, Robbie came out to greet us. The paps must have turned in, because nobody seemed to pick Jack out from the rest of the tuxedoed men roaming the streets in the dark February night.

How far was I willing to take my fantasy? If Jack was interested, was I prepared to sleep with him and finally close the circle we'd opened four years before? My mind filled with an image of him looming above me, all flashing eyes and powerful limbs.

"Good evening." Robbie said, haloed by the yellow light coming from the window of the lodge. "Don't you all look smart."

"Thank you, Robbie" we chorused.

"You look like the cat who caught the canary, Mr. Seary," Robbie said, with a wink that made me blush. I wasn't used to so many compliments on my appearance, even subtle ones like Robbie's. They made me realize now how desperately I'd yearned to be seen, and how hard it was going to be to revert back to my regular life after tonight.

"I *feel* like the cat who caught the canary." Jack cast me a hungry look that made the hairs on the back of my neck stand on end.

Robbie gave a slight nod to Jack. Jack gave one back.

We waved good night to our friends and headed for the staircase.

"What was all the nodding about?" I asked as Jack tightened his arm around me. I wondered yet again how his touch could feel entirely natural, yet completely electrifying.

He looked down at me, the corner of his lip twitching. "You'll see."

Liquid heat poured into my stomach. "Aren't we just heading to our rooms?" The staircase we were climbing didn't lead anywhere else.

Jack laughed and the long, hard muscles of his side vibrated against me. "Not really."

What did that mean? *Stop overthinking, Lucy. Just for tonight. Fairy tale. Remember?*

I'd been simmering all night for more of Jack, but now we were finally alone, my stomach clenched and my knees were wobbly. At the same time, in this dress, after this evening, I wanted the whole fantasy—all of Jack—every last crumb of pleasure.

Instead of veering right or left toward one of our doors at the top of the stairs, he stopped us in front of the third door in between. As far as I knew it was always locked. I'd always assumed it was a supply closet or something.

My eyes noticed a new detail—a key in the lock. Jack reached down and turned it.

"I had no idea that door even opened," I murmured, my heart in my throat. Where was he taking me?

"Really? What did you imagine was on the other side?"

"A janitorial closet."

He stopped. "You seriously thought for your surprise I was going to take you into a janitorial closet?"

I shrugged. "I definitely would've been surprised."

He quirked an eyebrow and pulled open the door. It creaked long and loud.

I peeked into the dark. As my eyes adjusted and with the help of the light from the landing, I saw a set of very old-looking stone stairs.

"See?" Jack said. "No cleaning supplies."

It smelled of old stone and disuse. "Maybe not, but there are for sure dead bodies up there."

He brushed a strand of hair that had fallen in front of my left eye and tucked it behind my ear. A million tiny fireworks exploded along the trail of his touch. "Do you trust me?"

That was the million-dollar question, wasn't it? Did I forgive his betrayal to the point I trusted him again? I'd certainly seen since we'd arrived at Beaufort that I didn't need to trust Jack to want him. Anyway, deciding that tonight wasn't part of my dream sequence. I pushed it to tomorrow's growing list of things future Lucy could figure out.

I tapped my lower lip with my fingers. "Enough to go up those dank, haunted old stairs?" I sidestepped his question. "I don't know if I trust anyone that much."

His lips dipped slightly. He saw my evasion for what it was.

Did he realize how hard this was for me? Trusting Jack meant trusting that life didn't always snatch away the things I loved. "I trust you enough for tonight."

His brows drew together. "We'll revisit that later." He squeezed my hand. "But for now, believe me when I say you can." He picked up a flashlight that had been set on the third step to light our way up.

"I can't believe you're not asking where I'm taking you." Jack's voice echoed off the narrow stone walls as we reached the first twist in the staircase.

"I'm trying to suspend disbelief this evening," I said. "Just tonight, though. Don't get used to it."

Our footsteps sounded hollow. "I wouldn't dare."

We finally reached a small arched wooden door with a key in it. We had to be up high, near roof level.

Jack unlocked it and swung the door open. He ducked and went through, holding tightly to my hand.

Why did my palm have to feel like it belonged in his? I wondered yet again why it only felt like this with one of the most famous men on earth instead of some regular Joe—an employee of Newfoundland fisheries and member of the local dodgeball league.

It felt like the universe was setting me up for a terrible long con with Jack. He'd let me down before. He was out of my league in every conceivable way. He was desired and feted, and our lives would go back to being completely incompatible once he left Oxford and rejoined Northern Junk.

I peeked around his broad back, and all those reasons excellent reasons to remain wary flamed out like falling flares in the star-spangled sky.

We were on a flat section of the roof of Beaufort, but someone had set up a bunch of blankets and pillows into a makeshift rooftop bed and surrounded it with candles. It looked something like a Bedouin tent in the middle of the desert, except without the tent part. A path of more candles, flickering in the sharp but clear February night, led to it.

An unstoppable smile grew on my face. "How?"

He led me toward the beginning of the candle path. "Let's just say it's fairies."

I remembered Robbie's nod. "Has Robbie grown wings?"

"Possibly. Do you seriously think anything happens at Beaufort that Robbie doesn't have a hand in?"

I shook my head, trying to absorb the magic in front of us. "It doesn't really matter. It's perfect." Desire and fear swirled together inside me.

"It's for star gazing." Jack waved his hand over the scene. "I thought we might look for shooting stars like we used to."

I was powerless against the nostalgia. The best hours of my life had been spent on the high school roof, with Jack pointing out constellations while I only half paid attention because my thoughts were consumed with wondering if we were ever going to kiss.

But Jack hadn't brought me up here just to star gaze ... had he? The potential humiliation of reading this situation terribly wrong made my skin prickle. Then I remembered the way he'd kissed me and told me I was the most beautiful thing he'd ever seen. If I was going to see this fairy tale through, I had to have faith and believe in my imaginary glass slippers for once in my life. "It's a bed, right?" I said, more a statement than a question.

His face looked both eager and nervous in the flickering candlelight. "Star-gazing doesn't work quite as well standing up." He angled himself toward me, took my other hand, and studied my face. "It's me, Luce. Jack the space nerd. I would never force you into anything."

"Like you could," I whispered, unable to resist.

"Exactly. I've seen you angry. I only want you to stay up here if you want to."

Jack and I had no future together—sure he was the astronomy geek, but he was also Jack Seary, for heaven's sake—but I deserved to throw my usual caution to the wind just this once. I'd earned it. Besides, it was a stronger woman than me who could resist Jack Seary standing in front of them in a tuxedo, begging. "I want to."

He let out a whoosh of air and tilted his head back as though he was thanking the stars. I caught him doing a little fist pump. "In that case, let's test this bed out." He led me down the candlelit path to the bed.

He pulled me down beside him onto the bed, flipped back the layers of duvets and quilts, and ushered me underneath.

I crawled in and felt deliciously warm.

"Is this duvet heated?" I asked.

"I think so," he said. "That's what I asked for, in any case."

"But how? There are no electrical sockets nearby."

He was so diligent about tucking me in that I was starting to feel like an Egyptian mummy. "Maybe magic?"

"No. There must be a battery pack in here somewhere."

He splayed his hands on either side of my shoulders and hovered above me, his eyes narrowed but with an amused tilt to his lips. "I thought you said you were going to suspend your disbelief tonight, Luce." He resumed fussing over my blankets.

He had a point. That was the goal of the evening, after all. "I'm trying." I sighed. "It's an ongoing process. Hey, I'm starting to feel like a sardine. How about you get in and warm me up?"

Jack froze mid-tuck. His eyes widened. "Really? I didn't want to rush you—"

A switch flipped inside me. "Stop stalling, Jack," I said softly.

He was under the covers and snatching me in his arms in record time, both of us still fully clothed in our formalwear. He smelled of fresh soap and that lemon scent from his guitar string oil that always lingered on his skin. I inhaled him in. *This was happening.* He rested his chin on the crown of my head as a tremor ran through his body.

"Are you cold?" I asked.

I could feel rather than see his head shake above me. "No."

"Panic attack?"

His laugh was shaky. "No. That would be seriously inconvenient." I loved how his chin rubbed across my hair as he talked. "But even if I did have a panic attack with you right now, I think I'd be okay."

His biceps flexed against my shoulders as he tightened his arms. It was growing toasty under the covers, the perfect contrast to the wintry air nipping my face. "It's hard to believe I'm a safe person for you. I either hold you at a distance or give you nonstop flack. I know I can be a nightmare."

He chuckled, and I squirmed closer to feel his chest vibrate with it. "Not my nightmare."

I wished, not for the first time, I could read his mind. He dropped a hand from behind my back and reached down for mine. His fingers trembled, despite the warmth of his palm.

"What's up then?" Just as I said it, I moved my leg slightly, and brushed up against the front of Jack's pants. My throat thickened with lust. Something was definitely up, even though it wasn't what I'd been talking about. The need to get him closer pulsed between my legs.

"I'm nervous." He squeezed tighter, his rigid cock unmistakable against my thigh. My head spun. *I did that.*

He'd been with so many beautiful women—models, singers, socialites .... It was me who should have been nervous, but weirdly I wasn't. "Why?"

He cleared his throat. "Do I really have to tell you?"

"Yes." This was the biggest risk I'd ever taken—I couldn't do it without total honesty.

"It's going to sound weird and maybe even presumptuous."

He was adorable nervous like this, but my impatience was getting the better of me. Now that I'd made the decision to take this night as far as it would go, my heart was doing backflips of anticipation, and zings of lust pinged through me. "Let me guess. You're a virgin."

He let out a funny choke of laughter. "No. I'm definitely not a virgin. I haven't been promiscuous either, but you know ... the normal amount."

"The normal amount for a rock star or the normal amount for a regular person?"

"Regular person."

"Then why the nerves? I need to know."

He arched his neck and groaned with frustration. Any straggling hesitation dissolved at the sound. "Okay. It's like this ..."

I waited ... and waited ... "I'm going to need more than that."

His hand ran up my neck until his fingers knotted into my hair. He tilted my head back so that my eyes met his, burning bright in the candlelight. "I've had sex with other women, but this will be the first time I've made love to the woman I love."

His fingers flexed in my hair as his words cracked my icy heart open and the world shifted on its axis. My brain raced to catch up, and also to preserve this perfect moment for me to use as a talisman until my final breath.

I propped myself up on my elbow so I could get a better view of his face. "You love me?"

He exhaled long and slow, the scent of red wine and whisky from the pub wafting through the air between us. "Yes, Lucy Snow. I have since the moment I met you in that grotty high school gym. I never stopped."

"You didn't?"

"No. Trust me. I tried."

My memories were reshuffling so fast my brain couldn't keep up. Still, something just didn't compute. "I know how I look tonight, Jack, but how could you have stayed in love with Saint Lucy the Martyr from back home? You're *you*. I'm just ... well, fairly boring."

He reared away from me then, his glittering eyes boring into mine. My breath hitched at their intensity. "Boring? I'm going to show you just how not boring you are, Lucy Snow."

My heart gave an odd thump. "Go ahead," I murmured, knowing I was giving permission as well as issuing a dare. "I'd like to see you try."

CHAPTER TWENTY-FOUR

Jack

I swept Lucy back against the makeshift bed, my need for her crushing and desperate.

She was perfect—soft and silky and glowing in the flickering candlelight. My cock had never been this hard. I wanted all of Lucy and I wanted her now.

I captured that stubborn mouth in a possessive kiss, sparks exploding behind my eyelids. I had to slow down, make this perfect for her, but this had been building for so long. The tight hold I'd been keeping on my desire was fraying fast with the feel of her struggling to get closer to me too.

She let out a small sound somewhere between a moan and a sigh, and I almost lost it altogether. "You are so fucking gorgeous," I murmured, my whole body shaking now from the effort of controlling myself. I had to take the time to make her understand how I felt about her.

I traced the luscious curve of her hip and thigh with a firm touch. She was so warm underneath me, so delicious. I could feel her body pulse under my touch. "I just can't imagine ever having my fill of you."

She blinked up at me, her beautiful eyes dark and not quite convinced. Dammit. I needed to make her understand how every inch of her was perfectly formed. She exuded this unyielding strength and yet there was such vulnerability behind it—I was helpless against the combination.

I tried to memorize her body, moving upwards, until I cradled the sweet curves of her face in my hands. "I can tell you don't believe me, but it doesn't matter. I'm going to show you."

Her body stiffened underneath mine, then released all at once and went pliant. Her lips brushed my ear. "Yes. Show me," she whispered. I had to draw back for a second so that I didn't come right then and there.

"I'll show you, all right," I gasped. I could hear the rush in my ears as the dam broke inside me. Her hips rose up to meet my erection, and my heart stopped for a few beats before lurching into action again.

With determined hands, she pushed off my tuxedo jacket and undid my bow tie, all without breaking our kiss. I reached up and yanked my tie off, throwing it over my shoulder. "You're terrifyingly efficient," I murmured.

"I know." Her hands dove under my dress shirt, and I groaned as she traced the planes of my muscles underneath. "Are you scared yet?" she asked.

"Only that something will interrupt us before I can slide into you." It was the truth.

I loved the sharp intake of her breath. A flame ran up my backbone. Oh God. Yes. *That.*

My hands slid down the front of her dress and into the promised land of her breasts. I cupped the right one and it felt even better than I'd fantasized—generous and velvety.

"So sexy," I murmured against her mouth. The pad of my thumb brushed over the hard, diamond point of her nipple. Her whole body convulsed. "So sumptuous." I brushed her nipple again and savored how she writhed under me in response.

I needed a taste of her. I dipped my head so my lips were near the swell of her cleavage. "You don't know how many times I've jerked off to this fantasy," I confessed.

She made a sound that was barely human. There was no sight more beautiful in the world than watching Lucy Snow come undone.

With my tongue, I traced the tight circle of her nipple.

She whimpered.

I needed more. I needed everything. I managed to fish out one of the condoms I'd tucked optimistically in the pocket of my pants. Our hands became frantic as she found my zipper and slipped my pants down over my hip bones, then my boxers, before I freed her of her dress and—be still my heart—her lacy confection of a bra.

I sucked hard and she arched underneath me. "More," she gasped. I almost passed out hearing the need in her plea.

We chucked our discarded clothes out beyond us into the flickering candlelight as we removed them. I spared a fleeting hope they wouldn't catch fire on one of the candles, but the whole college could go up in flames and it still couldn't stop me.

She wrapped her small but capable hand around my length and any coherent words scattered like light in the earth's atmosphere. I threw my head back, my breathing ragged.

She was perfect, and the weirdest thing of all was how *not* weird it felt to for Lucy to be sliding her hands up and down my cock and quickly driving me to the edge. "You're killing me, Lucy," I managed. "See what you do to me? Farthest thing from boring."

"Do you have a condom?" It sounded like the last gasp of practicality she had in her. I loved that I'd driven the rest of it out.

I grabbed the condom from where I'd shoved it underneath one of the pillows and lifted my fingers to show her.

"How did you manage that?" She sounded impressed.

"Took it out of the pocket of my pants before chucking them."

"Do you only have one?" she demanded, not pausing for a second on how she was working her fist up and down on my cock. God. She was glorious.

I shook my head. "I have several." I wanted as much as she could give me.

"I never considered foresight sexy." She grinned under me. "But here we are."

"Here we are." I ripped the package with my teeth and, with unsteady hands, eased my shaft away from Lucy's ardent grip long enough to roll on the condom.

In a snap I loomed above her, my body hard and ready to give her the most pleasure I possibly could. I needed to make her understand that she didn't need to be anyone for me except herself. That was already more riches than any man deserved in a lifetime.

I moved the duvet away from her so I could feast my eyes on her naked body. She was flushed and luscious. Perfection. "I knew it," I said. "You're a work of art naked." I dipped down and kissed her left breast reverently. "A masterpiece."

"I want you inside me," she said, her voice strained. "You've already made me wait far too long, Jack Seary."

"You waited?" I demanded. Why had we wasted the past four years not doing this? I reached down and stroked my fingers up and down her already slippery folds. Oh God, if I weren't already teetering on the edge, the feel of her would clinch it. "You're drenched, my Luce," I breathed. "Is that for me?"

She nodded, the trust in her eyes breaking through all those guarded parts of my soul.

"See?" My cock brushed against her entrance. "Not boring. In-candescent. My favorite dream of all time."

"Show me," she gasped. I was going to expire on the spot. "Show me hard."

There was no sound except the crackling candle wicks and our hitched breathing as I sank into her, inching in bit by bit to better savor the sensation. *Fuck.* She felt more perfect than anything.

Finally, I was fully inside her, thrust to the hilt, pressing against her tightness everywhere. A strange alchemy had replaced my blood with fire.

She bucked her hips slightly and I almost lost it.

I grabbed her shoulder. "Just ...," I gasped. "I need a second." I closed my eyes to master myself again. Gary's veneers, Cathy's helmet hair, the smell of old oil used for frying ....

Lucy stayed perfectly, torturously still under me. How did she manage to constantly have me balancing on the tightrope of orgasm?

"Sorry." I opened my eyes again. "You drive me wild, Lucy Snow."

Her mouth took on that mischievous tilt I adored. "I haven't even started yet."

I began to move inside her with deep, long strokes, caressing all of her secret places. The feel of our connection made me want to weep with joy.

It was even more than I'd imagined it would be. She was home. She was an irresistible dare. She was a crackling bonfire. We just *fit.*

"My shooting star," I murmured, drawing back and thrusting

into her again, so full of passion and love that my heart hummed with wonder.

It didn't take long for this thing between us to make us both explode together, like supernovas in the dark, starry night.

CHAPTER TWENTY-FIVE

Lucy

I woke up to the sky lightening from black to the darkest blue.

Jack and I were naked and intertwined under piles of blankets. My leg was hooked over his thigh, and my head rested on his bicep. Our experiments during the night proved that no matter which way our bodies melded together, they fit like puzzle pieces snapping into place.

The only part of me exposed to the frigid morning air was the top of my head, and it felt damp from the dew that meant the night was over. I wondered with a sinking stomach if that meant the magic would be too.

We'd made love three times—the first was a revelation. The second was fast, ragged, and completely wild. The third, in the early hours of the morning with the stars twinkling overhead, was slow and languorous—yet another of the seemingly inexhaustible ways we could be together.

I'd been deluded to think I could have Jack for one night and not want more. Time to face the truth: deep down, I was greedier than that.

Jack's head was flung back on one of the pillows. Even asleep, his arms held me tight against him. His upper lip was still stained slightly orange from our middle-of-the-night snack of Hawkin's Cheezies that his assistant had left beside the bed. They'd been the perfect fuel for more lovemaking.

I checked in with myself, fully expecting regrets, but ... nope. None. Was this what they called afterglow? Somehow waking up like this with him felt natural—maybe because last had made clear that Jack and I were always going to end up here sooner or later.

I couldn't imagine tiring of seeing him like this: spent, unguarded, relaxed in his sleep, keeping me close like I was the most precious thing in the world.

I leaned over and inhaled his warm vanilla morning scent, storing it away in a sacred memory compartment of my brain. I couldn't resist giving him a kiss on the chin, loving the intimate scrape of his coppery morning bristle against my lips.

He must be exhausted. We'd dozed only for a few snatches between making love and talking. Jack had pointed out constellations and entertained me with his theories on why the galaxy was in a constant state of expansion, like his love for me. We even saw two shooting stars.

Never in a million years would I have thought I could live a moment like this. My life was full of doing tedious things for other people; it was shocking just how much I enjoyed being selfish. I wasn't ready for it to end. Every atom of my being cried out *not yet.*

"Hm," he murmured, coming to the surface. "I'd like to wake up this way every day, please."

I chuckled, wanting to put off doing some hard thinking about my heart a little longer. "I can't believe we spent the whole night out here." The candles had guttered out hours before.

His eyes fluttered open—the same green as the feathery new needles of a fir tree. He gazed up at me, then we both looked over at the streak of pinky orange spreading across the horizon behind Beaufort's chapel steeple. "I would spend the rest of my life out here if I could."

I ran my index finger up the warm curve of his bicep, enjoying how his skin warmed under my touch. I started to hum, the sing, the shanty "Ramblin' Rover" while Jack stayed very still, a captive audience.

When I was done, he sighed. "I love that one. You were born to sing Lucy. It still kills me that I ruined that for you. I'll never forgive myself." He rubbed his eyes with the heels of his palms.

I shook his shoulder. "Hey. I didn't sing to make you sad."

"Your singing could never make me sad."

I shrugged. "It's probably for the best anyway." I couldn't possibly have Jack and singing—life would never let me have both, and seeing as I had to choose, I chose Jack. "I have to be practical."

I felt his chest expand. "Always the pragmatist, even when I've been inside you most of the night. We'll work on that."

A hot thrill ran between my thighs. I ached there, but I loved that physical reminder of our night. "Good luck with that." I hadn't told Jack the whole story about my dad's death, but if he knew he'd give up on trying to convince me to pursue singing again.

He traced the shell of my ear with his finger and all those bad memories disintegrated as I shivered under his touch. I loved how these caresses felt natural, like no thought went into them at all, just instinct. My heart somersaulted. Could I trust how real this felt?

He fingertips moved down each of my vertebrae as though he was memorizing them, then slipped up to my left breast. A shot of desire ricocheted through me. How did he *do* that?

Sore as I was, I would have him again in a heartbeat. I sucked in the frosty morning air, trying to clear my head. The thing was if I wasn't going to flunk out, I had to get up and read the thirty cases necessary to write a criminal law essay for my tutorial tomorrow. I didn't have enough hours as it was to do all that and sleep.

I let out a sound of frustration.

"What is it?" Jack's hand stilled on my breast, and he kissed my forehead. "I'm sorry, I can't help myself. I'm insatiable for you."

I shook my head. "It's not that. I love it when you touch me. It's just …." I sighed. "Reality."

He clicked his tongue. "By reality you mean law?"

I nodded against him. "I have to research and write a criminal law essay for tomorrow, then do a contract one for Wednesday, and Professor Speedman already thinks I'm a lost cause."

He propped himself up on his forearm, and the blankets over us slipped away, leaving his bare chest exposed, adorned with the tattoos that had hypnotized me when I'd found him shirtless in his room. There was one of a constellation on his shoulder I hadn't noticed before.

Surely my essay on causation and the case of R vs White could be delayed a few more seconds while I investigated.

He stopped breathing as I brushed my finger over the inky stars that splayed across his muscular shoulder. "Which constellation is that?"

He shook his head, then dropped a kiss on my lips. "Centaurus."

I did a quick calculation. My mom had always been into astrology, and I must have absorbed some of it by osmosis. "But you're not a Sagittarius. Why that one?"

LAURA BRADBURY

"I just like it." His eyes left mine briefly, then returned. "It's my favorite one."

"Any reason?"

"Guess which star lives in it?"

My hand continued up and over the sharp line of his jawbone. I loved how his eyelids dropped to better relish the feel of my fingers. If only I could memorize everything about him in this moment. "I'll take a wild guess. BPM 37093?"

His eyes flew open. "You remembered it!" He threw himself on top of me and kissed me thoroughly, his arm wrapping around and supporting my back.

"Jack!" I managed a feeble and completely insincere protest.

"You're already irresistible, but how can you expect me to control myself when you talk stars to me?"

"I memorized it the first time," I confessed. "I was just tormenting you a bit. You know, for fun."

"You think that's fun?" His face took on a look of determination. "I'll show you fun."

Things quickly progressed to the point where we were close to making love again, but the orange swaths lighting up the sky stopped me. The amount of work looming over my head became heavier as the daylight grew. I put my palm on his chest.

His breathing was heavy.

"I hate to do this," I said.

"Nooooo."

"Yes. No matter what my body wants and, believe me, it wants it all, I need to go to my room and work. I've put it off too long already. If we have sex again I for sure won't be able to string a coherent thought together."

He opened his mouth, then shut it again with a little grunt of discontent. "I guess you're right."

"I wish it wasn't," I said with feeling. Being a pragmatist sucked.

He splayed a hand on my right bum cheek and patted it gently. "It's probably for the best. We need to have a talk anyway."

"Oh?" I said airily. "About what?"

He squeezed. "About the state of cryptocurrency, of course."

I laughed. Combine that quirky sense of humor, those freckles, his gorgeous cock, and the hunger in his green eyes and ... if I didn't get up now, I was going to stay here all day.

I leaped up, then yowled at the frigid air. I snatched the top duvet and wrapped it around my shoulders. "Where are my clothes?" I demanded of the frigid February morning.

"I'll find them and bring them down to you."

If Jack came to my room, I knew there was no way I could stay focused on my reading. I wanted more than anything to be disturbed all day by him, but I couldn't put off real life any longer.

He dug into the blankets and held up my dress. "From the expression on your face, I'm guessing you don't want to be disturbed?"

"Are you a mind-reader?"

"I can read your face very well, Lucy Snow. I should, considering all the time I've spent staring at it."

I didn't know what to say, so I just filed it away in my "to-contemplate-later" drawer. It was getting stuffed to overflowing. I thought of my phone and the watch Jack had taken from me yesterday. Did that have something to do with why I'd felt so much lighter last night and this morning?

Guilt struck without warning. I needed to make sure my mom and Alice didn't need my help. I shouldn't have gone so long without being available. "Where's my phone and watch?"

"I left them on the desk in your bedroom."

I still didn't move. Jack all naked and tousled under the blanket was almost impossible to leave.

"Lucy?" He raised his left brow.

"I don't want to go," I said, to him or myself I wasn't sure. "But that's the only way I'll get any work done." Yet how could I possibly read boring cases when I could have him? Here. Like this.

"I understand. It's okay. Shoo. If it helps, I have to go to the observatory anyway and do some work on my research project. Professor Hayden agreed to come in and help me with some calculations."

I took a deep breath. "Okay. This is my final word. I'm going." I turned around and took a step toward the door that led to the staircase, the duvet dragging on the rooftop.

"Can I at least bring you dinner tonight?" he said. I turned around. My mind took a snapshot of him, his face and rumpled hair half hidden by a white pillow, the visible dimple carved deep.

Maybe it would motivate me to stay super focused knowing I would get a treat. Besides, I knew by then I'd by dying to see him. Even my willpower wasn't an inexhaustible thing.

"I guess I have to eat. I think I can let myself have a little visit if I get enough done."

"'Visit'? Is that a euphemism?"

I lifted a shoulder under my makeshift duvet cape. "We'll see."

His smile was brighter than the fuchsia and tangerine sky above us.

"Goodbye," I said, wishing there was an etiquette manual for this situation. There were no words for what the night had been for me. "Thank you for …".

He waited, patient.

"Thank you for you," I said simply.

"Lucy." He merely said my name but in a way that infused every syllable with everything else we'd shared.

I gave an awkward little nod and moved for the door to the staircase.

I turned the key and opened it. "Just...Lucy," he called from behind me.

I turned around slowly.

"I need you to know last night was the best night of my life."

I paused with my hand on the worn wooden door, everything inside me reaching out to him still deep in the covers. "It was for me too. Thanks for making it magic."

He shook his head. "*We* made it magic."

I shut the door to my room and made a beeline for the phone on my desk.

Shit. Ten missed calls from home.

My hands shook with fear as I held the duvet around my neck. Were they alright? I couldn't take my eyes off my responsibilities. Dialing my home number on speakerphone, I snapped my father's watch on. I'd never realized before how heavy it was on my wrist.

My mind flew immediately to the worst.

I didn't have to fill in much with my imagination. I would never forget the day the police and coast guard huddled in our rundown front hall, which always smelled faintly of fish scales, and told us my father had been calling Mayday when they lost emergency contact. That they were going to mount a search, but that given the storm, chances were slim.

My mother had collapsed to the floor. Alice, only a baby, had started crying. I picked her up, then hauled my mother off the floor with my free arm, pushing down my own terror and grief so I could carry theirs, like I'd promised my dad I would.

I'd settled Alice in her playpen in the kitchen and made everyone cups of strong coffee. After that, I had to do the next thing and the next thing and the next thing. Groceries. Cooking. Feeding Alice. Filling out paperwork on behalf of my mom. Forging her signature. I'd been eleven. And even then, I hadn't known the full truth that my dad had brought his death on himself.

The phone rang at home in our Newfoundland kitchen. Three rings. Four rings. Just when I thought my heart was going to beat out of my chest, Alice answered.

"Are you okay?" I demanded, not even bothering to keep the panic out of my voice.

"Yeah," Alice answered. "Why?"

"Is Mom all right? Did one of you have to go to the hospital?"

"No. Why would you think that?"

Trauma had showed me that the worst could—and did—happen. It had changed me for good, separating me from people like Jack who didn't carry that same awareness in every cell.

My heart started to slow down, but all that adrenaline transmuted into anger. I felt more annoyed than relieved. "Alice, you tried to call me ten times, and you didn't leave a single message. I'm a bit panicked."

"Sorry," she said, sounding indignant. "I was just excited."

Excited? "About what?"

"With the new talk-to-text thing my learning assistance teacher set up, I got ten out of ten on the creative short story I wrote at school!"

Satisfaction rushed through me. Alice might just be okay, thanks to Jack's money and my "favor" of pretending to be his girlfriend, although I certainly wasn't pretending anymore.

"That's amazing. How does it work?"

"I don't have time to tell you right now. Mom's taking me to my soccer practice. Bye!"

She hung up, and I was left staring down at my phone. Come to think of it, I hadn't heard from my mom in the past week. None of the usual desperate pleas for help or for me to come home.

I should have been happy, but instead worry wormed its way around my chest. What was going on over there?

CHAPTER TWENTY-SIX

Jack

When I returned to my room after tidying things up, I poured myself a hot bath and lit all my expensive candles. I had to leave for the observatory by noon.

Dinnertime with Lucy felt lightyears away.

Part of my mind couldn't comprehend last night had really happened. Was it wishful thinking, or did she seem open to us officially being a couple? The mere idea she might not want to be with me turned my shoulders to granite and filled my chest with a sick wooziness despite the tobacco and vanilla candles wafting around me.

It was enough, combined with a lack of sleep and the general unpredictability of my nervous system that I could sense a panic attack coming. It started slowly, with the sensation I couldn't expand my lungs. My breathing turned shallow and catchy.

No. I couldn't be having a panic attack again. They'd become so infrequent and mild when I wasn't exposed to anything Northern Junk-related—such as Cathy's impromptu 'visit'—that I'd begun to cautiously hope I was cured.

How could this be happening now, after finally getting what I'd dreamed about for the past four years? Disappointment and fear made my breathing come even more quickly.

I tried the cognitive behavioral mantras. *I knew what this was. I had survived so many of these and come out the other side.*

But doubts pinged frantically off my skull. What if this was the one that I wouldn't survive? Maybe they had all just been warnings, building up to this. The bathroom lurched as my head began to spin. Something was really wrong this time.

I crawled out of the bath and grabbed a towel, wrapped it around me, and lay down on the cold, tiled bathroom floor. Something terrible was happening. Numbness prickled through my limbs, and an anvil pressed down on my ribs. My heart was leaping and pumping like I was running up Everest. Everything was infused with an undeniable wrongness. Surviving felt impossible. The cruel irony was that after my night with Lucy I had so much to live for.

I squeezed my eyes shut and thought of her next door. Eventually, that calmed me enough that I managed to get to my bed. I set an alarm to leave for the astronomy lab in three hours and fell into an exhausted, defeated sleep.

I was still disoriented when I woke up and left my room. Panic attacks always left me spacey, disheartened, and confused. I couldn't figure out why I had to be like this.

When I was walking under the archway to the door out of Beaufort, Robbie called my name and ushered me into the lodge. He tilted his head and examined my face critically. "What's wrong with you this morning? Did last night not go as planned?"

I tried to shake away my panic hangover. "It went perfectly. Thank you so much. I'm sorry—"

He shook his head. "No time for that. I have to show you something."

"Is there a problem?" I asked as Robbie beckoned me to join him behind the glass separator by his desk.

He sighed. "I suppose it depends how you look at it, although I daresay you must be used to it by now."

He pulled out a handful of British tabloids—*The Sun*, *Daily Mail*, and the like, all specializing in character assassination and shady backroom alliances.

It took only a second to understand what had put those creases in Robbie's forehead. On the front page of every single one were photos of Lucy and me kissing in hall and later at the Turf, looking very much a couple in love. Thank god there were none of us on the rooftop—I'd started feeling so comfortable and safe within the walls of Beaufort that I stupidly hadn't even considered it a possibility.

We were a couple in love—at least I was—although the thought that she might not be on the same page made aftershocks of my earlier panic attack rumble through me. Even if things between us were slightly in limbo, they'd never been in limbo in my heart, even when I'd convinced myself I'd moved on from her. Were these photos going to freak her out and make her put up her walls again?

Tonight, we would have a serious talk. I didn't think my nervous system could handle waiting any longer.

I stared down at the tabloids again. That old distaste at being the object of so many people's attention felt like a vise around my throat.

Still, I couldn't help but smile to myself at seeing how beautiful Lucy was, and that she was on *my* arm, and that she had made love to *me*.

This was what I wanted, wasn't it? To show people I was wrapped up in romance rather than drugs and alcohol like the tabloids had implied—always stopping just short of defamation. The thing was there was nothing fake about it. I'd never been as serious about anything as I was about her.

Yet even if I'd fully expected and even wanted the media reveal, it left me feeling like I'd somehow cheapened what I felt for Lucy.

I dropped the tabloids back on the porter's desk. "Thanks for showing me, but I was expecting this. It was inevitable."

Robbie raised a black brow. "Goodness. You're reacting far better than Alfie ever did. He used to get apoplectic about the paps."

"Don't get me wrong, I hate them too, but Alfie had no choice about his father being notorious. I asked for it by joining Northern Junk in the first place."

Robbie frowned. "The kind of harassment the British tabloids dish out is vicious. Nobody deserves it."

I blinked as I digested Robbie's words. Gary and my bandmates, and even my parents, felt the press were allies rather than enemies and were to be courted and appeased. Gary always told us not to be hypocritical whiners when it came to media exposure of any kind. "That means a lot to me," I said finally.

Robbie bit back a smile. "Cedar bullied me into being nice to you to start with, but I've come to like you—and especially Miss Lucy." He took off his bowler hat for a moment and scratched his black hair, then put it back on. "I'd be remiss if I failed to remind you that although you may be used to this media attention, Lucy is not. She will need to know what to expect."

I should have been the first to think of that but, at the same time, I knew the slow softening of Professor Hayden toward me would be ruined if I was late. "You're right. I need to come up with a plan, but for now she's planning to say in her room to study all day." I pulled out my phone. "I'll text her right now."

"Are you off to the Bod?"

"No. I'm going to the observatory to do some research."

"No need to bother her. I'll be sure to watch for her and warn her if she decides to go out."

I doubted she would. When Lucy holed herself up to work, she generally didn't stir. She'd also made it clear she didn't want to be distracted before dinner—by texts or anything else. "You're a lifesaver, Robbie."

I made a move to leave, but Robbie grabbed my arm. "I'd suggest going out one of the secret doors." He was absolutely right—my brain was definitely not back online yet.

I managed to sneak out through one of Alfie's covert exits from the college basement and got as far as the foyer in the observatory undetected before being stopped by ... what the hell was Cathy doing waiting for me in the lobby of Green Templeton College?" I wondered for a wild second if my panic attack had predicted her appearance.

She barreled her way toward me, frumpy and scowling.

"Cathy?" I demanded. I couldn't for the life of me think of a reason why she would be here and not back in London with Gary.

"What have you done?" In contrast with her garishly patterned blouse, her face was white with suppressed emotion.

"Calm down. What are you talking about?" How had she known I was coming to the observatory?

She brandished a handful of the same tabloids Robbie had shown me. "This, of course!"

Wait. This was exactly the story Gary and Cathy had wanted to plant in the tabloids. "I'm doing exactly what Gary and you asked me to do so the press have an alternative to saying I'm a drug addict."

Hectic color flowed back into her cheeks. "Oh … oh, I see. When I saw these photos, Jack—"

"Why are you here?" I demanded. "I thought you and Gary would be thrilled."

Her shoulders dropped. "I am! I was just worried. I'm here to protect you, of course. Like I always do."

"I don't need protecting," I said, stirred to anger. They'd promised to leave me alone. "What I need is space and privacy." Cathy, with her appearance in my room and now this, was encroaching on my life. I needed to start putting up firm boundaries. How I felt about Lucy felt sacred, and I didn't want it tainted any further by their toxicity.

Cathy's breathing returned to normal. "Jack, a media mob is not the answer. It's far too messy. I will arrange a few exclusives with trusted sources. We need to find somewhere quiet where we can discuss strategy."

She was back at her attempts to stage manage my entire life. No more. The idea of going back to that felt unthinkable. "No. I have research to do."

"But, Jack! I insist. We need to talk."

"There is nothing to talk about." I left her standing there, her eyes narrowed.

My anxiety had finally released me from its clutches. It wasn't only because Professor Hayden had been even more enthusiastic and interested in my research than usual, but also because I now stood outside Lucy's door with several bags of steaming curry and copies of the tabloids to show her.

Please let this go well.

Even engrossed in astrophysics calculations, the memory of the way her neck smelled as I pushed inside her kept swirling back.

I awkwardly juggled the bags and knocked. She flung open the door. The hope she might have been waiting for me thrilled me ten times more than bringing the house down at Wembley. Even though the curry containers were scorching my fingers, all I could do was stand there and take in those clear blue eyes and how her hair was messily twisted up in a bun and anchored by a pencil.

She wore flowy pink pajama pants and a sweatshirt that read George Street Music Festival. The blood flowed straight to my cock as I remembered the heavenly curves and valleys underneath.

Her pouty lips were slightly open as she stared back at me. If only I could know what was going on in that complex mind of hers.

Lucy reached up, grabbed the collar of my hoodie, and dragged me into her room. "Be forewarned: you're about to be shamelessly used to quench my lust."

"Thank Christ," I exhaled, dropping the tabloids, curry, naan bread, and rice to the floor and picking her up. I was already hard, my body primed for hers in an instant.

I tossed Lucy on her bed, then leaped on top of her and set to kissing her with a hunger that she feverishly reciprocated. My heart raced with a sense of rightness like I'd never known. No wonder I'd had a panic attack at the mere thought of losing her.

"I've been counting the minutes until I could kiss you again," she gasped as she tugged off my top and the T-shirt underneath. How I adored her like this, eager and wanting. I'd always been obsessed by the sensual hedonist hidden behind Lucy's cautious exterior.

Bare-chested now, I flipped her over so she sprawled on top of me. Her pajama pants were all slippery and from what I had felt she hadn't bothered with a bra or underwear. A dream.

My hands roved over her silk-covered ass, cupping the glorious curves of her until she squirmed on top of me. "Fuck. You're going to be the death of me, Lucy Snow. I hope you're not too hungry yet, because I plan to take my time."

"I like a man who knows how to prioritize." She sighed in my ear. My dick twitched in approval.

"I need to get your jeans off." She'd already put her hands between us and started the job while I dealt with her sweatshirt and the silky pants.

"Finally," she whimpered as we pressed skin to skin.

I shuffled back against the bed and sat up, my back against her wall. I wanted to watch her, to see her, to drink in every expression that flitted across her face while we made love.

I lifted her so she straddled me. Her mouth curved up as she grasped me with a firm hand and then buried me in her to the hilt.

"Fuck, Lucy." The feel of her obliterated everything else. I reared up, she pressed down, and we burned hot and bright the way we seemed made to.

CHAPTER TWENTY-SEVEN

Lucy

We lay naked in my bed eating curry straight from the containers.

I ripped off a bite of soft, buttery naan with my teeth. "You know what? Curry tastes better eaten naked."

"In bed." Jack ate another forkful of Vindaloo. "With the person you've been obsessed with." He put down his curry container and kissed me. His hands ran over my hips, up my stomach, then lingered at my breasts while I hummed with pleasure.

My relationship with my body had evolved throughout my life. When I was a child, I was oblivious. My body just *was*—like the sky or the dark gray ocean or the white-and-blue icebergs. Then, when I started developing in middle school and realized I was much curvier than most of my classmates, I loathed it. Thanks to a lot of work, by the end of high school I viewed it with a resigned tolerance. It was what it was—at least it was functional.

In twenty-four hours, Jack transformed all that. He so clearly adored my body. How could I dislike anything that gave us such unmitigated pleasure?

"Really?" I murmured in his ear. "Your 'I never forgot you' story is for real?"

He pulled away far enough to stare down my skepticism. "How could you not have seen it? You're always so quick to pick up on things."

"I guess I never let myself go there." Even if I'd seen signs, I wouldn't have believed them. He was Jack Seary, and I was Lucy Snow. I certainly didn't feel like the same Lucy who had arrived at Oxford, but I didn't fully know who I was becoming yet either.

Could it finally be my turn to have good things happen to me? I had taken the leap to trust Jack again, but it was a whole other thing to trust life. My common-sense told me that I would be forced to give him up sooner rather than later, but since last night I couldn't help but feel it would be worth exchanging future pain for the extra memories.

"You didn't leave the college today, did you?" he asked out of the blue.

I shook my head. "I've been in my room the whole day."

He picked his curry up again and frowned into it. "I have something to tell you. Don't freak out."

Ice formed in my veins. I wasn't ready for the this to end yet—I needed more time with Jack. "What?" I managed to ask.

"There was a huge mob of paps outside the college doors—they've reconvened. I managed to trick them, but we need to make a plan for you." He got out of bed.

My whole body exhaled, and I couldn't help but feast my eyes on the view of his naked backside as he picked up the handful of newspapers he'd dropped to the floor when I'd tackled him.

He fanned them out on the duvet in front of us. "You need to have a look at these." His face was grim.

I stared down at the front pages. Jack and I were featured on every single one. My golden dress glowed in the table lamps of the hall, and I looked like I was floating on Jack's arm with a halo of light around me.

"Say something," he pleaded, his cinnamon brows drawn tightly together.

In the photos my eyes were an impossible shade of blue in the light of the flashes, and my lips held a secret smile. God, we hadn't even gone to the roof yet when these were taken. What would I look like the next time I got photographed, all blissful and sex drunk? I looked like I belonged on Jack Seary's arm, and he belonged on mine.

I shook my head, amazed. "I look fucking amazing."

Jack put down the piece of naan he'd picked up and stared at me. "You're not mad or—I don't know—upset?"

I searched inside myself. "It's kind of surreal to be on the cover of a newspaper, but I'm not angry about it." This was probably the closest I would ever get to fame.

Jack blinked. "Um, I wasn't prepared for this reaction."

"Can I keep them?" If everything blew up like it had before in my life, it would be nice to have a souvenir of a time when I'd felt gorgeous and happy.

He waved his hand in the air. "I'll arrange to get you as many copies as you want, but you need to know I've contacted my security people to discuss your protection."

"My what?" He was being paranoid. I could look after myself.

"The majority of my fans are fantastic, but a few are a bit overzealous."

I'd never even considered that. I couldn't believe Jack's fans would want to harm me. I was a nobody. "You mean a bit stalkerish?"

He scratched his cheekbone. "Yes. You haven't been approached by anyone, have you?"

My eyes shifted back to the front pages of the tabloids. I'd never considered myself female competition of any kind, but that girl in gold on Jack's arm—she was. "No."

Jack was just being overprotective. There was a novel sweetness to having someone worry about my well-being for a change, but it wasn't necessary. He used his fingers to comb my hair, which had gone berserk from our lovemaking, back from my forehead. I leaned into his touch.

"The idea of anything happening to you ...". His fingers ran along my hairline. "I couldn't bear it."

"It's not going to."

"My security team is coming up with a protection plan."

"It's not necessary."

"Will you at least agree to hear them out?"

I sighed. "Fine." I stared at the pile of law books on my desk. Our lovemaking had been worth the mess, but my butter chicken and aloo gobi were finished and I needed to get my land law essay written for eight o'clock the next day. I'd finished all the reading, but I hadn't even started the writing portion yet.

Jack watched me. "You're thinking about your law essay, aren't you?"

My eyes met his. "How did you know?"

"Your look of impending doom tipped me off."

I shuddered, thinking of the amount of work I had ahead of me. I would have to write all night, and even then, I wouldn't be able to produce more than a half-assed essay. Why was it so impossible to make myself care about law?

"Do you need me to go?" he asked.

I took in the wide set green eyes, those high cheekbones, those artfully scattered freckles across the bridge of his nose ... I didn't *want* that. "Jack—".

I get it." He sighed. "I wouldn't be able to keep my hands off you if I stayed anyway."

I used my fingertip to connect the stars on the Centaurus constellation scattered across his muscular shoulder, savoring the warmth of his skin underneath my fingertip. To be able to touch him like this was everything. "I think this is my favorite of your tattoos," I said. "Speaking of stars, how did your work at the observatory go today?"

His face lit up. I was always taken aback by how much Jack truly loved what he was studying here. "It was fantastic. Professor Hayden is getting more and more involved in my work on BPM 37093. He even suggested a few avenues of research I hadn't considered."

"That's exciting." If only I could feel that way about leaseholds.

"It is." His excitement carved his dimples deep. "When I think of the research possibilities ... they're *endless*, Luce.".

It was such a crying shame he had to go back to his rock star life in three weeks. "What would be your dream life if it weren't for Gary and your parents and the codicil?"

He stared at the Z-shaped crack on my plaster ceiling for a few moments. "I'd like to keep studying astronomy. I'd get some degrees here for real if I could. I'd love to be a professor of astronomy, even though I know that it would take a long time. You and I would be together."

My heart did an odd flip.

"We'd live in a small but cozy house with a fireplace, and we'd get a dog, maybe two. Same with kids if we were both on board. We'd cook delicious meals, and have our favorite restaurants, and friends who'd come around to share brunch on the weekends. We'd have a big, cozy bed, and I'd make you come several times a night."

My mouth went dry because I knew he could. Oh, could he ever. "You've obviously given this some thought," I said faintly.

He nodded. "I have. Eventually the media would forget about me, and I'd be that person some people vaguely recognized in the street and said to themselves, "'Hey, he kind of looks like that guy from that was in that band. What was its name again?'"

"Tell me again why you can't do that? Just tell Gary and your parents you're quitting, then hire good lawyers to deal with the codicil problem to make sure your parents don't get sued or anything. Hell, if any of this law I'm studying ever goes into my head, I could even try to help."

His hand fanned over my collarbone. I watched as a flare of hope shot up through his green eyes, then died away. "I've learned not to underestimate Gary. It's just too risky."

"But, surely—"

He brushed his thumb across my lower lip, sending an arrow of need straight between my thighs. "I want that dream so much it's painful to think about."

I understood that so viscerally all I could do was lean forward and kiss him. He kissed me back, his lips as gentle as butterfly wings, driving me wild. His arms pulled me tight against him.

We were rudely interrupted by the boom of the tower clock ringing eight times.

"Fuck," I muttered.

"You read my mind."

I groaned and collapsed back on the bed. "My goddamn essay."

He grimaced but slid off the bed and began to start tidying up, still buck naked. Strong, wide shoulders, those defined muscles running down the sides of his torso, that narrow waist .... I could lie here and happily feast my eyes on him forever.

There had to be a way to help him at least have a choice about going back to Northern Junk. "Can you get me a copy of that codicil?" I said. "Maybe I'll show it to Professor Speedman. She doesn't like me much, but she's scary brilliant with contracts."

"Sure." He shrugged, slipping his jeans on, commando. I knew what I was going to be fantasizing about when my concentration for law inevitably lapsed. "I'll get you a copy."

Ugh. Being responsible had never sucked this much. "I want you to stay." It felt crucial he understood how torturous this was for me too.

"I know." He blew me a kiss. "But you need me to go. Look, before I do, there is something I need to get off my chest."

"Uh oh." The only way I could deal with my fear that the other shoe was about to drop was to play it light. "Is this the cryptocurrency talk?"

His mouth quivered. "It is."

"Okay. Hit me."

He came back to the bed, carefully removed the duvet from my hands, and took them in his. His grip was warm and electric. "It's simple, really. I want to be with you Lucy. As far as I'm concerned, there is nothing fake about this thing between us. There never has been for me, if I'm being honest."

My heart felt like it was going to burst out of my body but now, more than ever, I needed to keep my wits about me and be realistic. "The future will be complicated," I warned. "I can't predict how it's going to play out."

"Nobody can." He squeezed my hands. "But one thing is certain. I love you, and it's not a new thing. How do you feel?"

He had no idea how scary this felt for me. I couldn't shake the feeling that if I tried to fly too close to the sun—and Jack was the sun by any definition—I would get burned. I needed to ration my time with him, and temper it with boring, tedious, and dutiful things like law so life would let me have him. I winced. "I love you too."

He came over and kissed me before collecting the curry containers. "I'm going to accept that and ignore that your face looked like you were being waterboarded while you said it."

"Wise."

SIXTH WEEK

CHAPTER TWENTY-EIGHT

Jack

On Tuesday evening I went to Lucy's room, ready to spring my romantic surprise on her.

We'd missed Valentine's Day as an official couple, but I was determined to make up for it. One advantage (maybe the only one?) of being a rich rock star instead of a poor but contented astronomist was I could spoil my girlfriend.

I reached the top of the stairs, the cozy familiarity of wood polish and old stone welcoming me. *Girlfriend.* Joy expanded my rib cage. *Lucy Snow was my girlfriend.*

I'd had fun contemplating different scenarios—everything from flying her to Paris for a dinner at Le Jules Verne in the Eiffel Tower or to the Roman Amphitheatre in Orange, Provence, where she could sing with just me as her audience. Finally, though, I'd opted for something smaller and more personal.

Standing on the landing, I vibrated with eagerness to see Lucy's generous lips curve into a smile when she opened the door. The idea of giving up this life at Oxford felt like a broadsword

255

through the heart.

I'd been at the astronomy lab all morning, thrilled as I analyzed the first concrete evidence that my crystallization theory was proving correct, supporting my thesis BPM 37093 was just as unique as I'd hypothesized.

I knocked on the door.

Lucy opened it up in jeans and a pale, butter yellow sweater. She reminded me of a daffodil.

"Hello stranger." She flung the door open and jumped into my arms. I kissed her mouth, her eyelids, her cheeks, wherever I could, basically.

My phone beeped and I put her down to check it. It was the driver my assistant had arranged, all ready to whisk us away to the secret location. "Are you ready?"

Her mouth dropped open. "We're leaving already? I'm not even dressed up or—".

I waved away her concern. "You look perfect. You always look perfect, but it doesn't matter what you're wearing. I'm hoping we won't be wearing clothes at all two hours from now."

She pulled away and cocked her head. "What?" I couldn't help but smile at the growing suspicion on her face.

"You'll see." I winked.

I managed to bundle her downstairs to one of the side exits and into the waiting black Land Rover. It took us only three minutes to reach Blackwell's, despite the fact that fluffy snowflakes had started to fall from the sky. I was thrilled to see that Broad Street was pretty much empty, and with the snow rapidly piling up looked like a fairyland.

Lucy remined completely silent, but her eyes were huge. I used the key they'd left me and led her inside.

I shut it behind us and turned to face her—the queen of Blackwell's bookstore for the entire night.

Her hair was adorned with snowflakes and there was one caught on her eyelashes. I leaned down and kissed it away. She melted against me, my very own ice princess.

After a long moment, she pulled back and narrowed her eyes at me. "Did we just break and enter? Not that I have any objections. Just curious."

"No." I took her hand and led her between the dark, silent stacks—the aroma of fresh paper and ink swirling around us.

We reached the bed on the floor set up between two shelves piled high with philosophy books on one side and history on the other. I'd asked my assistant to create a carbon copy of our rooftop star-watching bed, except with electric candles and fairy lights this time—the manager of Blackswell's had been adamant about no open flames.

I watched as her mouth opened. "How?" she asked, finally.

"Remember that first drink at the Turf just after we got here, and you had visited Blackwell's with Cedar? You said it was your fantasy to be locked in here overnight."

Lucy looked at me with huge eyes and nodded. "You remembered that?"

She was standing in front of a high, horizontal window, her disbelieving expression framed by the snowflakes falling outside in the streetlight. "I remember everything, Luce."

I sat on the bed and pulled her down beside me. "Champagne?" I asked her.

Her gaze went to the silver champagne bucket set up on my side of the bed, and her whole face lit up. "Just so you know, I don't drink champagne anymore."

What? "You don't?"

"No. Only Dom Perignon. Shaun taught me it's a completely

different thing than your run-of-the-mill champagne."

"Then you're in luck." I pulled out the perfectly chilled bottle of 2002 Dom Perignon Brut Rose and poured us each a flute.

"It's pink!"

"Happy Belated Valentine's Day, my Luce," I said.

"Happy Belated Valentine's Day, Jack." She leaned forward and we kissed. "This is amazing. Thank you."

"Having you to spoil is everything." I meant every word. I couldn't think of anything that made me happier—not even astronomy.

She snapped her fingers. "Before I forget, I gave the copy of the codicil you gave me to Professor Speedman to look at."

"She agreed?" I asked, shocked. From what Lucy said, it didn't sound like Professor Speedman was inclined to do Lucy any favors.

She shrugged. "I knew it would be awkward, but I couldn't live with myself if I didn't at least try to get her to help you. I know how much you want to stay."

I appreciated it, but wished yet again that Lucy would worry more about herself than others. "How did she react?"

She twitched her right shoulder. "She gave me that look of hers."

"What look?"

She frowned into her flute. "The look like she can't figure out how I got into Oxford in the first place, let alone her class. The look that lets me know she doesn't think I belong." She gnawed on her fingernail, her brows drawn together, then shook herself and looked at me. "But this is so romantic. You don't want to hear about that—".

"Are you upset about it?"

She sighed. "Yeah."

"Then I want to hear about it."

She didn't say anything for a while, but I relished being the one who could be here for her, even if it meant just quietly waiting for her to be ready to talk. It made me realize just how long I'd harbored the secret fantasy of being the person Lucy could turn to for help.

"Professor Speedman has a way of making me feel this big," She held her thumb and index finger no more than two millimeters apart. "I'm convinced she sees right through me and my fake enthusiasm for law."

I considered the logistics of hiring a hitman.

I grabbed her around the waist and then keeled both of us back so that she was half lying on top of me. I rested my chin on the crown of her head, enjoying the peppermint than lingered in her now-damp hair.

"Maybe she's not completely wrong about one thing ... if you followed your heart, would you be studying law?"

She stilled. "Like I said before, I'm not in situation where I can be selfish and follow my heart."

If that was an arrow at me, it was perfectly aimed. The difference between our responsibilities hit me in the center of my chest, but this was not the time to flinch or get defensive. For the first time, I saw how Lucy had been using anger to cover up that tender thing that lay beneath it—fear. Fear of what, though?

"Maybe it's not a question of you not being good enough for law, but rather law not being good enough for you."

"No." She took a shuddering breath. "That's not it."

But it was. I could hear the crunch of tires as a car drove slowly in the snow along Broad Street. I gestured at her to get under the duvet and I joined her, pulling it up over both of us. In seconds we were intertwined again, our bodies fitting together effortlessly.

The tall, crammed bookcases loomed above us, decorated with strands of sparkling white fairy lights. She didn't say anything for what felt like a long time.

"I can't quit Jack," she said, a few minutes later, against my neck.

I snaked my hand under her sweater and trailed my fingers up the curve of her lower back. Goosebumps appeared along the path of my touch. "Why not?"

"I don't quit things. This is the best way to support my family in the future. I mean, if I quit, who would support my mom and Alice? I'm all they've got now."

"Surely you didn't need to come all the way to Oxford for that," I said. "I love you, but I don't completely buy it."

She flipped on her back and covered her eyes with her hand. "It's true I can do this degree in three years somewhere else instead of two at Oxford, but when I learned about it being away from home—at Oxford, no less—I thought maybe this was a way I could take care of my family *and* do something for myself."

It was good she'd finally admitted that, but it still didn't feel like I was digging deep enough. I cleared my throat. "I'm convinced there's more to it than that—something you're not telling me about the promise you made to your dad—something that's stopping you from pursuing singing, even now."

She tensed against me. I hated that this was hard for her, but it meant I was getting close. A panicky pressure was growing behind my breastbone, but I tried not to pay attention I didn't have time for a panic attack right now. Lucy was the priority.

I squeezed her hip. "Just think of all the confessions and truths around us in these books."

She shifted against me. "I can't believe I'm considering talking about this."

"How does it feel—in your body?" I learned that from my group online therapy, and I'd always found it a good question, even though it hadn't miraculously cured my panic attacks.

"Like I'm being forced to hold an open flame in my hands and not drop it even though I'm being burned."

"Then it might feel good to share it with me."

She took a deep breath. "The night of the auditions for *Canada's Got Talent!* I came home after you bailed," she said. The delicate way she put it was new, but it made me feel more contrite than ever. "I bailed too," she continued. "You were right. I could have gone out there alone, but it was terrifying to possibly fail at the one of the only things I ever truly wanted."

"What else did you truly want?"

"Two things—for my dad to not be dead and for you to love me."

"But—" I began, but she put a finger over my lips, stilling me.

"This isn't easy. If I'm going to talk about this, I need to get it out quickly."

I nodded and kissed her fingertips.

"I went home, upset and crying. My mom was supposed to be out at an art therapy group thing I'd signed her up for, but she'd come home early. I couldn't hide from her, and maybe a childish part of me longed to have a parent I could confide in. I told her everything I'd been up to with the auditions and the rehearsals. I'd kept it all secret."

I thought of how I'd tried to push my parents out of that area of my life but how they'd stormed in regardless, intent on helping me achieve their version of success. If only I knew then what I knew now about how success *felt* rather than just how it looked. "How did she react?"

"She was furious. Angier than I'd ever seen her before—the"

kind of anger that's fueled by fear. She told me something that's been with me ever since—the full story of my dad's drowning."

Her right arm was near my face, and her dad's heavy watch clinked on her wrist. I stroked the nape of her neck, trying to soothe her through this. "Tell me."

"My dad wasn't at the pub with friends that night. He'd gone to a secret audition with a musical agent one of his cronies had set him up with. You know how those sea-shanty fishermen from Cornwall had so much success?"

"Yes."

"Well, he was hoping for something like that or even better. Everyone had always praised his voice, so it went to his head, according to my mom. He was impatient with fishing and being a father and husband. He wanted more."

Her breathing was catchy, erratic. Did the mere idea of wanting more make her that fearful?

I always thought of anxiety as what I had hard-wired into me—a hyperactive nervous system that catapulted me into fight or flight mode when it was completely unnecessary. For the first time, I considered that maybe what Lucy suffered from was just another form of the same wolf in sheep's clothing.

With all her unprocessed grief and PTSD around her father's death, no wonder she felt safer keeping her life small. Nausea rose up in me when I remembered that the one time she had reached for more, I'd betrayed her. I'd confirmed the very worst of her fears about life.

"Lucy, I'm so sorry," I said, trying to push the sledgehammer of guilt aside so I could continue to be a calm, safe place for her to lay her secrets to rest.

"It went well," she continued. "Even better than expected. He called my mom on the boat's CB as he left the dock. He'd been offered a contract, and he wanted to celebrate with us, despite the gale warning. He never would have gone on the ocean with that weather under normal circumstances. Getting his dream made him careless, reckless. He wouldn't have died if he'd been happy with an ordinary life."

It finally clicked—the final missing piece of the Lucy puzzle. No wonder the idea of Lucy reaching for a career of singing felt terrifying.

"You're not your father," I said, gently. That was the crux of the problem. Lucy was far too extraordinary to fit within the confines of the ordinary life her fear told her she had to live. I'd always sensed that, for her, playing it small, like struggling through her law degree, just didn't work.

"Maybe not, but there are parallels. He caused so much pain with his choice, so much loss—it taught me to stay in my lane, even more than when you bailed on our audition."

"Lucy, I'm so sorry I betrayed you like that. I will spend the rest of my life trying to make it up to you, I swear." I was groveling and I would do it for as long as it was needed, pride be damned. "I was so stupid and selfish—"

"Stop." Lucy shook her head against me. "You couldn't have known."

"I still should have kept my promise to you."

"You know what?" she said, burying her face in my neck so her voice came up to me muffled. "I think your misery in Northern Junk has been penance enough. I've seen you in the middle of a panic attack before going on stage at Wembley, remember?"

I dropped countless kisses on her head. I sure as hell didn't deserve her or her forgiveness, but I was going to take it. It was easy to reason why her father's history didn't apply to her, but I knew better than most people that fear never listened to logic.

"Does Alice know?"

She propped herself up on her elbow, her watch sliding down her arm. "God, no, I made sure of it. That knowledge feels like a concrete block my mom and I have to carry with us, day and night, knowing we can never set it down. I would never do that to Alice."

I sat up straight then, the duvet falling to my hips. "What can I do for you Lucy? Right now. Right this second in this bookstore."

She smiled a sad smile. "Please don't do that. I happen to like your soul."

"Then what?"

She looked up at me, blinking. "Make love to me."

She didn't need to ask twice.

SEVENTH WEEK

CHAPTER TWENTY-NINE

Lucy

It was Sunday, and Jack had convinced me to take a break from my ongoing essay-writing slog and join the skulk for a pint at a pub which, miraculously, wasn't the Turf.

Since our night at Blackwell's, he hadn't mentioned me singing again. His newfound restraint should've felt like a relief, but instead it disconcerted me. It made me realize just how tightly I clung to the dream I couldn't let myself have, even now.

The snow from the week before still stuck to the sidewalk, and fresh flakes were floating down from the sky. We were all wrapped up in our jackets, toques, and scarves. Everyone passing us was scurrying along with their heads down, trying not to slip on the icy sidewalks. Nobody was looking out for a certain famous musician in their midst.

"What's the name of this pub again?" I asked as Shaun led us down a tiny lane beside Worchester College.

"Jude the Obscure," he said. "It's in a neighborhood called Jericho. We're almost there."

"And why are we walking this far in the snow when the Turf is less than one hundred feet from Beaufort?"

Shaun looked over his shoulder at me. "I suppose you missed that part of the conversation. Jude the Obscure has a proper Ceilidh on Sundays, like in Ireland. The music is fantastic. I know law students at Oxford can forget such a thing as fun still exists, but I consider it my job to remind you."

"I object!" Jack squeezed my hand a little tighter. "I'm tons of fun for Lucy."

That was an understatement.

"I'm not talking about *that* kind of fun," Shaun scoffed. "The Turf will always be our second home, but I decided something different is essential to keeping the skulk from stagnating."

I had to give credit where credit was due. Shaun was a top-notch social coordinator.

Our friends kept Jack and me in the middle of our group—like we'd done on our way to matriculation.

That felt like a lifetime ago. We'd had so much time ahead of us then, but now ... The knowledge Jack had to leave Beaufort in two short weeks was a constant ache in my body. It was a terrible paradox—every day I spent with him was one day less with him.

Jack was still stressed about my reaction to his rabid fans, many of whom had apparently developed a hate-on for me now the news had broken I was Jack's official girlfriend and the reason he was "hiding out at Oxford," as the media called it.

Luckily, the online wrath couldn't happen to a more oblivious person than me. I had no free time to buy tabloids or surf the internet, and all my tutorials were in the college buildings. The impact on me was minimal—I was far too preoccupied with Jack and trying not to fail my classes.

Jack reached up with my hand in his and unzipped his jacket

despite the chill. He always ran hot—maybe it was all those long baths he indulged in.

"I like that sweater," I said, my voice unsteady. His cream cable knit turtleneck made me want to push him against the brick wall we had just passed and have my way with him against it, passers-by be damned.

"What? This?" He plucked at it. "Shaun called it an 'Aran Jumper'. I found it in the back of my closet. No idea where it came from."

Jack was already hard to resist wearing his space nerd gear, but I was powerless against him when he wore a cozy sweater and his heavy black glasses.

I buried my head against his cable-knitted chest for a moment—not easy to do as we were walking and trying to keep up with Shaun. Jack slowed down to help. God, it even smelled faintly citrusy like him. I finally lifted my head and met his eyes. "You wearing this sweater makes me very conflicted."

The corner of his mouth lifted. "How is that?"

"It makes me want to rip it off you and force you to make love to me wearing it at the same time."

Jack's green eyes flashed. "I can assure you there would be no forcing involved." He pulled me closer to his side. "You can even have it one way, then the other."

Why were we going to this pub again, instead of cozy in my bed with the door firmly shut, the snow falling outside my windowpane, and pigeons cooing on the window ledge?

I sighed. "I guess we have to go to this pub first, though, right? They would notice if we left?" I slipped a bit on the sidewalk, but he caught me.

"Reality check." He cast me an apologetic look. "Neither of us is powerful enough to resist Shaun's plans."

I sighed. "Nobody is."

We both looked at Shaun, marching ahead of the group as he held Raphael's hand. He turned his head again to check that his flock was keeping up.

"By the way, Alfie and Cedar," Shaun said as he focused in on them, walking arm in arm. "Norris was not included on my invitation."

Norris trotted along on his leash behind Cedar, as happy as a dog could be. I still found it hilarious that a purebred specimen like Alfie had such a complete mutt of a dog—against college rules, no less.

"Now, now, Shaun. No need for a strop about Norris," Alfie soothed. "They love dogs at Jude the Obscure. I've brought him there before and he gets thoroughly spoiled. They even keep liver treats behind the bar."

Shaun rolled his eyes. "You could at least own a less disreputable canine."

"He's not disreputable! Better than some inbred show dog," Cedar protested. "Mutts always do the best in the wild. Clever. Resourceful. Healthy."

"I'm not going to argue with you," Shaun said testily.

"Because you know you'll lose," piped up Binita from my left side, where she was chatting with Lachlan.

"Precisely," Shaun agreed as I spotted the sign for a pub hung over the sidewalk in the distance.

Jude the Obscure was true to its name—obscure. It took a few seconds for my pupils to adjust to its low ceilings and general lack of light.

Near the middle of the seating area, a bunch of grizzled men chatted loudly while they nursed pints and tuned their instruments—lots of fiddles, an accordion, what looked like a miniature set of bagpipes, and two flutes. I wondered if I would recognize any of the songs they played.

In Newfoundland our kitchen-party tradition meant most of us knew many of the old Irish songs, especially the sea shanties, by heart. Everyone sang them: on boats, in kitchens, in the courtyard at school. My heart clenched. They always made my heart ache for my dad.

Shaun quickly secured us a booth slung against the back wall with a view of the musicians. The whole place was wrapped in the comforting smell of spilled beer and wood polish.

I'd worn my backpack with some casebooks stuffed inside so I could take notes on the cases I needed to review for my most urgent essay.

That was part of my deal with Shaun. I'd tried to tell him I couldn't come because of schoolwork, but he told me he considered it his sacred duty to prevent me from languishing into the next Miss Havisham, and if I was determined not to have fun, I could just bloody well bring my books to the pub.

Anyway, I wasn't here to sing or do any more than listen to the Ceilidh. Loving Jack the way I did was already enough of a dream. That alone terrified me so much I could barely stand to think about it. Add singing? No. It was just too much.

Jack slid in beside me, and we watched as Alfie took Norris up to the bar, where the beefy bartender reached for him and cradled him in his arms like a newborn, gazing lovingly at his crooked ear and massive underbite. He reached under the bar and fed Norris something.

"Point to Alfie," Jack said in a low voice, just to me.

"Looks that way." I took three casebooks out of my backpack and put them in a pile on the table along with my notebook and pen. If I put them there, front and center, I figured the guilt would inevitably force me to crack them open.

Jack eyed them but didn't say anything. "I don't think anyone followed us here." He started to scan the room surreptitiously. "Shaun did a good job of taking a circuitous route."

"He'd make an excellent spy if he weren't so—"

"Noticeable?"

Shaun was dressed in head-to-toe blinding white, gorgeous against his mahogany skin. He looked like an haute couture James Bond in a remake of A View to Kill. "Yup."

Jack leaned against the back of the bottle-green leather booth. "Excellent. This place is outside the tourist center of town. Shaun said it's mainly used by older regulars. Nobody seems to be recognizing me."

I reached forward and plucked off Jack's toque, letting his auburn waves glow under the dim yellow lights of the pub. "Does that feel better?" I ran my hand through the silky strands, making sure my fingernails scraped against his scalp the way I knew he adored.

He made a sound that, combined with that sweater, made my heart do something odd.

"If you keep doing that—" he closed his eyes and smiled dreamily "—I will take you on top of this table. Fair warning."

Of course I wanted to, but my casebooks caught my eye, and I stared at them with loathing. "I hate estoppel."

"So do I," Jack said, his dreamy gaze landing on the books. "And I don't even know what the fuck it is."

It was too boring to explain. I sighed. "I should get to it."

Jack leaned toward me and whispered in my ear, "I will make it up to you when we get to your room. I promise." Sparks exploded all over at his warm breath and the feel of his lips as they brushed against my earlobe.

Alfie set down a round of drinks. He nodded at my books. "Crikey. Those books look just about as depressing as the novel *Jude the Obscure*."

"I haven't read it," I admitted. "Is it bad?"

"Dire," Alfie said. "I can't understand why some people love it so much—or anything Thomas Hardy wrote, for that matter. He would have made the most wretched company."

"How's Norris settling in?" I asked.

Alfie grinned. "He's behind the bar with a bowl of fresh water and delicious liver treats, being pampered within an inch of his life."

He headed back to the bar to pick up the remainder of the pints.

I cracked open *Law of Torts*. Better make some headway now so I could fully enjoy Jack in—and out—of that sweater when we got back to Beaufort.

After we'd made solid inroads on our pints, and I'd made headway on Hughes vs. Metropolitan Railway, the musicians struck up the first song.

It was an Irish love song I didn't know, slow and lyrical. I fought the desire to lean against Jack, who was resting his hand loosely on my knee. He was leaning back in the booth, nursing a Guinness and watching the musicians. I stopped reading and closed my eyes, savoring the sound of the men's voices as they rolled over me.

There were a few more like that, and then they struck up the sea shanty "Spanish Ladies," which had always been the one my dad sung if he really wanted to bring down the house. My heart twinged, but in a new way I didn't fully recognize. Since telling Jack the whole story of my father, some of my anger against his fatal lack of judgment had softened around the edges. I couldn't help but tap my foot as I blinked back tears.

"I've always loved this one," Jack groaned, then got up.

My shocked eyes followed him as he made his way to the front and joined in. Amazingly, nobody around us seemed to be taking any photos. He was wearing his black glasses and in the dim light looked like any another Oxford student. His green eyes flicked to me as he sang about being drunk and jolly, drowning melancholy, and true-hearted lasses. It was so wonderful to watch him actually enjoy singing again. I yearned to be up there beside him.

"What about 'The Ramblin' Rover'?" he asked the man who appeared to be the leader when they were finished. What was he up to? That had become *our* shanty—the one I'd sung for him on the roof.

My longing to sing was pushing hard against my better judgment. This song connected my father to me and me to Jack and all of us to Newfoundland. How could I not get up and sing?

I scanned the room again. Nobody seemed to have their phones out or be doing much besides chatting with friends, nursing their pints, and enjoying the music.

The lead musician shook his head. "It needs a female lead. I don't suppose any of your female friends over there can sing, can they?"

Jack's eyes locked with mine. He lifted a brow. He wouldn't make me do this. The decision was mine.

Maybe this singing thing was still niggling me because I needed closure. I had to sing with Jack one last time to close the circle we opened four years ago. This could be my swan song to the dream of being a singer.

I gave Jack a tiny nod, closed my law book and walked up to him. Out of the corner of my eye I saw Binita and Lachlan staring at me with wondering expressions. Right. None of our skulk had ever heard me sing before.

"I think my girlfriend, Lucy, knows that song," Jack said, while the other musicians tuned their instruments, unconcerned.

"You don't have to do this," Jack whispered to me. "I was planning on singing it for you, not forcing you into anything."

I shook my head. "I need to do this—just this once. You know, for closure."

"Can she hold a tune?" the man barked at Jack, as if I wasn't standing right there. Clearly, the Jude the Obscure Ceilidh was not amateur hour.

"More or less." Jack pursed his lips and shrugged with a mischievous twinkle in his eyes for me. "You'll have to judge for yourself."

I almost burst out laughing. Maybe I couldn't understand contract law, but I could definitely hold a tune.

The music stared tentatively, and the leader unceremoniously thrust a microphone in my hand.

I stared at Jack wide-eyed. Was I actually doing this? He nodded at me. I scanned the crowd. Even with Jack up here, nobody had their phones out and everyone was involved in their own conversations.

Our skulk was casting me curious looks and Alfie had an expression of grave concern on his face. Getting up to sing in a pub probably wasn't part of the code of conduct for British Lords.

The first notes of 'The Ramblin' Rover' began, and the music flowed through me, giving me that familiar rush I only ever felt singing in front of an audience and making love with Jack.

"Pretend it's just you and me," Jack said in a low voice. "Nobody here is paying attention anyway."

What Jack didn't know was that I wasn't scared—I was excited. I was possessed by the need to make all these pub-goers sit up and listen. I wanted to make goose bumps prickle down their arms and emotion rise up their throats. I wanted to use my voice to connect with them—not just any connection but one that was as deep, wide, and profound as the ocean.

This was the part of myself I had inherited from my father— that need to perform—the bigger the audience, the better. It was the part of me that scared me so much I stifled and denied it at all costs. I would light it on fire if I could and watch as it burned to ashes because it came with unacceptable risk.

But just this once, I wouldn't resist. This song wouldn't let me anyway. The words were fed to me by something brighter and more familiar than memory.

I opened my mouth and started singing. "We'll roam the country over, and together we'll face the world."

Jack's dimples deepened as I sang, and I was back in that high school music room in St. John's, lost in the incandescent joy of singing with him.

Everything else faded away—Jack's imminent departure, Professor Speedman, the sinking feeling of falling further and further behind on a path that had never been meant for me.

I sang of loss and heartache, of thwarted dreams and the ocean. I sang of joy and finally finding the person who made everyday life feel like an adventure and a dream. I sang because life was too short not to sing.

The acoustics were crappy, but it didn't matter. My voice filled the space and soared over Jack's and the other singers'. I unabashedly took up so much space when I sang. And singing with Jack, just like making love with him, felt like coming home.

The fiddle and flute notes finally died away, and the final echo of my voice faded into silence. I looked out at the crowd.

It took me a moment to snap back to reality, but when I did, I noticed no one was chatting now. You could have heard a proverbial pin drop. I'd made then stop and pay attention. Better than that, I was fairly certain I'd made them *feel*. Everyone was staring. Satisfaction ricocheted through me. I ventured a glance at our friends.

As I watched for a reaction from them, Shaun's pint glass slipped out of his hand in slow motion. He didn't even seem to notice, and I watched as it spilled all over our table. He didn't even move to get out of its path, despite his designer outfit.

The rest of them just stared at me with huge eyes, their mouths hanging open.

Finally, Cedar started to slow clap, then everyone joined in, then the noise of the applause got so loud it felt like it would blow off the pub roof.

Heat crawled up my chest and neck and I glanced at Jack.

He grinned at me. "That was too fun to stop now."

I couldn't resist drawing this joy out. "Do you know 'Bonnie Light Horseman'?" I asked the man who asked if I could hold a tune.

"Do I ever!" he shouted and immediately started playing it on his fiddle.

I spent the next hour singing along with the group, until my vocal cords started to catch and protest for a drink.

The musicians started to pack up, but first they all crowded around me, telling me I had to come back every Sunday, pumping my hand and praising my voice. One even knuckled tears from his eyes and told me I had the "bonniest voice" he ever did hear in a thick Irish Brogue.

Jack took my hand. "Ready for a drink?" he asked.

I nodded.

"You were sublime." He kissed me and led me back to our friends. I had barely sat down at the end of our booth when about ten pints were brought over by the grinning barman.

"How thirsty are you guys?" I asked my friends, confused. Everyone seemed to have drinks already.

The bartender shook his head. "These are all for you. Everyone in the bar wants to buy you a pint," he said. "But be careful because of alcohol poisoning, aye?"

"Never fear," Raphael said, reaching for two pints and giving one to Shaun, who was still gaping at me in shock. "We won't let that happen."

"Och, we certainly will not." Lachlan reached for one too and passed another to Binita.

"Such concern for my liver." I cocked my eyebrow at them.

"We live to serve." Lachlan smiled broadly.

Shaun gave himself a shake. "Lucy." He reached across the scratched and now sticky old pub table and grabbed my hand. "Where have you been hiding that voice?"

I shrugged. "I haven't been hiding it." That wasn't entirely true though, was it? I could have made countless opportunities to sing, with or without Jack.

"Why the hell are you studying law?" he demanded, incensed. "You *are* a singer."

Jack, tight beside me, squeezed my shoulder as if to say, *See?*

I was tempted. Of course I was. How could I not want more of the thing that made me happy? But pursuing it would make me feel too exposed, like I was set adrift in a rowboat during a vicious Atlantic storm in winter, defenseless.

If I claimed singing as my own, I couldn't shake the certainty anchored deep inside me that fate would take something away in return. Not knowing what would make it all the more agonizing. Alice? My mother? Jack?

Feeling the warmth of his solid form against my side drove home just how unsurvivable a second loss of him would feel. As for Alice and my mom, they depended on me. I couldn't risk it. "I just can't."

"We can make it happen," Shaun pressed on. I froze, fear icing up my ability to speak now that my dream felt closer than it had ever been. I had no doubt that Jack and Shaun could make this happen for me—all I had to do was reach out and take it. I couldn't seem to fill my lungs with enough air and my head swam with dizziness. Was this how Jack's panic attacks felt?

"No," I said, trying to put an end to the questions. I'd experienced firsthand the pain of where an unsafe path could lead.

"I don't get it." Binita shook her head.

"It's just not practical," I said lamely. How could I explain the twisted reasoning that made complete sense in my mind? "It's such a long shot, anyway. It would probably be a massive waste of time."

Binita eyed me. "Or you might get everything you ever wanted."

CHAPTER THIRTY

Jack

I was in the bath the next morning when I saw it.

After we'd returned from the pub yesterday, tipsy from beer and the joy of singing, we'd made love, then Lucy had banished me until she turned in her essay at one o'clock today.

I turned on the tap to add some more hot water. It had been exquisite torture to sing with Lucy at Jude the Obscure. She was so clearly meant to sing—Shaun had seen it instantly, as had everyone else in that pub. My problem was I couldn't figure out a way I could do something about it without betraying her confidence after her confession at Blackwell's. The decision had to be hers and hers alone.

I picked up my phone from the rim of the tub. It was foolhardy to scroll while I was in the bath, but I kept hoping for some sort of miraculous news like Gary had disbanded Northern Junk, or my parents had undergone a spiritual conversion and had decided to divest themselves of all worldly goods and live on a mountainside in Nepal.

The thought of going back to that rock star grind when I was deliriously happy here at Oxford felt so impossible my lungs couldn't fill with air, and I could sense panic circling me, ready to ambush. I had less than two weeks to find a way to leave without ruining my parents. The wild hope that I would find a solution was growing dimmer by the day.

My phone pinged—a text from one of my bandmates with a YouTube video attached. "What have you got up your sleeve?" it demanded in all caps. He'd always been a nasty piece of work.

I clicked open the video, and there was Lucy singing "Ramblin' Rover" at the pub, all glowing and transcendent. *Shit.*

Whoever had shot it had zoomed in on her, almost cutting me out except for my arm and shoulder, which honestly felt wonderful. The spotlight should've always been on Lucy. If only I could make her see that. It had never been meant for me, and I'd upset the natural order of things by letting my parents talk me into stealing it.

It already had over a million views. I checked the time on my phone. It had only been posted for an hour. It was entitled, "Jack's Gal Pal Can Sing!"

Who the hell had come up with the expression "gal pal"? It needed to be stripped from the English language.

I leaned my head against the cast-iron rim of the tub as I absorbed this new twist. The cat was out of the bag, and as much as I tried, I couldn't be sorry for it.

Maybe Lucy would finally see for herself now. I couldn't shake the conviction that she needed to sing to be truly fulfilled, as much I needed to be able to study space to my heart's content.

I couldn't let her be blindsided by this video. I had to go and show it to her—I checked the time on my phone. She was at her contract tutorial now. I would meet her outside Professor

Speedman's study.

I got out and tugged on a fresh T-shirt and hoodie, a flame of hope driving me on. Maybe this video could be the thing that would finally allow Lucy's confidence to gain the upper hand over her fear.

As if I was one to talk. Sure, I had fewer panic attacks than before Oxford, and less often, but they hadn't disappeared. I wanted to stay here at Oxford, finishing my research project and investigating the stars, but I had not one single feasible idea how I could actually make it happen. I appreciated that Lucy had tried to give the codicil to Professor Speedman, but I certainly wasn't getting my hopes up about that. She seemed like a very unlikely savior.

I checked the YouTube video of Lucy again. Everyone in the comments seemed to have an opinion. The video was discussed and pulled apart. Most people were exuberant in their praise, but a few had to slide in backhanded compliments as well, like, "she doesn't look like I expected the girlfriend of Jack Seary to look, but goddammit can she ever sing."

If they didn't see how fucking dazzling Lucy was, they needed their eyes checked.

I kept checking my phone as I waited in the hallway outside Professor Speedman's study. The college belltower rang three times. Lucy should be coming out soon.

After what felt like an eternity, the door cracked open. Two exhausted and young-looking students trudged out, black academic capes trailing limply behind them.

Then came Lucy, a pencil tucked behind her ear and her black academic robe flung over jeans paired with one of my favorite pink sweaters of hers. My heart stuttered. Lucy always looked like a walking fantasy to me.

Her shoulders were rolled forward and that divot was back between her brows, but her face brightened like a sunrise when she spotted me.

"Jack!" she said. "What are you—"

"Lucy," Professor Speedman called as she emerged from her office, dressed all in cobalt blue to match her piercing eyes. "I need to speak to you."

A shadow lowered over Lucy's features. I hated that I couldn't do anything in that moment to lift it again. "I'll leave," I said, aware that this conversation was not intended for my ears.

"No. You can stay." Lucy cast me a beseeching look. If that's what she wanted, nothing short of a nuclear blast could dislodge me.

"Mr. Seary." Professor Speedman looked down her long, patrician nose at me. "I didn't notice you there. That reminds me. Lucy gave me the codicil and your contract to review."

I couldn't imagine squirming under this woman's stare once a week. Lucy was made of strong stuff. "Thank you for looking at it," I said.

"I haven't yet in detail," she sniffed. "I'm a very busy person."

"I'm sure."

"But I did glance at the main contract. It didn't give me a very high opinion of your intelligence that you signed such a glaringly exploitive document."

Shame poured through me. "I was very young."

"You were very stupid," she corrected me.

Lucy stood frozen between me and her professor. Did professor

Speedman want me to refute that? I happened to heartily agree with her.

"Now Ms. Snow," she turned back to Lucy. I was sure her gaze could burn through metal. Instinctively, I reached out and grabbed Lucy's hand. "I'm going to be frank with you."

I couldn't imagine any scenario where this woman was anything but.

"Yes," Lucy managed. My brave girl.

"You are not cut out for law. You are wasting your time, and mine. You did slightly better in your last essay, but I have been a professor for years and I can tell your heart isn't in it. You are meant for other things. I know this sounds cruel, but I don't mean it that way." Her voice softened. "I think a few years from now you are going to look back and thank me for this."

A shudder ran through Lucy's body. "Are you kicking me out?" She blinked.

"No. Your grades don't justify that. It remains your choice."

"I'll work harder," Lucy said, unshed tears welling up in her eyes.

Professor Speedman pursed her lips. "I happen to think you are capable of a great many things, Lucy, but law is not one of them. If I didn't care, and like you as a person, I wouldn't bother telling you this."

I agreed with everything Professor Speedman was saying, if not the delivery. I wished someone had taken me and given me the unvarnished truth before I signed on with Northern Junk. My parents had been too blinded by their own ambition to think rationally. Still, I loved Lucy, so her pain was my pain.

"I have to do this degree," Lucy said in a faint voice.

Professor Speedman's lips thinned. "At least if you decide to remain you won't be able to say I didn't tell you.

"No," Lucy said, her chin wobbling slightly "I won't be able to say that."

Professor Speedman gave us a sharp nod of dismissal, went back inside her study, and shut the door behind her.

I wrapped my arms around Lucy, but for once she fought against me. Her hand clutched her throat. "I need to get out of here. I need to breathe."

I thought of a place—our rooftop. "Don't think yet," I said. "Just follow me."

Lucy blindly followed me up the circular stone stairs, but this time when we burst outside onto the roof, we were bathed in sunshine.

The sun had melted the snow and ushered in springlike weather in the matter of the last twenty-four hours.

Lucy started pacing around in a circle, gulping in the sweet air. She pressed her thumb and forefinger against her eyes to shove the tears back in.

"I'm so sorry, Luce," I said, remembering I still had to show her the video. "But can I show you something that might take some of the sting away?"

She crossed her arms in front of her. A swallow swooped in front of us, chirping. "I can't think of anything that would do that right now."

I cued up the video of her singing on my phone and passed it to her. "Watch this."

Her eyes got bigger and bigger as she did, her voice streaming out of my phone and sounding amazing even with the terrible sound quality.

She looked up at me from the phone when she was done. "How did this happen?"

I shook my head. "I'm not exactly sure. I didn't see anyone filming. Did you?"

"No! Of course not! When did you see this?" she asked, clutching my phone in her hand.

"Just before I came to meet you. You sound amazing, of course."

Her face took on an expression I couldn't fully interpret—was it excitement or fear? Maybe both. "I...after what Professor Speedman just said, I don't know what to think."

I crossed my fingers behind my back. Was this the turning point I had been hoping for her?

The sun warmed the top of my head and back, for the first time in months. I took it for a good omen—one that ushered in new beginnings. "Have you checked your email yet?"

Her forehead pleated. It took every bit of restraint not to kiss that worry away, but something told me I needed to let this moment unfold without my interference. "No. Why?"

I cleared my throat. "I can't know for sure, but I wouldn't be surprised if you've received some emails from music agents like Gary, maybe even from the media—"

"But that video was only just posted."

I slipped my phone out of her hand and checked it again. "Um. Lucy. Your video has three million likes already. You're going to have emails."

She blinked, with the roof of the Sheldonian and Bodleian in the distance as her backdrop. "My email address is private."

"I guarantee they've already found it."

She stiffened, then shook her head slowly, still gazing at the view of the Beaufort quad and then the spires of Oxford beyond. "It's only because I'm your girlfriend."

"No, Lucy," I said, my voice firm. "Maybe that was why the video was posted, but the reaction to your singing is due to your voice. I understand why your trauma still holds you back. Christ, I've earned a doctorate in fear myself, but you're too good to be ignored. Good enough to get three million views and more every second. That has nothing to do with me or anyone else."

Her shoulders, which had been up around her ears, dropped. "I know I'm good," she said finally. "That's what scares me."

"Check your emails, Luce," I said gently, gesturing with my chin.

She finally did—scrolling, scrolling, and scrolling some more.

"Five hundred new messages?" she murmured, the fight completely gone out of her now.

"Knew it." I pivoted so I could see her screen. There were 103 missed phone calls too. She started scrolling through her inbox again. I recognized names of record labels. Music agents. Media outlets. "We're going to have to get you a new phone—a private one."

As if on cue, her phone vibrated.

"Check who's calling before you answer. You don't have to talk to anyone right now."

She checked. "It's home. They must have seen it. Shit." Her face drained of color.

Dammit. Just when Lucy seemed like she might be giving in to the fact that the universe was setting up neon direction signs—complete with garish blinking lights—pointing towards a singing career, her mother was going to make her doubt herself yet again.

Lucy winced and answered with the speaker on.

"You're famous!" Alice's chirpy little voice came through.

"Check YouTube!"

"I just saw it," Lucy said, a faint smile on her lips. Her sister was her own little fan club. "I had no idea anyone was filming me. I didn't mean for this to happen."

I hated to hear her make apologies for her talent. She should never have to do that.

"I think it's awesome," Alice said stoutly. "I'm going to show all my friends at school tomorrow. Are you going to become famous and rich like Jack?"

"No, I don't think—" Lucy began, but Alice just barreled on.

"When you do a concert, I want VIP tickets for me and all my friends." Thank God for ten-year-olds with no phone manners or subtlety.

"Alice, wait—"

"Gotta go. Mom's breathing down my neck. She wants to talk to you."

There was a noisy clatter and then a sigh from Lucy's mother.

Lucy seemed to have forgotten how to breathe. I reached out and touched her hand to let her know I was in her corner—that I would always be in her corner.

"I guess you've seen the video?" Lucy said, her voice faint and riddled with guilt, as though she'd been caught abusing puppies instead of singing.

"Yes," her mom said. "You know, Alice and I are doing okay— far better than I thought, but *this*...," Lucy's mother's voice was unsteady with suppressed terror. "Have you forgotten about your father?"

How could she?

"Of course not," Lucy said in a lowered voice, her eyes downcast. "It's just a silly thing, Mom. They were playing music in a pub. Jack and I knew the shanties so we joined in. We had no idea anyone was filming us."

I hated how her mother guilted her into playing small. It was a weird flip on how my parents guilted me into playing big.

"Alice says this could make you famous," her mother said, suspicious.

"Don't be ridiculous." Lucy shook her head. "The internet has a very short memory. They'll be onto something else tomorrow."

"I'm scared," her mother confessed, and for the first time ever I felt a tug of sympathy for this woman, who had demanded far too much of her oldest daughter. "It reminds me of your father and—"

"I know," Lucy said, cutting her off. "It does for me too. I never meant for it to happen." Her voice sounded so resigned. Would she ever escape the limits her father's death had put on her capacity for happiness? The last thing she needed was for her mother to reinforce them. "You don't need to worry. I'm not going to chase the same crazy dreams as Dad."

"It's just … the idea of losing you too, or of something else happening—"

"I know."

My heart ached as I watched Lucy shutter up her dreams in front of me and lock them tight.

"We miss you," her mom said. "But now I can see the law thing makes sense. Just … stay grounded, okay? Don't fill your head with fame and fortune like your dad did."

A muscle twitched in Lucy's jaw. Was she angry? I hoped so, because I was fucking furious. "You have no reason to believe I'm not sensible, do you?"

"No, I don't. I realize now you're gone how much I've relied on you. You've been wonderful. I wish your father hadn't died without life insurance. I wish I'd been stronger. You never should have had to take on such responsibility at such a young age. I'm trying to make up for that now. I'll never stop being grateful for what you've done." Lucy's chin quivered. "But I also see so much of your father in you."

Was this the first time her mother had acknowledged what Lucy had sacrificed for her family? Even if it was, it was years too late, and it still wasn't enough. She had to release Lucy, and herself, from the chains of grief.

"That means a lot. Thanks, Mom. Bye."

She hung up and slipped her phone in her pocket without meeting my eyes.

CHAPTER THIRTY-ONE

Lucy

"You want to yell at me, don't you?" I finally said to Jack. I couldn't bear the unspoken tension between us since my mom's phone call.

He was sitting in front of the massive, specialized computer station in the observatory at Green Templeton college now. The screens and equipment were set up on a mammoth old desk pushed up against a solid section of wall.

He'd been inputting a series of astronomy calculations for his research. I stood nearby, in front of one of the huge vertical windows that punctuated the ancient space, watching him work.

I'd seen his lips press together after I hung up with my mom, stopping himself from saying all the things he wanted to—that I was being a coward, that I was turning my back on all the possibilities I'd always wanted because I was too damn scared.

The unspoken words now transformed the usually comforting silence between us into something heavy and thick.

"What?" He turned to me, his mouth a perfect 'O' of surprise.

His red hair was messy. It had grown over the past few weeks, and he had the tendency to twist it between his fingers when he was thinking hard. Love made my heart skip a beat despite the tension. I adored watching him nerd out. Was this what it was like for him when he heard me sing?

I hated the feeling that I had let him down as well as myself.

"You want to yell at me to just go for the singing thing, don't you?" I demanded. "And that I should stop being influenced by my mother."

He sat back in his wooden chair, steepled his fingers, and stared at the ceiling. He inhaled deeply.

I could see why Jack loved being up here in the observatory at the very top of the Green Templeton College buildings. The space was not only ancient, but gorgeous with its soaring spaciousness and an ornate twisted metal staircase leading up to the rooftop telescope. The detailing on the rounded ceiling was exquisite and made me feel as though I was standing inside a giant Faberge egg.

But, as beautiful as the ceiling was, Jack clearly wasn't finding an answer to my question up there. "Am I wrong?"

He stood up suddenly, sending his wheeled chair sliding across the floor. "Yes," he said, looking half stern, half amused. "You're completely wrong." Streaks of red stained his cheekbones as he came over to me.

"You're lying." I crossed my arms and stared at him. "You think I'm making a mistake, don't you?"

He nodded once. "Yes. I do."

He hadn't hesitated. If only I could borrow his certainty for the next little while. That was the core of my dilemma—the possibilities of the YouTube video lit me up inside, but that came with an aftertaste of doubt and fear. It felt like I was pushing against a stone wall that just wouldn't give way. I was beginning to see the wall for what it was, but I still had no clue about how to begin dismantling it. Still, none of this was Jack's fault.

"I'm sorry," I ducked my head. "I'm attacking you because I'm upset. You did nothing to deserve that except try and support me."

That big golden door I'd always hoped for was in front of me now—the only thing missing was my willingness to walk through. If only I wasn't paralyzed by my brain inextricably linking the pursuit of singing with impending doom. I couldn't quite convince myself that this opportunity wasn't a cruel trick I couldn't let myself fall for. "I can't explain it, I just … something is stopping me from taking that step."

Jack touched the toe of my boot with his shoe and sent me a sympathetic look. "I know it's hard," he said. "But I hate to see you stand in the way of your own happiness."

I frowned down at the floor. "Total happiness feels way more unsettling than struggle." I wondered now if that wasn't why I'd ended up in law even though it'd never interested me. Maybe that choice was a built-in safeguard, limiting my contentment so I could continue to feel safe.

Jack tilted his head. "I can understand how it can feel that way to you, but life is not a series of checks and balances."

Wasn't it? Could I actually have that much happiness—Jack and singing? It felt impossible. Greedy.

"I do want to yell." Jack rubbed his crooked pinky with his thumb. "But not at you. Never that."

I looked back up at his face. "Then at who?"

"At your fear. It's a liar, and I want to drown it out by screaming how much I believe in you, and how much I love you, and how you deserve all the happiness in the world."

I wished I could do that for Jack too when he was struggling with his anxiety and panic. The last of my anger melted away. "You say that because you love me."

"I say that because it's what everyone deserves ... well, except maybe Gary."

A movement outside caught my eye. The only light out there came from the windows in our perch here above the world, but ... was that a person darting behind one of the pruned topiaries in the college gardens below?

"I think someone is out there," I pressed my palm flat against the glass. I caught a glint of dark hair, then the shadow dropped to the ground.

"What?" Jack came over stood with his fingers resting on the nape of my neck, peering outside with me.

I tapped the windowpane, slick with the damp cold of early March. "I think I see someone lurking around outside." I looked again.

I saw another movement as they ran from behind one topiary to another. "There!" I pointed. "I just saw them again. Did you see it?"

"No, but whoever they are, they're not going to get very far." Jack's thumb lazily traced circles on my nape, softening every part of me. "They need a key to get in the building. We're safe up here. My computer needs about twenty minutes to work on a calculation," he said, continuing his circles. I lowered my chin to give him better access. "Let's move away from these windows and over to the couch."

His caresses had put me into a trance. "Mmmmm. Okay." He led me over and sat me down.

"Can I make you a coffee?" He pointed at an ancient-looking coffee maker on the scratched wooden table beside the beat-up sofa. "I know it looks like it's survived World War Two, but I promise it makes a surprisingly good cup of Joe."

"Most people don't drink coffee at midnight, but yes."

Jack chuckled as he busied himself with coffee filters and a dented can. The rich, dark scent of ground coffee beans floated in the air as he opened the lid. "Maybe not, but we're Newfound-landers—descendants of fisherman and pirates. Coffee at midnight is our birthright."

He was right. There was no bad time to have coffee back home.

He flicked it on. The machine noisily shuddered to life.

"That sounds like a 747 taking off."

"Part of the charm." He flopped on the couch beside me, then pulled me in for one of his searing kisses, desperate as a shore-man on leave.

His lips burned me with an intensity that left me breathless and pushed everything else out of my head—the fear that made decisions for me, the upcoming set of law exams next week, called "collections," that I was sure I was going to fail, the fact Jack was due to rejoin Northern Junk ...

His fingers tangled in my hair as he deepened the kiss. I could never get enough of him. He was a force of nature, like the super-novas he studied, consuming every particle of my soul.

"See, no yelling at you," he whispered as his mouth slid closer to my earlobe, making all the tiny hairs on my arms stand up on end.

The coffee maker made a series of shrill beeps.

He pulled away on a muttered swear and brought back full mugs. The heat soaked into my palm. Mine had a chip out of the rim and a "Trinity College" crest on it.

Relationships faded, but that wasn't going to happen with Jack and me, was it? We burned so bright it felt impossible. Still, unless a miracle occurred, he would soon be back on tour with Northern

Junk. I wasn't naive. That would change things. It had to.

"You're not the only one who feels stuck." He frowned down at his mug. "I don't want to leave, Luce. Turns out I didn't just need a break—I needed a whole new life."

Seeing him here, with his glasses and NASA hoodie and the astronomy faculty mug in his hands, it drove home that he really did belong in this observatory studying space and not on center stage at Wembley. "Do you think you'll be able to finish your project before you leave?"

I'd always believed Jack's ability to do all sorts of different things incredibly well was a gift, but it was clear to me now that it could be a curse too. It made it too easy for him get waylaid from his true interests.

"Not the way I want to finish it." He took a deep breath. "We need to talk about me leaving. We've both been putting it off."

My heart lurched. "I can barely let myself think about it." I stretched my legs over his thighs, and he used his free hand to knead my feet. I groaned.

"When you groan like that, it makes me want to—"

"A-OK by me."

"—but that would be putting off the hard stuff."

I blew out a puff of air between my teeth. "How annoying."

He nodded but kept massaging. "All right, so here goes. I hate the fact I'm leaving. It gives me an instant panic attack to even think about it. Even now my heart is picking up pace, and I have that unsettled sensation in my chest I know well."

I wanted to soothe those creases pleating his forehead. "There's no way you can refuse to go back? You deserve to have the life you want, Jack."

He grimaced. "Just like you. Just like everybody." He slid me a look. "But ... my parents."

I understood. I'd been so apoplectic about how my mom and Alice were going to cope without me, but now I realized they were doing fine. Better than fine, actually. Me being out of the way seemed to allow my mother to finally step into a maternal role for Alice. I felt stupid now for being so convinced my sacrifice had been necessary for their well-being. Maybe it had for the first little while, but after that I should've taken a step back.

I took his hand in mine. "I'm seeing for myself that sometimes it's best to just do the thing and then let people get used to it. For too long I was waiting for the change to come from someone else. My mom and Alice are doing just fine without me. I never would've realized it was even a possibility if I hadn't left."

He gave me a penetrating look. "It's what I've always tried to get you to understand—going after our dreams doesn't need to be earned. We all deserve the right just by virtue of being."

"Being what?"

"Just being. Most of the elements of our bodies were formed in stars over the course of billions of years and multiple star lifetimes. We're all star stuff. We were all meant to shine."

This was such a revolutionary idea that I didn't say anything for a long moment. "I need to let that sink in."

Jack raked his hand through his hair. "We both have lot to consider, and fast." The timer went off on his phone. "Let's see what came out with my calculations."

I set my coffee down on the arm of the couch, and he pulled me back to the computer. "What were you trying to calculate?"

"The composition of BPM 37093 using her frequency spectra with this technique called stellar seismology."

"Wow. Okay. Her?"

"I always think of BPM 37093 as female."

"Why?"

"I can't explain it. I just do." He let go of my hand and rubbed his together with anticipation as he sat down in front of the computer. "The moment of truth."

He started reading the output filling up the screen. "Carbon," he whispered. "I knew it! At least ninety percent carbon."

"That's good?" I guessed.

He whooped and leaped out of his chair, dancing me around in circles. "It's better than good! It's incredible! Oh my God, do you know how close I am to proving my theory is correct? I need to start outlining a paper and ... there is so much else I want to do."

I squeezed him back, and we danced around a little more. His excitement was contagious.

"You can't leave this," I finally burst out. "You and stars, Jack. Even as a rock star, you couldn't forget them. The way you sing 'Stars in Her Eyes' is different from any other song you play with the band." I was in his arms, both of us panting slightly from the dancing.

He laughed. "I never connected that, but it's true. It's the only one I wrote, but that's not the only reason it's still my favorite."

My mind flew to what I had learned about intellectual property from Professor Speedman. "Did you get song writing credit for it?"

"I did. Gary wasn't pleased, but he had no choice. We worked with other musicians on the instrumentalization, so I had witnesses."

"Have you ever been paid royalties on it? Not just for performing it, but for writing it?" Miraculous that I'd thought of this. Maybe my contract law course had taught me something after all.

"I'd have to check," he said.

"You should." Jealousy made me lower my eyes from his. I was back to standing in the wings at Wembley, watching him perform it. Who was the lucky girl he'd written about? One of the hal-ter-top groupies? "That girl you wrote about—I hope she realizes how lucky she is to be immortalized like that." I tried to swallow past the lump that had formed in my throat. "You must have re-ally loved her."

Jack's fingers were warm under my chin. "Haven't you realized yet?"

I blinked. God, he was beautiful. The idea another woman had captured his heart was burning me. "Realized what?"

"I wrote that song about you, Luce."

"What?" My heart throbbed with joy. I briefly entertained the idea he was telling me a kind lie, but his eyes had room for only truth. "I—I don't know what to say."

"Just kiss me, dammit."

I did, and before we knew it we'd flung off each other's clothes in full view of the windows. I thought briefly of the movement I'd seen outside, but as Jack lowered his head and kissed my breasts, his lips as gentle as butterfly wings, I could no longer make my-self care.

CHAPTER THIRTY-TWO

Jack

The next morning, I was eager to return to the observatory to check the calculations I'd set up to run overnight to verify my findings.

I'd hoped maybe yesterday was the turning point for Lucy, but she'd dutifully gone to her land law tutorial this morning. Professor Speedman's harsh words, the video of her singing that was racking up more views by the second, and our conversation in the observatory still hadn't overpowered her doubt. I'd started to doubt that anything could.

My jaw ached from clenching it with frustration, not just over her situation, but mine. Our conversation last night left me wondering—would my parents eventually accept my decision if I left Northern Junk? Even if they didn't, was I just being a coward by staying?

I crossed the quad with my hands deep in my pockets. Two robins hopped around the perfectly manicured grass, chirping. Everything around me felt poised for new beginnings.

Even after this project was finished, there were so many more stars to study. I could research them all my life and never get to the end of things I wanted to discover.

I entered under the archway that led to the lodge and out of college, and it wasn't until my eyes adjusted to the dim light that I noticed two familiar figures stood in the shadows. *Shit. There was no way this could be good.*

"Jack!" An all-too-familiar voice bellowed my name. I paused for a second, cowardly wondering if I could turn on my heel and run in the other direction.

"Don't pretend you didn't hear me," Gary snapped as I got closer.

Cathy was beside him, wringing her hands. "Jack! We have to talk to you."

I wouldn't put it past them to make a scene if I didn't. I needed out of this life—away from these toxic people. My mind whirred, but it kept coming back up against that horrendous contract and my parents' liability.

When I got closer, I saw Gary was grinning. His bleached teeth generated their own light. Cathy's smile was strained.

"I still have a week left," I said as a greeting.

Gary waved his hand, his gold signet ring heavy on his index finger. "You may be able to stay longer than that if you play your cards right."

Hope sparked in me despite my better judgement. *The things I could do with another term.* I could build on my research and maybe start writing a paper with Professor Hayden's oversight. Maybe it could even be considered as part of a degree here. More days and nights with Lucy ...

Cathy clutched Gary's arm. "Gary, you know what I think—"

"And you know I don't care," Gary snapped back. He had always treated her like she was mud on his shoe, but they rarely disagreed. This was new.

"He needs to come back," Cathy insisted. "Now. With us. Otherwise, we'll lose him. We can't let that happen."

Gary made an impatient gesture. "We won't lose him. Not with the contract he signed."

He loved holding this over me as much as I hated it. "Why are you here Gary?"

"To propose a deal."

He would never let me have something for nothing. "What deal?"

Cathy was shaking her head. "You can't do this, Gary. Don't you see—"

He flicked his hand in her direction in the way you would swat a buzzing mosquito. "I'm here to offer an extension on your stay here at Oxford."

Was I hearing him properly? "How long?"

"Another term."

I tried to smother the flame of hope between my ribs. I couldn't let myself be drawn in. Gary would always be Gary. "What do you want in return?"

He grinned. "I saw the video of your 'girlfriend.'" He made air quotes around the word, and I clenched my fists, ready to punch him if he didn't get Lucy's name out of his mouth. "I need your help convincing her to sign with me. I've sent her emails and called her, but no response. The extra term here at Oxford will be in lieu of your commission."

I wanted Lucy to have a singing career, but sign with Gary? "Over my dead body."

Cathy went limp. "Thank God." After a few breaths, her brow furrowed. "Why?" she demanded.

"Why what?"

"I've been up all night worrying that you would jump at this offer. Why do you care what happens to your fake girlfriend?"

My glare made her take a step back. "Lucy is not just my fake girlfriend."

Cathy plucked at her floral top. "Well, I'm not surprised you're sleeping with her. I mean, of course she would try to make the most out of your arrangement."

"Don't talk about Lucy like that," I said, my voice low and throbbing. "Ever."

She gasped and took a step back as though I'd slapped her. "But, Jack—"

"I love her."

She covered her mouth with her hand. "No."

"Yes." I drove the facts home, implacable. "I've loved Lucy since before I joined Northern Junk."

Her eyes went wide, and her hands started shaking. "You don't mean that."

"With every fiber of my being."

Gary rolled his eyes. "Enough of this. Unlike Cathy, I couldn't care less about your little love affairs. What I want to know is why Lucy won't sign with me? Has she signed with someone else?"

How could I have forgotten Gary's biggest fear in life was having someone be even more devious than him?

"She's not signing with anybody." Maybe that would make Gary leave her alone. "She's continuing her law degree."

"But that's impossible," he spluttered. "There is no way she could possibly let that voice go to waste."

It was a very unsettling sensation to be on the same page about something as him. "Not everyone runs after celebrity."

He shook his head. "Yes they do."

"No, they don't. Me, for example. Signing that contract was the biggest mistake of my life."

That snakelike expression sharpened in Gary's face. "You truly are a spoiled little boy."

That wasn't going to work on me anymore. No more being manipulated with guilt trips. I could hardly encourage Lucy to stand up to her mother if I wasn't willing to take a stand in my own life. "Shut up."

His face flushed a florid red. "You are living the dream of millions of people around the world, and you're still not happy?" He stabbed his finger in my direction as he talked. "You ungrateful little shit."

Before Oxford and Lucy, this familiar move of his would've shut me up. No more.

That familiar panic rolled through my cells, but I wouldn't let the anxiety monster stop me this time. Of course it was showing up now. There was so much uncertainty involved in leaping into the unknown. I had no idea if the net would appear or whether I would crash into a bloody heap on the ground. Regardless, I had to leap.

It took courage to let go of a life not meant for you and swap a sure road for an uncharted one—that was the fear Lucy and I both struggled with—and it was a real, tangible thing. Still, if I didn't let go of what made me miserable, I could never make room for what I truly loved.

"I'm not happy. The rock-star life is not for me."

Cathy made a strange sound, somewhere between a yelp and a squeal.

"But your parents!" Gary stabbed his finger some more. "They have invested everything in you. If you threw all this away, they would never recover."

"My parents will eventually get over it ... or not. That's up to them." My voice held a confidence that I didn't exactly feel but it was high time they got back to being parents instead of living vicariously through me. If I waited for them to come to their senses, I would be waiting for the rest of my life. I was finally living a life aligned with my actual self instead of the golden boy my parents wanted me to be and it made me so much happier.

Cathy tried to touch me, but I leaned back so she couldn't. "Don't say such things. That Lucy girl has been manipulating you—"

"Cathy!" Gary snapped. "Stop moaning about Jack leaving. It's not going to happen. I made sure of it. Let's get back to the reason we came here. Jack, I know you have influence over Lucy. She's besotted with you."

"It's mutual," I said, smug.

"I'm certain you could change her mind."

I laughed. If Gary only knew just how hard I'd tried, and failed, to do just that, he'd be astounded. He'd also be shocked—and probably secretly impressed—at Lucy's stubbornness. "Fuck, you're exhausting. It's not going to happen."

"Then I need you to come back to Northern Junk, effective immediately. Enough recess. It's time you got back to your obligations. You have a contract, and I can choose to enforce it at any time."

I shook my head. "Do your worst. I quit."

Cathy's face drained of color.

"I know you'll try to sue me and my parents into oblivion," I continued. "But I'll fight back."

I was going to have to make a difficult phone call to my parents. I'd been putting off the conversation for three years, but I was determined to have it today. I'd call them on my way to the observatory.

I would make sure my parents were okay, but I wouldn't live their dream life instead of mine for one second longer. Maybe sometime in the future they could start dreaming for themselves instead of me.

"Oh, I will do my worst," Gary hissed.

"Bring it on." I had a life I loved to protect now, and that made all the difference.

Cathy managed to grab my arm, but I shook free and stalked out the front door of the college and off to the astronomy lab, a smattering of paparazzi in my wake.

I pulled the phone out of my pocket, took a big gulp of air, and dialed my parents' number.

EIGHTH WEEK

CHAPTER THIRTY-THREE

Lucy

Why was I even here? The usually noisy hall echoed with monastic silence as I waited for our contract exam to begin. This was the first of my four in-college "collections" to gauge how me and my fellow students were performing in our degree.

Oxford seemed to purposely ramp up the formality of exams to maximize the intimidation factor. I was wearing formal sub fusc like all my fellow exam takers, and fidgeted in my black skirt, white blouse, and black academic gown. My regulation black silk tie had never felt so suffocating around my throat. At least nobody seemed to be wearing their mortarboards, so mine held my pens on the hall table in front of me.

The bench was hard under my bum and my hands shook with nerves. My brain was telling me that I should just leave but my body couldn't seem to move.

Jack's decision to quit Northern Junk deepened my doubts about sitting here right now. I adored seeing him so elated and free, but it made me feel even more stuck by comparison.

I hated this. I'd crammed until five minutes ago, but still felt as though I was drowning. The material just wouldn't stick in my brain no matter how hard I worked.

In two hours, I'd be meeting my friends at the Turf. I just had to survive this.

But survive what exactly? Survive until the next tutorial, the next essay, the next exam ... more and more I wondered if life shouldn't feel like so much more than just a series of crises to endure.

I should just stand up and walk out of here right this instant. I couldn't explain what was stopping me, except that somehow, since my dad died, suffering had always felt like the safest option. Happiness felt foreign—dangerous.

Besides, if I had everything I wanted, I would be more vulnerable than ever before, I could lose it all, and already having Jack felt like so much—sometimes too much.

Jack had taken the leap, and the results were anything but simple. His parents were so angry they refused to take any further calls since the first one. Gary, true to his promise, had lost no time in starting the legal procedures to sue Jack. Yet, somehow, none of that made a dent in his incandescent happiness.

Professor Speedman paced around my table, eyes fixed on an ornate pocket watch. She was dressed a tailored black pantsuit, like a very chic grim reaper. "You may now turn over your papers," she said.

I read the exam the whole way through. It was impossible. Simply sadistic. A girl further down the table began to quietly weep. A bubble of laughter rose in my throat. What was I even doing here?

"Is there a problem, Miss Snow?" Professor Speedman materialized behind me. She hadn't mentioned our conversation in the hall again, but it was there in every questioning look she gave me—and she gave me plenty of those.

Yes. Massive problem. I don't even know what in God's green fuck I'm doing here. But instinct kicked in. "No. None at all."

I started writing on automatic pilot. For better or worse, I wasn't going to give in without a fight. But give in to what? It made no sense that I was fighting to make myself even more miserable.

Two hours later, disheartened and sweaty, I left the hall after seven pages of complete garbage answers. Maybe this was how it would end—the decision to quit law would be made for me.

All I wanted to do was get outside as fast as possible and fill my lungs with fresh air. I mentally planned my route as the hall door banged behind me. I would leave via the cloisters where I could exit through one of the secret basement doors to get to the Turf. I longed to collapse in Jack's arms. I needed the laughter and support of our friends.

I felt like I was walking away from a car crash. As I went down the stairs from the hall, I couldn't feel my fingertips. I hadn't been able to remember a single one of the cases we were asked to contrast and compare.

The medieval cloisters were empty when I got there—thank God. Birds were chirping, and pale green leaves had started to bud on the gnarled oak tree set just outside them.

My pace slowed as I sucked in the fresh spring air. Should I just quit law and follow Jack's lead? Jack's new motto was that we couldn't wait on other people's permission to step into the life we were meant for. I agreed, except it got complicated when you were waiting for permission from a dead person. I rubbed the face of my dad's watch with my thumb.

Fear and frustration spun like a tornado in my head. I went

around the first corner of the square cloisters and stopped in my tracks. Someone was standing there.

Was that Cathy? It was. The garishly floral top was a dead give-away. What the hell was she doing back here?

"Hi, Cathy," I said. Maybe she had a few loose ends to tie up with Jack, although I couldn't imagine what those would be. "What's up?"

She didn't answer, just stared at me with narrowed eyes. I'd always thought she was an odd person, but ultimately unthreatening. Now, though, there was something different in her expression that made me wonder if she was actually as harmless as I'd assumed. Nah. My ears were still ringing after that exam—I was probably just imagining things.

"How did you get in?" If Robbie had been manning the front door, I was certain she wouldn't have gotten past him. Her hands were fiddling with something behind her back.

"I have my ways," she said, with a smug tilt to her mouth.

"Were you looking for Jack?"

She blinked slowly... creepily. "Jack has to come back to North-ern Junk." Her voice was strangely monotone.

A wave of ickiness rolled through my stomach. "He quit. He told me you were there when he did."

"He quit because of you."

I shook my head. I was, predictably, blamed by the media over Jack's decision to leave, but he'd given an interview to straighten out that misconception. "Actually, no."

She shook her head. "I don't believe it."

I was sure she wasn't the only one, but I couldn't care less. How had Jack put up with her meddling ways for so long? "It doesn't matter what you believe. It's the truth."

"You think you're his home now? You're wrong." A bit of spittle stuck to her cheek. That, more than anything else, sounded alarm bells in my brain. "*I've* been his home these past four years. He didn't need anyone else. You brainwashed him."

A prickle of fear crept up my spine. She was acting like a jealous lover. "Cathy." I kept my voice firm. "You shouldn't be on college grounds. You need to leave."

"What I need to do is get rid of you, so Jack rejoins the band and comes back to me. Only I can take care of him."

I could tell from her expression that in her mind her logic made complete sense. *Get rid of me.* Did she honestly think I wouldn't fight back? She was gravely mistaken about that. I could—and would—take her on. "I don't intimidate easily," I warned.

A distant shout echoed from the quad beyond. Her eyes flicked in its direction, then back to me. "You're going to leave with me right now."

I snorted in disbelief. "Like hell I am."

She brought her hands from behind her back. The bright sunlight coming in through the open carvings in the cloisters flashed on the silver handgun she held in them.

My knees wobbled. *A gun?* I tried to convince myself she wouldn't actually shoot me, but from that wild look in her eyes I realized—too late—that I couldn't predict what Cathy would or wouldn't do.

The irony. I'd sought out safety in such convoluted ways since my dad died, and denied myself so much, and this was where it got me. Part of me—the old, faulty wiring in my brain—decided this was life's retribution for the happiness of being with Jack.

But a bigger part of me could no longer buy into that lie. Jack was right. Life wasn't a set of checks and balances. Life wasn't out to punish me anymore than it was out to reward me. It was far more random and lawless than that. Any attempt to control it was doomed to failure.

Even rigid with fear, I felt the wall between me and the life I truly dreamed about crumble to the ground.

I didn't want to be a martyr like Cathy anymore. I was going to fight for my happiness with everything I had.

"What do you plan to do with that?" I demanded, nodding at the gun. My voice remained steady considering my heart was flapping around like a caged bird.

"Shoot you if necessary."

I could tell she meant it. "Inside the college grounds? You'll never get out again."

She shook her head. "People always underestimate me. That's my superpower, you see. Gary, you, even Jack—you don't realize just how ruthless I can be in fighting for the things I love."

She was right about one thing—I had underestimated her—everybody had. "Do you honestly think shooting me will make Jack rejoin Northern Junk?"

"Yes." Her tone didn't hold one shred of doubt.

"You're wrong." I knew I shouldn't be baiting her, but keeping the conversation going was what I was supposed to do in a hostage situation, wasn't it? Besides, it distracted me from the lethal-looking metal of her handgun, still pointing at me.

"Even if I am, at least you'll be out of the picture for good."

Desperation clawed inside me. I couldn't die. I wanted more of Jack, of joy, of life … suddenly I was absolutely fine with my greediness. "So, what's your plan?"

"You're going to walk in front of me. I will follow closely behind, the gun will be hidden by my coat over my arm. I'll keep it pointed at your back at all times, plenty close enough to put a bullet in your back. If you so much as make a move against me, or try to escape, I will shoot you, then I will wander away and melt into the crowd. No one will even know I was here. There are advantages to being invisible, you see."

I clenched my jaw to keep my teeth from clattering together. As much as I hated to admit it, her plan wasn't completely terrible. Cathy wasn't someone who attracted notice, and she did blend into the crowd. She also didn't exactly fit the profile of a cold-blooded murderer.

Sweat trickled down my spine. She jerked her head to indicate I walk in front of her—a perfect target.

I had no choice but to do what she said—for now—even as my brain ran through ways to escape. All I could do for the moment was try and buy time. "Fine."

I started walking. A spot burned between my shoulder blades where I knew, even without looking, she had her gun pointed.

I led the way out of the cloisters, thinking longingly about my phone in the pocket of my black sub fusc skirt. How could I reach for it without Cathy noticing?

"Where are you planning on taking me?" I asked. My only hope was crossing paths with somebody I knew and telegraphing with my eyes that I was in trouble. *Please let it be Jack.* Of all people, he would recognize Cathy and know right away something was wrong.

"We're going to leave through the basement door of the Holywell building."

That was one of our secret doors. It led to a side street that fed into New College Lane. Alfie had showed it to us, but it was almost never used except by the maintenance staff. "How do you know about that?"

"Underestimating me again? I know all the entrances and exits of this college. I visit often."

I thought of the shadowy figure I'd seen the other night at the observatory. "Was that you creeping around the garden under the observatory?" I simultaneously did and didn't want to know.

"Yes." Her voice was smug. "I've been around a lot, watching. You were disgusting with Jack that night, taking advantage of him in full view of the windows."

Nausea rose in my throat. She'd watched that?

"That was when I knew I had to remove you from the equation."

I started shaking so much I could barely walk. We'd exited the cloisters—the clear, sunny sky a cruel contrast to the fear coursing through my body. I led down the stairs to the basement of Holywell, where I made my way through its maze of empty paint cans, spare lawnmowers, and ladders until I opened the door to the lane.

"Where do we go from here?" I asked. The college belltower rang three times. Three o'clock. How much longer did I have on this earth, and why the fuck had I been wasting so much time not singing, not really living, these past ten years? It was horrible to contemplate dying with so many regrets.

"We're going to the Radcliffe Camera."

She was planning to do away with me at the most picturesque building in Oxford. "Why there?"

"Did you know underneath the Radcliffe is a warren of tunnels connecting it to the Bodleian and beyond? Some of them are very old and unused." Her voice was almost conversational. "I've done my research and found the perfect little spot to take care of my business with you. Nobody will find you for a while. I know exactly what I'm doing."

I believed her now. As much as I hated her, I felt a little tug of understanding—I knew what it was to be ignored and underestimated. Maybe Cathy was a cautionary tale of what happened when you played small. Did it eventually eat away at you, like it

obviously had with her, until there was nothing left but a maca-
bre version of yourself?

"You're a dark horse, Cathy," I said. It felt less scary to hear
her talking than to have her silent with her finger on the trigger
behind me.

"So are you," she said. "I thought by suggesting you as Jack's
fake girlfriend, I was safe."

Keep her talking. "Safe from what?"

"Safe from him falling in love with anyone. I never thought
he'd fall for you."

"Why not?" Jack still felt like my own personal miracle, but the
idea of us being in love no longer felt anything but natural.

"The way you look," she continued. "You're not the type of girl
men like Jack tend to fall in love with. I didn't see you as a threat.
I'd like to know what tricks you have up your sleeve."

Anger took hold. I was so much more than my clothing size.
Jack had just shown me the beauty in me that I'd been blind too
for so long. He made me feel like a goddess, and somewhere along
the line, I had started to see myself that way too.

I wasn't going to just accept death—I wanted to live. I wanted
a big life, full of Jack and singing for massive audiences—the bigger, the better. I thought I'd been playing it safe, but in fact I'd
been doing the riskiest thing of all—wasting my days listening
to fear.

I had to find away to escape before Cathy got me underneath
the Radcliffe Camera. Once she forced me into those tunnels it
would be over.

We walked down New College Lane. The sunshine meant the
lane was bustling with people soaking in the springlike weather.
My eyes roved over the crowd. Should I take a chance and make
my move now? I wanted to believe Cathy wouldn't do something

LAURA BRADBURY

as stupid as shoot me in a crowd of people, but I didn't know if she had limits—I suspected she might not when it came to Jack.

Adrenaline zinged sickeningly in my veins. With every step I took, I was closer to the Radcliffe Camera and the Bodleian tunnels.

I didn't recognize anyone. Cathy was right. No one was taking a second glance at her—or me, for that matter, without Jack. We were about to pass under the Bridge of Sighs when, in the small passage leading to the Turf, I saw Raphael.

I couldn't motion with my hands without risking being shot, but I made huge eyes with him, pleading, and tilted my chin back, indicating he look behind me.

His eyes went to Cathy and the folded over coat over her arm. Would he notice something was off with how closely and intently she was following me? He nodded once, but then disappeared back in the lane again towards the Turf. Had he misunderstood? Why had he gone back to the pub?

I kept walking, thinking of all the ways I could disable Cathy and get her to drop the gun without shooting me. Even if I took a bullet to the shoulder or leg, I would probably be okay. If only I could predict how good her aim was—very good, I suspected. I'd misjudged her so much already. I couldn't underestimate her now.

It was only now everything became crystal clear. Life was a crapshoot—a wild ride with wildcards like Cathy and my dad's death that no human could predict or understand. I didn't control anything, and trying to was the path to madness. All I could do was fearlessly go toward the things I loved.

Yet at the exact moment I finally opened myself up to life, I was walking toward my death. Too little, too late.

316

Alfie, Cedar, Binita, and I were sitting at an outdoor bench against the back wall of the Turf, having a midday pint as we waited for Lucy to join us after her exam.

The sunshine warmed my face. All was right with the world— or it would be if Lucy wasn't writing that stressful contract law collection thing right now under the disapproving eye of Professor Speedman. I checked the time on my phone. She should be finishing right about now. I leaned my head back and smiled to myself. *My girlfriend would be here soon.*

The Turf managers had grown protective of me, and had blocked both entrances off so the paparazzi couldn't get in. The security people knew Lucy, so she'd have no problem getting through.

"Doesn't it bother you that the media are so rabid right now?"

Alfie asked me.

I was feeling surprisingly philosophical about this final burst of tabloid interest. "It'll pass." I waved my hand. "When they realize I've left Northern Junk for good, the story will become old news and they'll move on to someone else."

"As long as it's not me." Alfie grinned. "But my father has been keeping a surprisingly low profile, so for the moment I'm good."

Raphael had left to meet Shaun under the Bridge of Sighs, but he burst back out of the alley and ran towards us, without his boyfriend. His broad chest was heaving.

"I just saw Lucy." He pointed back towards the alleyway. "I think she might be in trouble."

I jumped up, spilling my pint all over the bench. The exam must have gone horribly. My muscles pulsed with urgency. I had to get to her. "Where?"

"Under the Bridge of Sighs. She was being followed by a woman who looked weirdly focused on Lucy's back." Raphael frowned. "She was wearing an awful top."

Cathy. Fuck. I had no idea what she could be up to, but I had a sinking premonition it couldn't be good—anything to do with Northern Junk couldn't be good. "Where were they headed?"

"To the Sheldonian via Catte Street."

"We'll help," Cedar said, and my friends all nodded and stood up.

My mind spun. "Okay. You four go out the Holywell Street exit and try to head them off near the Sheldonian. I'll go through the lane and try to reach them from behind." My lungs clogged with panic, but for once it was completely appropriate. "I can't have Cathy see me. I don't know what she would do. No sudden movements—nothing to jeopardize Lucy's safety."

"Got it," Binita said, and they sped off.

I pulled my hoodie tight around my face and ran out the alley and under the Bridge of Sighs, sneaking past the paps who were searching for a flash of my red hair.

Why were there so many people out on the street today? On Catte Street I scanned the heads wildly, looking for Lucy's blonde waves and black sub fusc. My chest squeezed with urgency. I had to make sure Lucy was okay—she'd become my heart.

I skirted along the edges of the buildings that lined the road to avoid being spotted. The absolute worst thing would be to be swarmed by paps or fans and have Cathy turn around and notice me before I could help Lucy.

There! I'd recognize Lucy's ethereal blond waves anywhere. And there was Cathy, looking stiff and holding her hand at a strange angle in front of herself. Instinct told me she was hiding something underneath that coat of hers.

They'd almost reached the Radcliffe Camera. Blood rushed in my ears, and it took every last shred of my willpower to restrain myself from calling out to Lucy—to let her know I wasn't going to let Cathy hurt her.

I caught sight of my friends coming from the other direction. Lucy and Cathy were between them and me. I motioned at them to wait. They tried to look inconspicuous by chatting among themselves, but I could tell from their body language they were ready to pounce on my signal.

Cathy walked closely behind Lucy as they entered the gated enclosure and reached the base of the front steps into the building, which were flanked by huge stone bannisters.

Lucy turned and I saw the exact moment she caught sight of me. Her eyes widened and she tilted her head towards where Cathy walked behind her. I watched as she said something that made Cathy pivot and take her hand out from beneath her coat.

What was that in Cathy's hand? I stopped breathing and my bone marrow turned to ice. It was that moment I knew fear—real fear. Cathy was pointing a handgun at my Luce. It glinted mockingly in the afternoon light.

Lucy's eyes connected with mine then, and she gave me an infinitesimal nod.

What was she going to do? My heart clenched and time slowed to almost a standstill. I started walking faster toward them, then broke into a run.

It happened in a flash. I saw Lucy's lips move as she said something else. Cathy whipped around to look behind her. My Luce pounced, grabbing Cathy's wrist with both hands. She twisted and banged Cathy's hand and the gun hard against the stone of the banister.

A gunshot exploded through the air.

Cathy dropped the gun and it clattered on the ground. She tried to lunge for it, but Lucy was quicker. Moving like quicksilver, she brought her knee up under Cathy's chin. Blood spurted everywhere as she kicked the gun out of Cathy's reach. I got to them just in time to snatch it up off the ground.

"Jack!" Cathy was holding her chin as blood flowed out between her fingers. Lucy's knee had split it open.

But I only had eyes for Lucy. Still holding the gun, I pulled her against me with my free arm.

"Jack!" Cathy pleaded. "I had to. You left me no choice."

Our friends grouped around us, except for Raphael who held Cathy back with an iron grip.

Cedar removed the gun from my hand so I could tighten my grip around Lucy. She promptly opened it and emptied it of bullets. "Thank God the gun was pointing up at the sky when Cathy fired," Cedar said in a matter-of-fact way that took the edge off my panic.

"How do you know how to unload a gun?" Binita asked her in disbelief.

"Forest. Bears. You know." Cedar shrugged, unflappable.

"Can you call the police?" I asked Alfie.

Cathy struggled pointlessly against Raphael's massive arms. I'd been right that he'd make an excellent bodyguard if he ever wanted an alternative to medieval literature. Alfie took his phone out and dialed. He walked a few feet away to talk to the police. Being a Lord wouldn't hurt in getting them to get here fast to arrest Cathy.

Lucy's face was buried against my chest, and we were both shaking. "I'm not dreaming, right?" I murmured in her ear, soaking in the warm, familiar peppermint smell of her. "You're okay?"

She nodded against me. After a while she lifted her head slightly and stared at the ground beside the stairs. "My Dad's watch," she murmured.

I followed her gaze down to the gravel on the ground. There, shattered, was her father's watch.

I reluctantly let her go and went to pick it up. I knew how sentimental it was for her. "Don't worry. I'll get it fixed for you." I wasn't sure exactly how though. The glass face was smashed and a pebble was lodged in its hinge, warping the two arms.

She took it from my hands and threw it over her shoulder. "Don't bother. I don't need it anymore. I got my dad's ability to sing. That's all I need to remember him."

Before I could react, Binita squeezed Lucy's shoulder. "You should give self-defense classes. That knee move was impressive."

"You were a heroine," Raphael added, still holding back a struggling Cathy.

"Yeah, your own heroine." Cedar winked at her. "The best kind."

"I was, wasn't I?" Lucy said, an amazed look in her clear blue eyes. A full body tremor ran through her—the after effect of all that adrenaline coursing through her system, no doubt.

I smoothed my hands over her arms, her back, her hips, trying to calm her nerves. "This never should have happened," I said. "I should have seen it coming. I failed to keep you safe and—"

Lucy put her fingers against my mouth. "I'm not so interested in playing safe anymore,"

"Jack, I didn't mean it," Cathy wheedled. "I was just trying to scare her."

I examined Cathy's face for the first time. Even though I felt pity for her unbalanced mind, I would never forgive her for what she had just done. "You need serious help, Cathy." My lip curled. "I'm getting a restraining order against you. If you contact me or Lucy, or if you so much as breathe the same air as my girlfriend, I will make you regret it for the rest of your life."

"Jack!" Cathy's eyes were huge.

Sirens grew closer, then stopped. The police had arrived.

Lucy and I both gave our statements while Cedar handed one of the bobbies the empty gun and bullets. We all watched as two bobbies put handcuffs on Cathy and led her to their police van.

Finally, it was just us and our friends standing there. On the other side of the black iron gate surrounding the building, paps were starting to close in. I hadn't even noticed them until now.

"Cover for us?" I asked Alfie.

He nodded.

"Scram." Cedar smiled. "We've got your back."

We quickly hugged, then I took Lucy's hand and pulled her to where the paps couldn't follow, inside the Radcliffe Camera. I hurried her through the Gladstone tunnel underneath until we were inside the main Bodleian library building, then I made a beeline for one of the side doors. The horror of what could have been was quickly hijacking my thoughts.

I had to stop and get Lucy alone for a moment so I could convince myself she was still here with me, unharmed.

I spotted an old red phone booth on the street corner—it must have been one of the last few remaining in Oxford. I led her towards it, opened the door, and pulled her inside. My eyes flew over her. Her lips were pale and her eyes were far too big for her face.

"Did that r-r-really happen?" Her teeth chattered over the words as the stress worked its way through her nervous system. I had plenty personal experience with how this process worked.

"My Luce," I murmured, tracing her familiar face with unsteady hands. There was the silky skin I loved feeling under my fingers. There was that softly rounded curve to her jaw that I adored from every angle. I rubbed the deep crease between her brows with my thumb, then finally peppered it with soft kisses, to try and ease the tension there.

"Please tell me you're okay and that I'm not dreaming," I said between kisses.

Lucy bit her lip. "I think I'm all right, but everything feels far away ... except you."

"It's called dissociation. Completely normal. It'll pass." My hands and lips moved carefully over her, checking out every inch. "From now on I'm going to keep you safe. I promise."

Her mouth turned up the tiniest bit at the corners. "I learned something today. Nothing can protect me from life. I shouldn't want that anyway. I've been so obsessed with trying to stay emotionally and physically safe for the past ten years that I forgot how to actually live." She kissed me firmly—a seal on her words.

Finally. I wish with my whole self that it hadn't taken Cathy and her gun, but my whole body loosened with relief. I groaned, my hands knotting into Lucy's hair. "I love you."

"More than BPM 37093?" She laughed shakily.

"Lightyears more. You were such a badass my Luce. I'm so sorry I brought this on you."

She shook her head. "Nobody is responsible except Cathy. It was nothing we did or didn't do. I realized that about life when I was walking along with a gun to my back. Things just happen, and we can't do anything but react the best we can in the moment."

I blinked, trying to adjust to her dramatic pivot. "And love each other," I added.

"Definitely that." She slipped her hands around my jacket and under my hoodie. They were icy cold, but I wanted nothing more at that moment than to be her sun and warm her up.

"Jack," she said, "you may have already figured this out, but I'm quitting law. I'm going to sing until my voice gives out. Will you help me?"

"You don't even have to ask." I opened the buttons on her coat and slipped my hands inside, pulling all her fierceness as tightly against me as possible. "And when you become rich and famous, will you be okay with having a geeky astronomer covered in chalk dust on your arm?"

She pretended to give it some thought. "Yeah," she said softly. "That sounds perfect, actually."

Our kisses became urgent and desperate, but we needed more reassurance than we could get in an old red phone booth in broad daylight. No more wasting time. We both needed everything.

"Do you still want to go to the Turf with the others?" I asked. I wanted to give Lucy all the time she needed to come back down from her emotions. "We can get you something to eat there or a kebab on our way?"

She shook her head. "I'm feeling hungrier than that."

"Oh?"

"I want to wrap myself up in you—preferably in my bed. Besides, I may have some Hawkins Cheezies stashed in my room for sustenance."

"Lead the way."

CHAPTER THIRTY-FIVE

Lucy

Three Months Later

My new assistant had arranged for a black Land Rover to take me
from the AIR recording studio in London, where I was recording
my first album, to Templeton Green college, where Jack was pre-
senting his preliminary findings on BPM 37093 in the observatory under Professor Hayden's oversight.

The traffic getting out of London had been horrendous but
there was no way I was going to be late. This was a huge day for
Jack—his first step towards carving a place for himself in Oxford's
astronomy department.

I checked my phone as we pulled up in front of the college with
only a couple of minutes to spare. I'd started using it for time
since I'd broken my dad's watch when I twisted the gun out of
Cathy's hand.

Luckily, we didn't need to worry about her anymore. Jack had taken out a restraining order against her the very next day and the police had told us she was in a treatment center somewhere in Scotland now.

"Thanks!" I shouted at the driver as I prepared to launch myself out of the car.

"Do you want me to wait here for you?" he asked.

"No thanks. I'll be staying in Oxford for the next few days."

I'd been right about Jack's writing royalties for "Stars in Your Eyes"—Gary had been holding them back all along and embezzling them for himself.

With the first payment Professor Speedman secured for Jack, he'd bought an adorable little cottage behind big walls just on the outskirts of Oxford for the two of us. The past few weeks we'd even been scouring online for a rescue dog to adopt who had the right temperament to spend long hours at the observatory while Jack did his research. I took Jack's dreams as seriously as he took mine.

The plan after Jack's presentation today was to head over to the Turf with the skulk to celebrate over a pint or several, then go back to our house for a curry take-out and yet another viewing of his beloved Apollo 11 documentary.

I needed to plan a time to meet with Jack and Professor Speedman over the next couple of days too. We got along now I'd dropped out of law, and both Jack and I owed her so much.

She'd been so incensed with Jack's iniquitous contract with Gary that she'd taken on his high-profile case—which was rapidly raising her public and academic profile—to argue that a new precedent needed to be set to protect musicians signing on with agents and managers.

I charged through the front doors of the college and up the many, *many* stairs to the observatory. Thank god I knew the way up.

I cracked open the door, worried Jack may have started speaking already.

The normally echoing space was humming with chatter. Folding wooden chairs were set up in neat rows. They were mostly occupied by important looking academics in their black robes with variously colored silk sashes and a lot of ermine. I spotted the heads of our skulk in the second row.

Whew. I'd made it in time.

Professor Hayden cleared his throat and introduced Jack. My boyfriend was unusually pale and formal in his freshly ironed black and white sub fusc. In contrast, the cinnamon and copper waves of his hair glowed wildly in the sunlight from the observatory's many windows. I'd never get tired of looking at him.

I resisted the urge to go up and hold his hand while he talked. We'd talked this through last night on the phone, and I knew how tough this public presentation was for him with his anxiety. He'd been terrified about having a panic attack at the lectern, but I was so proud of him—he'd made the brave decision to do his best, well aware that his anxiety would no doubt be going along for the ride.

His panic hadn't disappeared—and he'd accepted now that it probably never would completely—but thanks to weekly in-person therapy sessions and a daily dose of medication he told me it had shrunk from a predatory monster to an annoying acquaintance.

His eyes met mine and the entire audience swiveled in their seats to see who had earned those blinding dimples. His Northern Junk fans would probably weep with jealousy, but not for long. He was losing followers as fast as I was gaining them.

I blew him a kiss and gave him a thumbs up. The dimples deepened.

I made my way to the front and slid in beside Lachlan. I leaned forward and gave our skulk a little wave. They were all there—Cedar and Alfie at the end, then Shaun and Raphael, then finally Binita and Lachlan next to me.

It was good we had this new friend family because Jack's parents had only just started speaking to him again. They were still bitter and angry. Things were far better with Mom and Alice. They were doing great and I'd just bought tickets for them to fly over and visit us next month.

Professor Hayden ushered Jack to the lectern. I leaned forward to listen to what he had to say about this star that fascinated him so much.

"First, I'd like to go back," Jack began said, "and tell you about how BPM 37093 captured my interested in the first place."

As Jack expounded on carbon and hydrogen and pulsations and seismic astronomy, I watched his anxiety evaporate in real time, leaving behind the sparkling reality of a man who was finally living a life he adored.

Jack's charisma meant that he lit up every room he entered, so he was keeping his audience just as riveted here as he had at Wembley. His fans complained he was wasting his talent in the astronomy department at Oxford, but I disagreed. For the first time ever, Jack was following his two passions with all his heart—the stars and me.

He always brightened my days and ... wow ... the nights. Heat crept up my neck.

"So, as you see, BPM 37093 is quite simply a white dwarf, but is it that simple?" Jack asked with that mischievous quirk of his mouth, waiting several beats to keep his fans in suspense. "Of course not. Nothing is that simple, is it, in space or in life? Beneath the humdrum exterior of BPM 37093 shines its core, which my preliminary findings have proved is the biggest diamond ever identified."

There was an audible gasp.

"I calculate it to be the equivalent of ten billion trillion carats."

I laughed with delight, and I was far from the only one.

So BPM 37093 had been a massive diamond all this time? Unbelievable. Jack would never stop astonishing me.

His speech went on for twenty minutes more. Afterwards he was peppered with questions from the audience. The final one was: "Have you decided to give this star a common name besides BPM 37093?"

"Yes." Jack looked over the heads of everyone else and his sage eyes locked on mine. "I'm calling it Lucy."

THE BONUS EPILOGUE

Would you like to read the bonus epilogue for Oxford Star featuring another Wembley concert with the whole skulk?

Just go to **mailchi.mp/laurabradbury.com/oxfordstarepilogue** to get yours!

THE GRAPEVINE

Interested in receiving sneak peeks at Laura's new work, as well as exclusive contests and giveaways, insider news, plus countless other goodies? Sign up for Laura's Grapevine newsletter and join our fantastique community. Just go to **www.bit.ly/LauraBradburyNewsletter.**

Thank you

I have many people to thank for Oxford Star, as I do for all my books.

First of all, a massive thank you to all my readers who have been with me through thick and thin (including several trans-Atlantic moves and a liver transplant!). I couldn't and wouldn't do this without you.

Special thank you to my insider team on my Patreon page. I adore this small, intimate little community and truly see it as my "inner circle". Beth, Chris, Marisa, Brad, Tricia, Debra, Lisa S, Aly, Harriet, Lisa B., Ivy, Tracy, Cindy, Lucy, Mike & Katie THANK YOU for being the fuel in my tank. I don't know if Oxford Star would be here without your support and insights. You can join my Patreon community at **patreon.com/LauraBradbury**.

I owe a massive debt to Judy who completely saved my derriere and applied her amazing editing skills and eagle eye to every sentence of Oxford Star. I cannot adequately express my thanks.

Huge thanks to Jolene Perry for her amazing developmental editing, and actually seeming cheerful (!) to receive my half-baked manuscript in the early stages. Sally Glover (check out her wonderful new book, The Farthest Star) did an amazing copy edit and Britt Taylor for a fantastic proofread.

Enni Amanda in New Zealand at Yummy Book Covers created another beautiful cover for this story. This really is my favorite—

until the next time.

The lovely Julie Christianson and Jennie Goutet are my blurb whisperers. I thank the heavens for them, as I'd rather write an entire novel than a blurb. My fellow writers are seriously the best.

Thank you always to Trish Preston for being the most amazing unicorn of an assistant.

As always, thanks to my husband and my daughters for not caring at all about my writing, and for constantly getting me away from my laptop. Life is never boring with the four of you.

Thank you to Nyssa for giving me life with her courageous decision to give me a large chunk of her liver almost six years ago. I never take one second of my bonus time for granted.

About Laura

Laura Bradbury is the author of the transplant romance, *Unlikely Match*, *Oxford Wild*, and the Winemakers Series. She also wrote the bestselling Grape Series of memoirs, and the award-winning cookbook *Bisous and Brioche*.

She earned a law degree from Keble College, Oxford (with a respectable Upper Second thankyouverymuch) but Laura's true love was always writing. She married a Frenchman and ran off to France after graduation so she would have something to write about. Sign up for her beloved monthly Grapevine at www.bit.ly/LauraBradburyNewsletter, her Patreon community at patreon.com/LauraBradbury or find her on IG at laurabradburywriter, Tik-Tok laurabradburyromance or on her website at www.laurabradbury.com.

Author's Note

Writing *Oxford Star* was pure fun. After writing *Unlikely Match*—which mined my own illness and transplant experience—I wanted to write a book that was packed with fantasy fulfillment.

Jack Seary and Lucy Snow popped into my head fully formed, and I knew immediately that Jack was a Harry-Styles famous rock star who suffered from something I knew firsthand—anxiety and panic disorder. He's also a space geek (*ahem* I may share that trait). Nothing is as sexy to me as a hot nerd.

I've had anxiety and panic attacks for as long as I can remember. Like Jack, it began very, very young, As I got older (and more importantly, into therapy) I came to accept this was just the way I'm wired. With the help of therapy, designing a more sustainable life for myself, and a daily dose of anti-anxiety meds I have come to a real place of peace with it.

To all the anxiety and panic people out there—I see how brave you are every single day.

Lucy fulfills my dream of having an amazing singing voice—it is one of my greatest regrets that I can't carry a tune in a bucket. If a genie every granted me three wishes, that would be one of them. I get goosebumps when I hear amazing singers covey so much emotion and beauty with their talent.

I also happen to know something about feeling frightened by happiness. Somewhere along the line I had internalized the belief that it had to be earned through suffering, hard work, or general martyrdom. Like Lucy, I blithely assumed that life was a system of checks and balances. I'm trying to change that. I love Jack's theory that joy is the birthright of all human beings because—ask any scientist—we are indeed made of stardust.

Lucy goes through the world as a size 16 woman, which is exactly what I do every day. Like me, she has reached a place of acceptance about it most of the time, but is often made to feel that she doesn't quite fit in the world. Luckily, I'm married to a guy who looks at me the way Jack looks at Lucy (bonus—he's French).

It's always super nostalgic and fun to revisit Oxford and my years there. Thanks for coming along for the ride!

FIND LAURA ONLINE

BOOKS BY LAURA BRADBURY

OXFORD SERIES

Oxford Wild

TRANSPLANT ROMANCE

Unlikely Match

THE WINEMAKERS TRILOGY

A Vineyard for Two

Love in the Vineyards

Return to the Vineyards

~ MEMOIRS ~

GRAPE SERIES

My Grape Year

My Grape Québec

My Grape Christmas

My Grape Paris

My Grape Wedding

My Grape Escape

My Grape Village

My Grape Cellar

Made in United States
Troutdale, OR
03/30/2024